BLUECOAT WARRIORS

As the dragoon detachment cantered across the prairie, Jeffries rode far enough ahead to be able to give ample warning if the situation with Running Wolf's renegade Kiwota war party turned nasty. The anticipation of a fight was keeping the blue-coated cavalrymen keyed up and alert.

"Major Devlin!" Standish shouted, suddenly pointing ahead. "Here come Jeffries riding hell-for-leather and waving his arms!"

Devlin wasted no time. "Detachment! Form as skirmishers left and right, at a trot, yo!"

As the two lines of the patrol split up to form one rank facing outward, Jeffries galloped in and came to a dust-billowing halt.

"It's the Kiwotas, Major!" he shouted. "Just over the rise!"

"Draw pistols!" Devlin ordered.

With revolvers held in their right hands, the dragoons moved over the rise. When they topped the high ground, they could see the Kiwota war party a couple of hundred yards ahead.

Wishing he had a bugler, Devlin took a deep breath and bellowed, "Charge!"

ZEBRA'S HEADING WEST!

with GILES, LEGG, PARKINSON, LAKE, KAMMEN, and MANNING

KANSAS TRAIL (3517, $3.50/$4.50)
by Hascal Giles
After the Civil War ruined his life, Bennett Kell threw in his lot with a gang of thievin' guntoughs who rode the Texas-Kansas border. But there was one thing he couldn't steal—fact was, Ada McKittridge had stolen his heart.

GUNFIGHT IN MESCALITO (3601, $3.50/$4.50)
by John Legg
Jubal Crockett was a young man with a bright future—until that Mescalito jury found him guilty of murder and sentenced him to hang. Jubal'd been railroaded good and the only writ of habeus corpus was a stolen key to the jailhouse door and a fast horse!

DRIFTER'S LUCK (3396, $3.95/$4.95)
by Dan Parkinson
Byron Stillwell was a drifter who never went lookin' for trouble, but trouble always had a way of findin' him. Like the time he set that little fire up near Kansas to head off a rogue herd owned by a cattle baron named Dawes. Now Dawes figures Stillwell owes him something . . . at the least, his life.

MOUNTAIN MAN'S VENGEANCE (3619, $3.50/$4.50)
by Robert Lake
The high, rugged mountain made John Henry Trapp happy. But then a pack of gunsels thundered across his land, burned his hut, and murdered his squaw woman. Trapp hit the vengeance trail and ended up in jail. Now he's back and how that mountain has changed!

BIG HORN HELLRIDERS (3449, $3.50/$4.50)
by Robert Kammen
Wyoming was a tough land and toughness was required to tame it. Reporter Jim Haskins knew the Wyoming tinderbox was about to explode but he didn't know he was about to be thrown smack-dab in the middle of one of the bloodiest range wars ever.

TEXAS BLOOD KILL (3577, $3.50/$4.50)
by Jason Manning
Ol' Ma Foley and her band of outlaw sons were cold killers and most folks in Shelby County, Texas knew it. But Federal Marshal Jim Gantry was no local lawman and he had his guns cocked and ready when he rode into town with one of the Foley boys as his prisoner.

Available wherever paperbacks are sold, or order direct from the Publisher. Send cover price plus 50¢ per copy for mailing and handling to Zebra Books, Dept. 4299, 475 Park Avenue South, New York, N.Y. 10016. Residents of New York and Tennessee must include sales tax. DO NOT SEND CASH. For a free Zebra/Pinnacle catalog please write to the above address.

PATRICK E. ANDREWS

BUFFALO WAR

**ZEBRA BOOKS
KENSINGTON PUBLISHING CORP.**

This book is dedicated to:
BILL FIELDHOUSE
(Wherever he may be)

ZEBRA BOOKS are published by

Kensington Publishing Corp.
475 Park Avenue South
New York, NY 10016

Copyright © 1993 by Patrick E. Andrews

All rights reserved. No part of this book may be reproduced in any form or by any means without the prior written consent of the Publisher, excepting brief quotes used in reviews.

If you purchased this book without a cover you should be aware that this book is stolen property. It was reported as "unsold and destroyed" to the Publisher and neither the Author nor the Publisher has received any payment for this "stripped book."

Zebra and the Z logo are trademarks of Kensington Publishing Corp.

First Printing: September, 1993

Printed in the United States of America

Prologue

The raiding party, made up of two dozen warriors, rode down the hill at a full gallop. They bellowed no triumphant war cries, instead riding with grim expressions on their faces.

One of their number, painted with white stripes across his face and upper arms, galloped a few strides ahead of the group, leading them in the direction he had chosen to go. The others followed him out of a combination of respect and habit.

This man's name was War Heart. He was an experienced fighter in his thirties, who had proven himself a clever and successful battle leader on countless occasions. Directly behind him, casting angry glances toward the rear over their fellow tribesmen, was a young firebrand called Running Wolf.

War Heart headed for a ford in the creek that lay just within sight. As he urged his horse into an even faster pace, he suddenly caught sight of soldiers coming out of the trees to the north. The mounted dragoons, sensing victory, galloped and hollered as they closed in on the Indians.

Following their leader, the warriors made a turn toward the south, but another group of dragoons appeared from that direction. Now the Indians were pinned in and badly outnumbered by the troops. War Heart returned to his original direction, going straight for the creek.

Shots exploded from the surrounding soldiers. Bullets split the air, and a couple of warriors lost their seating and slipped from the backs of their horses to bounce and roll into undignified positions of death.

At the exact moment the hooves of the Indians' horses hit the water, a third unit of dismounted soldiers suddenly rose out of the grass to the direct front. Bellowing smoke from the simultaneous volley they fired appeared an instant before the sound of gunfire reached the warriors. Ten of the Indians were knocked to the ground, killed or wounded by the swarm of close-packed bullets.

War Heart, bellowing in frustrated fury, pulled on the rawhide reins of his horse. He circled several times while vainly looking for a way out. But he and his tribesmen had ridden into a situation where they were surrounded by a well-armed, determined enemy who would grant them no quarter.

The Indian leader leaped from his horse and ran down the creek, seeking the cover of the trees that grew along the bank. Good concealment was available where the elms and spruce dipped their limbs into the slow-flowing water. War Heart's dozen companions followed his example, splashing after him. More shots, these from mounted troopers just arriving on the scene, killed three additional warriors.

The surviving Indians had no more ammunition. They went to their bows and arrows, readying them for possible targets as the one-sided battle rolled on.

"Look!" Running Wolf hollered, grabbing War Heart's arm. "Some of the bluecoats have left their horses and chase us on foot along the bank!"

War Heart said nothing. He stopped long enough to

loose three arrows, then turned and continued through the water that was now waist deep.

Shots from ahead and the sound of army horses on both sides of the narrow waterway gave heartbreaking evidence to the warriors that no escape was available to them. One man, a warrior known for his recklessness, began singing his death song. Throwing away his bow and arrows, he grabbed the trading store hatchet he carried, and scrambled out of the water into the thick vegetation on the bank. A fusillade of shots detonated, and he fell back into the creek, his final shudder kicking up a scarlet foam in the water.

War Heart looked around in his fury, trying to make sense of the situation. Running Wolf, his battle spirit soaring, shouted defiance at the soldiers who were now so close they could be heard shouting to each other.

The soldiers began shooting in their fashion that always seemed so strange to the undisciplined Indian warriors. Taking turns, and reacting to the shouted commands of their officers, the dragoons sent several highly coordinated volleys of carbine fire slashing and slamming into the huddled Indians. When the gunfire ended, only War Heart, Running Wolf, and a warrior named White Elk stood in the bloody water.

White Elk wiped at his face, smearing the war paint, and said, "I will sing my death song now." He looked at War Heart to see what he would say.

But another voice sounded from behind the trees on the bank before War Heart could respond.

"Looks Ahead has told me he will not kill you if you surrender!"

The voice was in the language of the Indians. Slightly accented, the words came from the black man called Night Face by the members of the tribe.

Running Wolf, panting and tired, joined White Elk in waiting to see what War Heart would do.

War Heart sighed and looked at his companions. "I am going to surrender."

"Why?" Running Wolf asked. "It is better to die a warrior than an old man."

"We cannot think of ourselves now," War Heart said. "What we do at this moment will determine the fate of the women and children."

"Do you think Looks Ahead will go and kill them if we keep fighting?" White Elk asked.

"If he doesn't, another white man will," War Heart said.

"Yah!" Running Wolf snarled. "It is a good day to die."

Once more Night Face's voice called out, saying, "Looks Ahead will not kill you if you surrender to him."

War Heart said, "You two do as you please. I have to trust Looks Ahead." He pushed against the water as he waded to the bank.

Running Wolf and White Elk looked at each other for only a moment before following after the veteran warrior they allowed to lead them.

Moments later, the three surviving warriors stepped through the bushes to stand in front of the leveled carbines of angry-faced soldiers. The Indians dropped their weapons.

One of the soldiers strode forward. He spoke through the black man, saying, "Do you surrender, War Heart?"

"Yes, Looks Ahead," War Heart said. "Your fighting medicine has been too strong for us."

The dragoon they called Looks Ahead peered into the trees along the bank. "Where are the other warriors?"

"You killed them all," War Heart said.

Running Wolf growled, "But there are more in the village."

"Do you surrender, Running Wolf?" Looks Ahead asked.

Running Wolf, with water pinkish from blood dripping off him, said, "I do what War Heart does."

"And I," White Elk echoed.

"Our war has gone on long enough," War Heart said. "I think it is over."

"As do I," Looks Ahead replied with a tone of relief in his voice.

Chapter 1

The gathering of men under the elm trees appeared almost gaudy in the somber mood that dominated the event. This was a meeting sanctioned by the federal government between Indians of the Kiwota tribe and the United States of America. The session had come about after three years of fierce fighting between the Indian warriors and soldiers of the U.S. Dragoons.

Although the civilians were rather nondescript, the blue-and-yellow of the horse troopers in attendance, along with the accoutrements of the Indian warriors, made splashes of color in the shady area. The attenders sat almost motionless except for occasionally stretching or standing up to relieve cramped limbs after long hours of talk in the warm autumn weather.

The non-soldiers among the whites were all official representatives from the U.S. Government. Some had come out to the treaty powwow as a lark, while others had real business to attend to. By then, for most of them, the week spent in the prairie wilderness had reached the point of montony and discomfort. They were in an obvious hurry to wrap things up and get back to the luxuries of civilization where good food, comfortable living quarters, families, and other physical pleasures awaited them.

The most unique person in attendance was a black man named Fred Jeffries, and he was also the busiest. Not one bit of the business could have been conducted without him. Called Night Face by the Indians, he acted as the interpreter for the session.

Jeffries was an experienced and expert frontiersman who served as scout for the dragoon squadron under the command of Major Matt Devlin. The army officer was called, most respectfully, Looks Ahead by the tribe now gathered for this treaty talk. His successes in battle had at first dismayed the tribe who struggled against him. Several victories later, they had grown despondent and discouraged, thinking him invincible. In time, they believed his personal medicine strong enough to allow him to look into the future, thus the name Looks Ahead.

The Indians were represented by their most popular war chief, a somber, dignified and handsome man named War Heart. His wives had seen to it that he was magnificently arrayed in buckskin moccasins, leggings and jacket decorated with intricate beadwork. War Heart also sported a war bonnet of eagle feathers. To show his intentions were peaceful, rather than carry a weapon, his right hand held a fan made from the tail of an owl.

His tribe was called the Kiwotas only by the whites. They referred to themselves as the People in their own language as was common among most indigenous groups in America. Although their nomadic culture emphasized hunting and war making, they also had a deeply religious and spiritual aspect to their tribal life that was based on a dedicated and sacred rapport with nature. The arrival of the horse in their culture had enhanced these practices by making hunting easier, thus giving them more time to develop their intellectual and philosophical tendencies rather than spending endless days on desperate hunts, but also provided more time and mobility to war making.

Their shaman had concentrated on making special medicine to assure success in the powwow with the whites. Now a lull in those talks followed the final agreements made in the negotiations, and everyone's impatience had increased to the point that it was obvious the end of the proceedings was at hand.

After conferring with Major Devlin, a small, bald, plump man stood up. Wheeler Coburn had been appointed by the Indian Bureau in Washington to take over what was to become the Buffalo Agency, which would administer to the Kiwotas.

Jeffries, in his role as translator, clapped his hands loudly to attract everyone's attention. He spoke to the Indians. "Your new agent, Coburn, now wants to recite the treaty for the last time."

Coburn held up a document of several pages that ended with signatures by the whites and duly witnessed marks made there by the Indians.

"This is our treaty," he said through Jeffries. "You have a copy and we have one. If any other white men come to you, you may show them this paper to prove you have made peace with the Great White Father and no longer fight or kill his people."

War Heart appeared impassive, sitting cross-legged and leaning forward slightly as he listened to the message changed into his language by Fred Jeffries. The warrior glanced at the rolled-up paper sitting in front of him. He had seen the strange, orderly inscriptions on it and had made his mark as prescribed by the white men's instructions to him.

"As it states, we have all agreed that peace must exist between the Kiwotas and the whites," Coburn continued. "This can only be done if you stay on the reservation that is agreed upon to be your land. The north limit is Medicine Hills. Your land continues to the south until Bear Gap is reached. The eastern side is bordered by the Des Lacs River, and on the west, you must go no farther than Greasy Flats. That is the entire area called Buffalo Steppes."

War Heart looked up. "That is not enough land to hold the number of buffalo we must have to eat."

"Goddamn it!" Coburn swore angrily. He nudged Jeffries. "Tell that stupid redskin we already talked about the fact the hunting won't be so good. That's why the U.S. of A. government is giving these useless bastards quarterly issues of beef cattle."

The interpreter was more diplomatic as he translated the words. War Heart remained silent, once more staring at the ground.

Coburn was still upset. "While you're at it, tell that stupid son of a bitch that the Kiwotas is getting six hundred square miles o' prime prairie land as it is."

Jeffries shrugged. "They ain't got no numbers or measurement like that."

"Then, tell 'em it's a heap lot o' land or however you're supposed to say it," Coburn said. "You might throw in the fact that there's plenty o' white farmers that'd give their left balls to be able to push a plow into this dirt."

After Jeffries spoke, War Heart replied, saying, "Do you promise to keep other whites away from us?"

"Yes!" Coburn exclaimed. "We're gonna build an agency and trading post right here. This is the onliest place where you're gonna see white folks. The army is even setting up a fort nearby to make sure nobody bothers you damn Injuns. You agreed to that already. You remember, don't you?"

War Heart nodded yes.

"Is there anything else you want to ask about before we break up this pow wow?" Coburn asked.

"Who will be the soldier chief here?" War Heart inquired.

"It will be Looks Ahead," Jeffries answered.

Now War Heart got to his feet. He looked at the whites for several long moments, particularly studying the stern face of Major Matt Devlin of the U.S. Dragoons.

"We have given up much of our land," War Heart said. "It is where the People have lived and hunted since the beginning of the earth. But the whites are too many, and their soldier chief, Looks Ahead, can tell what we are going to do in a fight before we even do it. How can we beat him? I do not want to see more of our young men die or the young women weep. So I tell you now that I will agree to stay on this Land of the Buffalo or whatever you call it."

The whites began to get restless. As far as they were concerned the job at hand was over. Hot food at the camp and a few good slugs of whiskey would make a fine ending to a fine day. They were all anxious for the Indian to shut up so that they could get to the social side of the situation.

"I hope that there will be no more reason for the People to go on the warpath," War Heart said. "All I can ask is that I be left to hunt buffalo and eat well and live in peace with my wives and my children. I think we are finished here. Goodbye."

War Heart knelt down and picked up the rolled-up treaty, then abruptly turned, walking away. The other Kiwotas followed him, leaving their side of the clearing completely vacant.

Coburn and the whites watched the Indians go over to their horses and mount up. After the Kiwotas had cleared the area, the government representatives and the soldiers got to their feet to begin the short walk back to their camp. Major Devlin and Coburn walked together.

The Indian agent glanced up into the face of the taller man. "Looks like you and me is gonna see a lot o' each other, Major."

"I suppose," Devlin said thoughtfully. A tall, muscular man, he was considered handsome by the ladies, he was a distinguished-looking officer with gray in the temples of his brown hair. He sported a moustache, turned down at the corners, which he kept meticulously clipped even when in the field.

Coburn grinned. "Y'know, you're a hard man to judge, Major. I can't tell if you're happy about this treaty or not."

"I'm happy, believe me," Devlin replied. "After three years of fighting War Heart, I'm more than glad to see the hostilities come to an end."

"Sort o' sounded to me like them Injuns is plenty scared o' you," Coburn said.

"The feeling is mutual," Devlin said.

Another civilian joined them. DeWitt Planter was the official surveyor who had laid out the boundaries of the Buffalo Agency for the legal papers to be filed with the government.

"D'you think them damn redskins is gonna stay on the up and up?" Planter asked.

"War Heart will if he's not provoked," Devlin said. "I can't speak for the others in the tribe any more than he can."

"What're you talking about?" Coburn asked. "Them Kiwotas'll do what he tells 'em, won't they? He's the chief."

"The Kiwotas don't have any leadership like we know it," Devlin explained. "As long as a warrior brings about successes in the war parties he leads, he is listened to and obeyed most of the time. But if some hotheads among the tribe's fighting men decide to forget the treaty and go back to raiding, there isn't much he can do about it."

"Then, he didn't have no business signing that damn treaty!" Planter said.

Coburn chuckled. "That don't mean nothing, DeWitt. If them Kiwotas even look cross-eyed at somebody, this here hunk o' paper gives us the legal right to turn Major Devlin and his dragoons loose on 'em!"

Devlin had noticed the two men during the treaty talks. "Were you gentlemen acquainted with each other before?" he asked.

"Sure," Coburn said. "We're both from the same county in our home state. We knowed each other as tads."

"You bet," Planter said. "And we was appointed to the Injun Bureau by Senator Osmond Torrance hisself."

"His family runs things where we're from," Coburn said. "We kinda helped him in the elections now and again. So we got these good jobs out of it."

"The positions you gentlemen have seem rather challenging," Devlin observed. "You may not think you've been done any favors before all this is said and done." He glanced at Planter. "Didn't one of your surveying party fall to his death during your work out there?"

"Sure did," Planter said. "It was a geologist. The feller went too far on the edge o' one o' them cliffs up in the Medicine Hills." He shook his head. "Maybe them Injuns got a curse put on the place."

"I wouldn't doubt it," Devlin said.

The three men and the others of the party reached the campground. Sturdy wall tents had been set up for the civilian officials while the dragoons lived in more humble circumstances a half mile away. Numerous cooks and servants kept the government men from having to dirty their hands with common camp chores.

"I'll leave you gentlemen until in the morning," Devlin said. "Tomorrow we're going to have to begin building our new garrison and agency."

"Why don't you move over here with us?" Coburn asked. "We got plenty o' room for you and your cap'ns and lieutenants."

"Thank you very much, but I must decline," Devlin said. "My officers and I have developed a closeness with the men. We prefer to share their lifestyle as we do the danger we all face. Thank you again, and good evening."

The major continued his walk across the prairie country until he reached the dragoon camp. After exchanging a salute and a few words with a seasoned trooper on guard duty, he went to his tent, where the captains who commanded the two companies in his squadron waited.

Captain Bernie Blanchard, a dark Louisianian who commanded Company A, greeted him with a lazy grin. "Are we at peace, sir?"

The other captain, a lanky fellow named Paul Teasedale, led Company B. Like Blanchard, he relaxed in a camp chair while sipping coffee.

"Yes, sir. Tell us the truth, Major," Teasedale requested. "May we unload our carbines now?"

"We're technically at peace, but I wouldn't clear those weapons yet," Devlin said. He took an empty chair. "War Heart has the fight out of him for right now. But if something goes wrong, then we're going to be right back where we started."

Devlin's orderly got a cup of coffee for his commanding officer. He limped over and served the hot brew. "I don't give a damn what he does, as long as we get a permanent garrison set up, sir." He was an old, rheumatic-ridden soldier named Thomas Kubelsky.

"We'll see that you have a comfortable winter, don't worry, Tommy," Devlin assured him.

"The army pays next to nothing to old troopers like me," Kubelsky lamented. "The least it can do is see that I got a warm place to sleep."

The orderly's complaints and disrespectful comments were tolerated by the officers because of his faithful and meritorious past service prior to being crippled by the disease that racked his joints. Another reason was the gastronomic miracles he could produce even on the limited field rations provided by a stingy government to an over-worked, spread-out little army on the frontier.

Blanchard glanced toward the pot simmering on the fire. "What's for supper tonight, Tommy?"

"Sage hen and rabbit stew," Kubelsky answered. "And I got some bread baked outta flour I got from one o' them civvie cooks over in the other camp."

"You're a miracle worker, Tommy," Teasedale said.

"All us dragoons got to be," Kubelsky said, limping back to tend to his cooking. "This damn army's been running on short rations since the Revolution, I reckon."

"I'll bet you were at Valley Forge, Tommy," Blanchard remarked with a grin.

"Hell, sir! Even I ain't been in the army that long," Tommy said as he went about his chores.

Blanchard took out his pipe and began filling the bowl. As he applied a match, he looked through the smoke at the commanding officer. "You haven't said much, sir. What's your conception of the situation we have out here on the Buffalo Steppes now?"

"It's precarious," Devlin said. "Even after we've

established our garrison and the men and horses have a chance to rest up, there is still a good chance that we'll see plenty of action by the time next summer is on us."

"So you're expecting a quiet winter at least, are you?" Teasedale asked.

"I think so," Devlin remarked. "As far as I can determine, the primary issue of beef to the Kiwotas is going to be a most generous one. That meat combined with what they've garnered from this year's buffalo hunts means they can pass the cold months in relative comfort."

"With both the Indians and Tommy Kubelsky wintering well, we can all be at ease," Blanchard said with a laugh. He took a few puffs off his pipe. "I have to admit I'll be glad to be in permanent quarters for a change."

"Amen!" Teasedale said. "What about the Indian agent? What's his name—Coburn?"

"Wheeler Coburn," Devlin said. "He's a political appointee, but so are all the people running the agencies. So I don't suppose we'll be any the worse for that. The funny thing is that the surveyor for the treaty boundaries and Coburn were sent up by the same man, a senator with plenty of influence. I hope that doesn't mean the politician has got a special hold on the Indian Bureau. Somebody with that much power who is far away can be neglectful. Or worse yet, manipulative."

"No matter, we'll still have to be good little soldiers," Blanchard said.

Over by the pot, Tommy Kubelsky hollered out, "Hot chow in another fifteen minutes."

With the thought of a good meal now dominating their thoughts, the three officers settled back in their chairs and waited for their supper.

Chapter 2

The United States was slightly more than fifty years old at the time the treaty with the Kiwota Indians was signed, making it an infant among the other nations of the world. Unfortunately, its capital city, being even younger, was an ill-planned, worse-built, and poorly located community.

Rather than establish their seat of government in an existing city, the squabbling politicians of early America compromised by decreeing that the seat of government should be newly built. Thus, Washington, D.C.—known as Washington City in those days—had been laid out in the wilderness along the Potomac River.

The final selection of the site had been made by the first president, George Washington. He'd liked the location because the waterway was navigable to Georgetown, a community that was an important tobacco market at the time. Also, a canal had been planned that would go from the new city across the Cumberland Gap to give access to the wide-open frontier in the West.

What resulted, unfortunately, was a crude settlement with a swamp in the middle, numerous huts and other rustic buildings, and a reputation as a "mud hole'' among the people living and serving their government in the area. The road to becoming a beautiful, thriving metropolis would prove to be a long and bumpy one. Needless to say, foreign diplomats were not pleased with their postings to the locale. They considered such an assignment an exile to hell itself.

When the surveyor DeWitt Planter arrived in the capital on a fall mid-morning a couple of weeks following the signing of the treaty with War Heart of the Kiwotas, Washington City could boast many unfinished public works with great promise and damned little else. But Planter scarcely took notice of his surroundings as he hurried across dirt and cobblestone streets and past unattractive buildings on his way to visit Senator Osmond Torrance's office in the Willard Hotel.

His arrival at the senator's chambers was not unexpected because of a telegram he'd sent at the first opportunity when he reached Minneapolis after leaving the wilds of Dakota Territory. The politico's secretary, a rather effeminate, well-dressed young man named Harvey Puffer, responded quickly when Planter presented himself.

"The senator said to notify him immediately when you arrived, Mr. Planter," the secretary said. "Please have a seat while I inform him you are here."

Planter didn't bother to make himself comfortable. He was too agitated. He paced back and forth, glancing toward the office door during the ten minutes he waited.

Finally, Puffer reappeared, saying, "The senator asks you to step inside, Mr. Planter."

Planter rushed past the startled young man, slamming the door shut to ensure privacy. He found the senator seated at a writing desk facing the window.

"Damn, Senator!" Planter exclaimed. "I got news!"

Osmond Torrance turned and looked at his guest. The politician was a portly man, with mutton whiskers growing thickly from his heavy jowls. Bald, with thick eyebrows and a scowl on his face that would only disappear through conscious effort, Torrance was not a man to be trifled with. He found excited constituents a source of irritation and threats to his political career.

"I received your telegram, DeWitt," Torrance said. He reached in his pocket and retrieved the crumpled missive. "I'll be damned and double-damned if I can understand what you're trying to tell me in it. As far as I can see, you've said practically nothing here."

"Well, sir—"

"You got to speak up plain and loud, son," Torrance said. "Or, in this case, write it out plain and simple. I have a lot on my mind. If you're upset about something, you'll have to come right to the point."

"Senator—"

"A plain and simple approach gets things done, son," Torrance said. "You can't do a thing if folks don't know what sort of information you're trying to send on to them. I'm a busy man, DeWitt, and I don't have the time to spare trying to solve an enigmatic telegram sent by you."

Yes, sir," Planter said. "I'm—"

"Now simmer down and tell me what this is all about," Torrance said. "I can tell from looking at you that you're still flustered as hell. Choose your words carefully, DeWitt, and enlighten me as to what you wish me to know."

Planter took a deep breath, then forced himself to speak as deliberately as he could. "There's gold in the hills where them Kiwota Injuns got land in that treaty and I know 'cause I seen it and I couldn't say nothing about it in the telegram because I didn't want nobody else to find out about it."

Torrance smiled, now speaking even slower than his normal drawl. "Well, sit down, DeWitt! Take a load off your dawgs. Gold is a hell of a subject to talk about, DeWitt. That's a precious mineral that can make fortunes for folks that handle the situation right."

"Goddamn! I know that, Senator!" Planter exclaimed.

"Do you understand that talk about new gold—the kind that nobody else knows about—is something that calls for the strongest regard to secrecy?" the senator asked.

"I do, I do!" Planter said. "Oh, indeed, I do!" He rushed to a chair across the room and dragged it over in front of the senator. He plopped down on it and said again, "There's gold in the hills that them Kiwotas got in the treaty."

"I understood you to say that," Torrance said. When he sensed something important, he always became most attentive and careful. "You're talking about the agency where I got ol' Wheeler Coburn a job, are you not?"

"Yes, sir," Planter said. "And where you had me sent to survey the place to mark out the boundaries for the treaty."

"I understand, DeWitt," Torrance said. "Now get on with what you want to tell me."

"Well, sir, I had just set up my crew to take sightings and note azimuths and was able to step back and watch the work progress. The geologist—"

"Geologist? What geologist?" Torrance interrupted.

"The one that came along to write up his own report for the Department of the Interior," Planter explained. "When he saw I was pretty much caught up and didn't have much to do at the time, he invited me to go along with him while he did some exploring and note taking."

"I didn't send a geologist," Torrance said.

"Listen to me, Senator," Planter pleaded. "I just told you he was assigned to the job by the Department of the Interior. He was supposed to write out a report on the type of rocks and dirt in the area, and all that sort of stuff. Him and me become sort o' friendly over the course of the job."

"It's not good to have an outsider in on something like this," Torrance said. "It can complicate matters."

"I knew that from the start, Senator," Planter assured him.

"That's good to hear, DeWitt," Torrance said. "Get on with what happened, please."

Planter related how he and the geologist tramped around most of the morning while the fellow gathered rock samples and bits of earth to take back to Washington City for his report. Things were pretty uneventful up to the time they took a rest to eat the food they'd brought with them. After sitting around a bit and smoking their pipes, they went back to exploring the terrain.

"Toward the end of the afternoon, he found a rock formation that really caught his attention," Planter said. "He took that li'l ol' hammer o' his and started chipping away at the side of a hill near the edge of a cliff."

"Did he make any particular remarks?" Torrance asked.

"Not for a few minutes, but he was getting agitated as hell," Planter said. "Then he held some of the stuff in his hand and turned to me and said, 'By God, Planter! This is gold!' I walked over and he showed me. I asked him if there was much."

Torrance slowly rubbed his hands together. "Just what did he answer, DeWitt?"

"He said it appeared to him that the yield in that mountain was enough to make ten thousand men rich beyond their wildest dreams," Planter said. "That's when I thought o' you."

"How's that?" Torrance asked.

"Well, Senator, there wouldn't be no way I could swing getting that gold out on my own," Planter said. "Especially since it was on Injun land give 'em by treaty. I knowed if there was one feller that could work out the details to make him and me rich, it would be you."

"That was real intelligent of you, DeWitt," Torrance said in a tone of approval. "But don't forget that geologist friend of yours."

"He died," Planter said. He hesitated, searching for words, finally saying, "He kind o' slipped and fell off'n that cliff right after he told me about the gold."

"I see, DeWitt," Torrance said in a calm manner. "I take it you didn't tell anyone else about the lucky find."

"I sure didn't, Senator," Planter assured him. "Not even Wheeler Coburn. You and me're the onliest people that know about it."

Torrance smiled. "You did good, DeWitt." Then he was silent for a few moments as he mulled over the information just relayed to him. "Could you find the place again?"

"I can do better'n that, Senator," Planter said. He reached in his pocket and pulled out a sheaf of papers. "I went back up there with surveying instruments and laid out the exact location by latitude and longitude, and wrote her down on one o' them government land claim forms we got to carry around with us."

Torrance took the document and studied it. "In order to claim this land, we must simply file this form at the proper government land office, true?"

"It'd prob'ly work out better if it was in your name, Senator," Planter said. "If my name is on it, somebody would figger out something wasn't quite the way it should be."

"That's good thinking on your part because eventually, after a while and the news of the gold got out, someone might even get suspicious about the geologist's death, DeWitt," Torrance said.

"Yeah, that's another reason for it to be in your name," Planter said. "O' course, it might not do us any good anyhow since that land is part o' the Buffalo Steppes treaty."

"Yes it is, but I don't believe the government ever meant any agreement with savages to be permanently binding," Torrance said. "So action can still be taken." He reached over and tinkled the bell on his desk.

The door opened, and the secretary stepped inside. "Yes, sir?"

"Harvey, I wish to file a claim on some land out west," Torrance said. "Bring me a pen and ink so I might sign the proper government form."

"Right away, Senator," the secretary said. He went back outside and returned with the writing instruments.

"Use that fancy handwriting of yours to put my name at the top in the proper place, Harvey; then I'll sign the document," Torrance instructed.

The politician and the surveyor watched as the secretary tended to the chore. When he finished, the senator signed the document with a flourish.

"Now take this down to Frederick Mullhouse's office in the Department of the Interior, Harvey," Torrance said. "Tell him it is a claim that I wish to file on land in the Dakota Territory. Tell Mr. Mullhouse that we would appreciate it if the job was done quickly, quietly, and with the utmost discretion. Do you understand, Harvey?"

"I understand perfectly, Senator," Harvey replied. "Don't worry, sir. I'll see to it immediately."

The young man made a hurried exit. Planter watched him leave, then turned to the senator. "Just how're you planning on working this?"

"Well, the claim will go through in spite of the fact that the land is on Indian territory," Torrance explained. "There would be no trouble there unless we went out to the place and started to occupy it."

"Then, how in the hell are we gonna be able to get that gold outta there without the Injuns and ever'body else finding out what we're doing?" Planter asked.

"The answer is obvious, DeWitt," Torrance said. "We must take the land away from the Indians, mustn't we?"

"I don't see how you're gonna get them hills away from the Kiwota tribe, Senator," Planter said.

"Quite simply, DeWitt, by getting those redskin rascals to break the treaty," Torrance said.

Planter smiled as the idea slowly began to dawn on him. "You aim to stir them Injuns up, don't you, Senator?"

"Stir them up? That is an understatement, DeWitt," Torrance said.

"If they go on the warpath, the dragoons'll move in and wipe 'em out," Planter said. "That Major Devlin whipped War Heart once, and he can sure as hell do it again."

"Of course. Remember, however, we must drive those Indians into raiding outside their territory, too," Torrance said. "There're plenty of farms and little towns in Minnesota and Kansas Territory that would prove tempting to enraged savages."

"A lot o' folks might die," Planter said.

"A lot of folks *will* die, DeWitt," Torrance said. I believe a certain geologist already has."

"I reckon it'll be worth it to be rich and be able to have anything you want, huh?" Planter said.

"I believe you are right," Torrance said.

"I'd like to buy me a cotton plantation and have carriages and slaves and a real beautiful wife," Planter said.

"Oh, why bother with a plantation when you can have a mansion and lots of land without worrying about crops and weather and all that, DeWitt?" Torrance said.

"By God, Senator!" Planter said. "I believe you're right. I ain't gonna have to work at nothing, will I?"

"That's right, DeWitt," Torrance assured him. "The money is just going to be rolling in. Why, it'll come so fast you won't be able to count it."

"Oh, Lord!" Planter happily exclaimed.

"Now, let's get down to some more business," Torrance said. "We're going to have to pull in someone else to help us out, but he's not to know of the gold."

Planter continued to grin. "I know who—Ned Wheatfall, right?"

"Right!" Torrance answered. "He has plenty of experience out west, and I know he's growing restless down there in Georgia since his return after that unpleasantness with the farmers in Missouri."

"I reckon some folks just don't believe in keeping slaves," Planter remarked.

"That's something that's going to come to a head real quick with those damned Yankees," Torrance said. "But that's another problem. Right now, I want to get ahold of Ned as quickly as possible."

"He knows the Buffalo Steppes, Senator," Planter said. "He used to deal with French trappers outta Canada up there."

"I remember that as well," Torrance said. "I think our old friend Ned has just the talents we're looking for when it comes to stirring up Indians. I'll have Harvey telegraph him right away."

"Do you need anything else from me today, Senator?" Planter asked. "All of a sudden, I'm powerful tired. I got to tell you that I been agitated as hell from holding this news inside. What I really got a hankering for is a room and to get some sleep for a while."

"There's a boardinghouse over on North Capitol Street," Torrance said. "It's run by a lady named Mrs. Murphy."

Planter frowned. "North Capitol Street? That ain't a good part o' town, Senator!"

"We can't have you staying on here at the Willard or the National," Torrance said. "We got to keep you outta sight. Don't worry. I know the landlady real well. Just tell her that I sent you over, and everything will be fine. Another thing, DeWitt, I don't want you coming back here 'til I send Harvey over to fetch you, understand?"

"I sure do, Senator," Planter said. He stood up, saying, "I'm going now. I'll wait for you to send for me."

The men shook hands, and Torrance again complimented the surveyor on his wise handling of the gold he'd learned about on Kiwota land. Planter left the office and hailed a hansom cab. The driver wouldn't take him all the way to his destination for fear of being robbed. When Planter stepped out of the vehicle, he walked as fast as he could down North Capitol Street in the rough neighborhood until he reached the boardinghouse.

At first the landlady was suspicious of him. Most of her clientele were not the sort who wore decent clothes and carried a fine leather suitcase. But when he mentioned Senator Torrance's name, Mrs. Murphy beamed.

"Why, sure then and it's welcome y'are, sir!" she said, holding the door open for him. "And I'll be giving ye the best room in the rear o' the house. The fights on the street won't bother ye near as much back there."

"Thank you kindly, I'm sure." Planter said.

The surveyor found the room small, dingy, and with dirty windows. But, out of respect for the senator, he settled in as best he could. He spent the rest of the afternoon and into the evening lying on the lumpy bed, biding his time. In spite of his fatigue, he could only sleep in short, fitful naps.

Mrs. Murphy called him down for a supper of stew and corn bread. The rest of the boarders looked at him with sullen suspicion, then went back to slurping up their food. Planter finished as quickly as he could and retreated back to his room.

The evening passed, and darkness descended on the city. Noise increased on the streets as drunken shouts and other disturbances ranged up and down the avenue. With no lantern in his room, Planter sat in the gloom feeling miserable until he drifted off to a restless sleep.

The knock on the door startled him to wakefulness. He looked around and noted where he was. It was quieter now, so Planter knew the hour was late. Once more someone pounded on the door.

"Who is it?" Planter asked.

"The senator sent me," a voice said.

Planter leaped out of bed and happily rushed over to answer the summons. He opened the flimsy portal and could see the shadowy figures of two men in the hall.

One moved quickly forward with a swing of his hand. Planter didn't realize the icy sensation he felt in his belly was a knife thrust, but by the time the second man sliced him across the throat, he knew it was an attack.

The assailants stabbed and cut numerous times until the surveyor was dead on the floor, his blood flowing slowly across the room to drip down through a crack in the boards.

"That's that, then," one of the men said in a husky voice. "An easy fifty dollars, Tim."

"I wonder what this was all about," the second man remarked.

"Sure now and I don't know any more than the skinny runt paid me the money and told me where this bucko was," the first said. "All we had to say was that the senator sent us and he'd open the door."

Then, thinking of all the whiskey they could buy along with bedding a decent-looking whore, the two killers eased the door shut and snuck through the house back to North Capitol Street.

Chapter 3

During the remainder of the fall season working on the Buffalo Steppes Agency, the squadron of dragoons stationed there did very little drilling or other military activities. Most of their working days, rather than being spent as soldiers, found them toiling as carpenters, masons, and laborers. The pressure of the coming Dakota winter made work schedules long in the relentless drive to get the job done as quickly as possible.

Only a few absolutely necessary martial duties such as guard and patrolling took the troops away from the very important chores of building both the trading post and the fort that would administer the Kiwota Indian treaty.

Most of the men grumbled about the hard work since many had enlisted in the army to avoid the drudgery of manual labor. But they had to admit to themselves that with the harsh Dakota winter coming on, lives would depend on strong, blizzard-resistant buildings in which to live and work.

By late October the job was done. Fort Buffalo, with four one-story barracks buildings, officers' quarters, a headquarters building, stables, latrines, and a line of small houses called soapsuds row where the married sergeants lived, was an established and working army post.

The Buffalo Steppes Agency consisted of one large building that served as a trading store, agency office, and residence of Mr. Wheeler Coburn, the government agent.

The Kiwotas passing by the place during hunting forays were amazed at the change in the area. What had once been empty prairie was filled with the white men's structures and activities. The Indians were particularly astonished by the fact that a couple of the buildings were used for the sole purpose of tending to nature's call and to bathe. They considered the quicklime dumped down into the holes periodically by the soldiers to be a very strong medicine. Nothing less would take away the smell of feces. The Kiwotas simply moved away from an area when it became so fouled as to offend the sense of smell. They didn't return to that spot for a few seasons, waiting for the passage of time to diminish the odors until it was a fit place to camp again.

In early November, just before the first snows came, a flurry of excitement swept across the place. Soldiers' families, who had been waiting back in Fort Snelling, Minnesota, arrived. The Indians, especially the women, made an appearance at this event. They had rarely seen white men with white women and were curious as to how the couples lived. The children, in particular, were a source of gentle curiosity to the Kiwotas who indulged their own offspring when very young.

But the tribe's interest in the army families came to a quick close at the arrival of the first quarterly beef issue of two hundred head of cattle to be given to them as part of the treaty agreement. While the Indians prepared to draw their meat-on-the-hoof, the married soldiers enjoyed being able to renew their domestic existence and live again with their wives and children. The post commander, Major Matt Devlin, was no exception.

During her fourteen years of marriage to Matt, Beth Devlin had given birth to five children. Two had died in infancy, but three had survived the health-threatening climates and environs of frontier army posts. Twelve-year-old Freddie, his sister Mattie of eight years, and their five-year-old brother Bobby were among the worst hellions of a breed of misbehaving, mischievous, and devious youngsters known as "army brats." When the children and numerous dogs of the post caused any disturbance or outright physical damage, the Devlin kids were sure to be in the middle of the fracas with Freddie in the vanguard.

While the adults settled into their new quarters, the children broke away to begin exploring their new battleground, quickly acquiring additional allies in their adolescent campaigns of terror and turmoil—the youngsters of the Kiwota tribe.

The busy occurrence of the issue of the cattle brought all the children together. Acquaintances and friendships were quickly formed in spite of the language barrier. For the girls it was an opportunity to learn about each other's clothing and toys. The Kiwota lasses had their own form of dolls usually made for them by grandmothers. The white girls, on the other hand, had more realistic store-bought varieties. A bit of trading went on in which trinkets, bracelets, and necklaces were exchanged as games of baby caring spontaneously began.

The Kiwota girls showed the soldiers' daughters how to make a miniature village in which make-believe chores were done. The white lasses reciprocated with their own versions of playing house. This playtime was filled with wonderful and tender moments between the girls.

The boys' relationships, on the other hand, began on a less-than-friendly level. Unspoken challenges resulted in wrestling matches, foot races, and other physical activities that finally settled down to some serious exchanges of pocketknives and other boy-type toys and possessions after bartering and grunting at each other. A few of the youngsters paired off as friendships developed. Freddie Devlin became pals with a Kiwota boy of his age named Swift Rabbit. But this came about only after testing each other in a series of rough-and-tumble wrestling matches that didn't come to an end until both boys were nearly exhausted.

The children's games broke up as the Indians took possession of the two hundred head of cattle that would help see them through the winter. The Indians boys had herding chores to attend to, and they made an abrupt exit following the guttural commands of their fathers and uncles. The Kiwota girls would be helping with the butchering when the beef reached their village, so they, too, were obliged to break off the play session and prepare for serious work.

A week later, the established rapport between the children picked up where it left off. Many hours were spent together in the quickly shortening daylight hours until the first snows arrived. At that point, things slowed down, and everyone lapsed into a winter routine as the cruel winds of the north brought activity on the Buffalo Steppes to a frigid standstill.

The dragoons spent a lot of time in barracks, going out only for the most necessary of chores such as tending to their horses in the stables or guard duty, along with housekeeping tasks that were essential in keeping Fort Buffalo running smoothly in spite of the awful weather.

Out on the prairie, the Kiwotas settled into their lodges, content with the dried beef and buffalo meat that would see them through the unpleasant months ahead. Some of the camp dogs would eventually give their lives to add fresh meat to the menu now and again during those days of no hunting, but mostly the People dined on the preserved variety of animal flesh.

War Heart shared his tepee with his two wives, children, and a few nieces and nephews. His first wife, Summer Wind, was the one he had chosen and courted in the fashion of the People. His second wife, called Medicine Woman, was the widow of his brother killed in battle against the Crows. War Heart, as was the custom, had taken her and her children into his lodge. She had two children by her first husband and had already been impregnated by War Heart before the winter actually arrived.

The chief, like the other warriors and boys, ventured out to do some trapping when the weather gentled enough. This was due to Wheeler Coburn offering them knives, hatchets, and trinkets in exchange for beaver and otter pelts. The practice was not entirely legal, since the Indian agent was not to embark on any commercial activities. But Coburn took advantage of all opportunities to make some extra cash.

The black scout and interpreter, Fred Jeffries, lived with his Cheyenne wife, Moon Deer. Their habitat was situated as he preferred it to be, separated from both the Indian village and the military post. He had a sturdy, comfortable soddie dwelling constructed of chunks of prairie earth. The roof was alternating layers of logs and more earth. Its natural insulation required little heat, so a small stove with its pipe sticking high above the roof to keep it out of the deep snow was all that was required for health and comfort. With his own dried meat and being able to purchase goods at the trading post from his army pay, Jeffries and Moon Deer enjoyed a comfortable, virtually carefree life in their small quarters.

Jeffries had come out out the Dakota Territory as a young boy. He couldn't remember if he had been employed by or a slave of an itinerant white trader who moved among the Indians selling and trading whiskey, guns, and other goods in demand by the tribes.

Eventually tiring of the wandering life, the man had set up a trading post and enjoyed moderate success in the venture. By the time the old fellow died, Jeffries had grown an expert in several Indian languages and could also boast of an intimate knowledge of the Buffalo Steppes and surrounding territory. Never much of a shopkeeper, Jeffries had drifted into trapping jobs until his skills had come into demand by the U.S. Dragoons. He'd become a contract scout for the army a couple of years after rescuing his wife from a Lakota raiding party. The Indian woman had settled in with him, and they had been living together ever since.

While the people on the Buffalo Steppes wintered as best they could, a half continent away in Washington City, a meeting between two men was held on a cloudy afternoon in the latter part of January.

Senator Osmond Torrance had spent a frantic four months trying to locate one of his constituents, an enigmatic man named Ned Wheatfall. One of the reasons for the difficulty in finding an individual like Wheatfall was the fact that he was not entirely welcome in a lot of places. In others, he was very much wanted—not for his charming company, but to face charges on felonies that ranged from armed robbery to murder. Wheatfall had extensive Indian-fighting experience through working as a guide for wagon trains. He had also served five years in the army from which he surprisingly received an honorable discharge in the rank of sergeant. Along with those lines of work, he had trapped fur-bearing animals in the Rocky Mountains and done a lot of buffalo hunting on the plains.

Wheatfall's latest project had gotten him into serious trouble. He signed on as a hired gun with a pro-slavery faction trying to move into a county in Missouri where the majority of residents were abolitionists. The end result of this invasion was a bloody war in which assassination, robbery, rape, and lynchings ran riot. Before the slavers were defeated, Ned Wheatfall had increased his reputation as a cold-blooded killer to such an extent that a five-thousand-dollar reward was offered for him dead and a thousand to anyone who brought him in alive.

When Senator Torrance's secretary, Harvey Puffer, informed him of Wheatfall's predicament, the politician wasn't surprised that his old friend Ned would be difficult or even impossible to find. But Puffer's persistent efforts finally paid off when Wheatfall was discovered working as an overseer on a Mississippi cotton plantation.

When Wheatfall arrived in Washington City, unlike the unfortunate DeWitt Planter, he was put in one of the better hotels. Torrance even advanced the man some cash to enjoy the pleasures of the flesh offered in the metropolis's brothels and saloons. After a week of celebration and debauchery, Wheatfall was ready to settle down to business and find out why the senator had summoned him all the way from Mississippi.

They met in Torrance's private chambers in the Willard Hotel, down the hall from his office. Harvey Puffer arranged to have coffee, a bottle of good bourbon, and plenty of good cigars handy for the two men. When the pair had settled in, Puffer withdrew to tend to his administrative duties.

Wheatfall took a sip from the cup that was half-coffee

and half-bourbon. "It's mighty good to see you again, Senator."

"Why, thank you, Ned, and it's a real pleasure to be talking to you, too," Torrance said. He took time to light a cigar and study the man sitting across from him.

Wheatfall was a bit over six feet tall, rail thin, with a long, black beard. His gray eyes were cold and without emotion to match the tone of his voice. Although gaunt-looking, the man gave the appearance of physical strength and well-being.

Wheatfall glanced out at the bleak, wintry day. "It seems mighty cold, or maybe it's because I just come up from Mississippi."

"It's cold, don't try to fool yourself," Torrance said. "It's a hell of a lot colder up north where I have a job for you, but you needn't worry about that. Your work won't start until the springtime."

"What kind o' work you got for me, Senator?" Wheatfall asked. It was already assumed by both men that whatever Torrance wanted, Torrance got. "I been mighty curious about that when I found you was bringing me all this way."

"I want you to go buffalo hunting," Torrance said. "You've done that before, ain't you?"

"Sure," Wheatfall answered. "I killed a few for food, a few for their hides, and a few just for the hell of it. How come you want me to go back into that line o' work?"

"I need to starve a bunch of Indians in the Dakotas," Torrance said. "If they don't have buffalo to feed on, then they'll starve."

Wheatfall laughed. "Lord have mercy, Senator! I could go out there with a thousand fellers and shoot a thousand buffalo for a thousand days, and there'd still be plenty for Injuns to feed on."

Torrance leaned forward. "These Indians are on a reservation."

Wheatfall shrugged. "So what? If they get hungry enough, they won't starve. They'll just ride off the reservation and hunt."

Torrance smiled. "That's exactly what I want them to do."

Wheatfall got up and fixed himself another coffee-and-bourbon. He went back and sat down, spending a few moments in thought. Finally, he asked, "Are you trying to start a Injun war, Senator?"

"I sure as hell am," Torrance said. "I believe you're familiar with the Buffalo Steppes, are you not?"

"I sure am," Wheatfall assured him. "I used to work with Frenchie trappers from Canada up there. There's a particular mean bunch o' redskins called the Kiwotas that claim the steppes as their personal property."

"Well, a few months ago they signed a treaty, giving up a lot of land in exchange for beef issues and the promise that white folks would stay away from them," Torrance said.

Wheatfall nodded. "It might be a good idea to mess up that beef, too," he suggested. "If they can't get buffalo and there ain't enough cattle given to 'em, they'll really get riled."

"I plan on seeing to that," Torrance said. "By the way, Wheeler Coburn is the Indian agent on the reservation."

Wheatfall burst into laughter. "That horse thief? I'll bet you got him the job, didn't you, Senator?"

"He's proven particularly helpful in recent elections, Ned," Torrance said. "Things started to get a little hot for him down home, so I figured it was time to give him a reward. He'll be able to make some extra money if he works the job right."

"Oh, he'll work it right, no need to ponder that," Wheatfall said. "If anybody can starve them Kiwotas, it's Wheeler Coburn."

"He's good, but not that good," Torrance said. "That's why I'm going to want you and a big group of hunters up there on the steppes slaughtering buffalo early this spring."

"All you got to do is give me the time and money, and I'll round up gang of the meanest son of a bitches that ever drawed bead on a buffalo or an Injun," Wheatfall said. "I think we'll need about fifty fellers, if we ain't gonna get massacred while doing the job."

"That's fine, Ned," Torrance said. "I have all the faith in the world in you."

"By the way, Senator," Wheatfall said. "I take it this is all going to happen 'cause you or a friend o' yours wants that land on the steppes. Do I need to know why?"

"No," Torrance answered abruptly.

"Yes, sir," Wheatfall said.

"Do you think you'll have any trouble lining up enough guns to take with you?" Torrance asked.

"No, sir," Wheatfall replied. "I got plenty of time. Just keep in mind that I may have to sign on a few early. That means they'll have to go on the payroll right quick, or they'll drift away. It could get expensive."

"That's no problem," Torrance said.

"We could make some money by selling the hides of the buffalo we kill," Wheatfall said. "You might get some o' that extry expense back by the end o' summer."

"That's not important," Torrance said.

"Then, I'll give the hides to the boys as a bonus," Wheatfall said. "We're gonna have to fix them buffalo carcasses so they ain't worth shit to them redskins."

"I'm going to leave that all up to you, Ned," Torrance said. He tossed his cigar butt into a spittoon beside the table and stood up. "I must attend to other business now, Ned. I'll send Harvey down here to work out the details on what you'll need."

"And when I'll need it," Wheatfall added.

"Of course," the senator said. He held out his hand. "It was indeed nice seeing you again, Ned, and a pleasure to be working with you again."

"Same here, Senator," Wheatfall said, rising.

The hunter waited until the politician left, then fixed himself another drink. He downed it in several swallows, then began to prepare another as he mulled over what had just been discussed. He caught his reflection in a mirror on the wall, and raised the cup in a toast.

"Here's to hell-on-earth!" Wheatfall said. "There's gonna be more'n buffalo blood flowing out there on the steppes afore this is all said and done."

Chapter 4

After months of cruel winter weather, the coming of spring to the Buffalo Steppes was first discovered through the sensitive rapport that a twelve-year-old boy of the Kiwota tribe had with the world in which he had been raised.

His name was Swift Rabbit, and on that morning he had reluctantly left the warmth of his buffalo robes to pull on leggings, shirt, and moccasins to tend to watering his father's horses. After wrapping a blanket around him, he picked up a wooden staff he used to urge the animals to do his bidding. The boy stepped outside into an early, but bright sunny morning. It seemed crisp and cold, but the boy felt a difference somehow. He wasn't sure what it was, but the smells and feel of things seemed different to him.

Now experiencing an unexpected vigor in his own being, Swift Rabbit hurried across the crusty snow to the herd. After gathering up the three mounts, he drove them down to the brook that ran past the village, urging them on with sharp whacks from the stick.

When he reached the little creek, he stabbed at the ice with the staff. The glazed sheet across the water was thinner than usual and easily gave way to the sharp blows. Swift Rabbit continued breaking it up until enough was cleared away to allow the horses to begin slaking their thirst.

While Swift Rabbit waited, he glanced around noting that the ice, now weaker, had given way in spots to the creek's current, and was cracking close to the banks. The boy took pains to study the sun, appreciating the fact that it seemed warmer that particular morning. Another glance toward the bare limbs of the trees gave him the pleasant view of the ice on them slowly melting, letting small droplets of water fall to the snow.

An old woman came down to the creek to get a potful of water for her lodge. She nodded a silent greeting to the boy and squatted down to tend to her chore.

"You will not have to hit the ice hard, Grandmother," Swift Rabbit said, using the respectful address for an elderly woman as was the custom of the People. "It has grown thin under the sun that now shines stronger. I think the Moon of Awakening is now pushing against the Moon of Cold Hunger."

The woman, with the experience of many years of outdoor living, glanced up and judged both the angle and warmth of the sun. Then she sniffed the air and smiled.

"Ah! You are right, Grandson. I smell life." She cocked her head slightly. "I think I hear the new grass trying to push through the ground and the snow. It wants to feed the hungry buffalo."

"How far away is the first hunt?" Swift Rabbit asked. He hungered for fresh meat other than dog.

She laughed. "At least another moon will pass across the sky before the ground begins to grow firm enough for the men to ride their horses fast enough to catch buffalo."

Swift Rabbit was glad for the coming of the Moon of Awakening and the warm days to follow. As the old woman said, it wouldn't be long before the warriors and older boys would seek out one of the herds roaming the reborn prairie. He couldn't wait for his first taste of raw buffalo liver. Swift Rabbit smiled to himself as he thought of the good times ahead.

Meanwhile, he and the rest of the tribe would begin preparing for the days to come. Arrows had to be made, bows restrung, lances sharpened, and the lighter clothing for the warm weather unpacked and prepared.

Weeks later, over at Fort Buffalo, the residents had scarcely noticed any change at all. But their awareness was sharpened when the melting of the snows began to produce mud. Then the cursing, struggling soldiers went about their duties in quagmires of the gooey stuff that stuck to boots and horses' hooves with maddening tenacity.

Finally, in April, the intensity of the sun brought about a drying phase that even occasional showers could not affect. The ground firmed up, green shoots of new grass appeared, leaves on trees emerged, and the first blossoms of wildflowers dotted the prairie country in patternless spreads of color.

The Kiwotas had received a mid-winter issue of cattle. This influx of fresh meat other than camp dogs made the people happy and satisfied. Perhaps, they reasoned among themselves, the treaty to which War Heart had led them was not such a bad thing after all. Now, with the warm weather upon them, more beef was due the tribe. But the buffalo had already had several weeks to fatten up on the fresh growth of grass. The tribal shaman had a vision that told him it was time for the first hunt of those mighty bison. His announcement caused a flurry of activity in the village as the warriors prepared for their first kills of the new season.

Extra effort was taken on personal medicine charms. The Kiwotas believed that if the first hunt was a bad one, the rest of the year would be filled with disasters of many kinds. Their enemies, the Crows and the Pawnees, would be able to come and steal horses and women to their hearts' content. Therefore, the preliminary foray into the buffalo herds called for very special preparations.

Each hunter showed up at the appointed time to honor the animals they were about to slaughter. The medicine man went through an elaborate ceremony that would cause the bison to move closer to the village. A dancer, wearing a fur cap with buffalo horns, went through a short but elaborate dance imitating a fierce bull. This was meant to show respect for the prey, making the herd feel honored to fall before the weapons of Kiwota warriors.

When the preparations were finished, no more time was wasted. The warriors quickly mounted their favorite horses and rode out of the village to track down the first buffalo of the season.

War Heart and his young friend Running Wolf rode side by side in the hunt as they did in war. White Elk, another friend who had shared many adventures on the warpath with them, had gone on ahead of the others. In a nation of excellent trackers, White Elk was considered to be among the very best.

That morning proved to be a completely unique one the likes of which no other group of Kiwota hunters had ever experienced. White Elk's first contact with the buffalo was not through a spoor or trail left across the sea of prairie grass. Instead, a sickly, rotten smell assailed his nostrils. He knew it was buffalo because he had come across the rotting carcass of one of the great animals before. But never had the odor filled his nostrils with such a stench. A few minutes later, as he pressed on with his tribesmen a few hundred yards behind him, White Elk noted black specks circling in the sky. After a few more moments he could hear the obscene call of hundreds of crows. When he topped a rise and could see across a wide expanse of the steppes, he pulled on the rawhide reins of his horse, bringing it to a quick halt.

In a sweeping panorama that went from horizon to horizon, the Indian could see countless dead buffalo rotting in the mid-morning sun. Overfed crows, stuffed with fetid meat, still gorged themselves. Most could barely fight their way into the air as White Elk rode down to take a closer look. He turned and saw the other hunters now approaching with War Heart and Running Wolf in the lead.

The Kiwotas could not believe what they saw. None spoke as they looked at each other between long bouts of gazing at the obscene waste that spread out before them. Only the hides had been taken from a few of the buffalo that were so decomposed they offered nothing except their bones. Not one shred of the putrid meat or hides on the remainder would serve any useful purpose.

War Heart, his fingers clamped over his nose, rode slowly through the expanse of stinking corruption. Suddenly he stopped, looking at the tracks that suddenly appeared on the ground. They were the shoed hooves of horses—white men's horses. More markings on the ground showed the prints of booted feet.

Running Wolf joined him. "What do you see, War Heart?"

"Look," War Heart said, pointing. "White men stopped here."

"Many white men," Running Wolf added.

"They stood here and shot the buffalo," War Heart

said. "See the gun flints and the burned paper and cloth?"

"But why would they shoot so many buffalo for nothing?" Running Wolf asked. "They did not kill them all for food or for things to make from the hides and bones. There is no reason for it."

"Maybe the whites think of the buffalo as they do the land," War Heart said. "They do not want the Indians to have any. Let us follow these tracks and see where they came from."

As the hunting party rode slowly to the east, the number of dead animals began to decrease. Finally they reached a point where several ruts were cut deep in the prairie dirt.

"They had rolling boxes with them," War Heart said. "Those are pulled by the long-eared horses. See the hoofprints?"

"When the whites have rolling boxes, that means they carry much food and bullets," Running Wolf said. "Let us find these whites and kill them all. Then we can have their food to take back to the village."

"Don't be a fool!" War heart admonished him. "Can you not see there are many whites? They are more than we number in this hunting party. They would kill us all."

"Are you saying we can do nothing?" Running Wolf said.

"Let us go see the agent Bear Belly," War Heart said.

"I do not want to see that fat man with no scalp!" Running Wolf exclaimed.

"Then, do not come with me," War Heart said. "The treaty we have with the whites says the soldiers must keep other whites off Kiwota land. I will tell him what has happened. The soldiers will fight these hunters."

"They are not hunters!" Running Wolf shouted. "Hunters only kill what they need to eat!"

"No matter," War Heart replied. "Looks Ahead is pledged to keep this thing from happening. If it does, he is pledged to punish the white men who do it. I will tell Bear Belly to have that thing done."

The chief turned his horse and began riding toward the agency. Within moments all the other Kiwotas, including Running Wolf, followed after him.

It took the group an hour to reach the agency. They glanced over at the army fort as they rode past, noting the soldiers engaged in various activities that appeared to be pointless drudgery to the nomadic spirits of the free-roaming Kiwotas.

War Heart slid off his horse's back and handed the reins to White Elk. He strode up to the agency door and stepped inside. The scout Fred Jeffries, purchasing some items, turned and nodded to the Indian.

"Greetings, War Heart," Jeffries said in the Kiwota tongue.

"Night Face, I wish to speak to Bear Belly," War Heart said, referring to Wheeler Coburn.

Jeffries, not having heard the Indians' name for the agent, grinned and looked at Coburn. "War Heart wants to talk to you, Mr. Coburn."

Coburn, entering the scout's purchases into his ledger, frowned. "Tell the son of a bitch to wait 'til I'm finished here." He snorted. "As if he could recognize a man doing real work."

A full five minutes passed before the agent walked over. "What's he want?"

War Heart said to Jeffries, "Tell him we have gone on our first hunt for buffalo. We found many buffalo killed and left to rot. Hardly anything was taken, very few hides, very little meat. They were killed and that was all. We found tracks of white men and their horses.

Also, there are marks from the rolling boxes they use to carry things. This is not supposed to be. The treaty said white men are not supposed to walk on Kiwota land. Our first hunt has failed, and this makes bad medicine for the People."

Jeffries quickly translated, adding, "This is damn serious, Mr. Coburn. The Kiwotas think that bad luck on the first hunt means big trouble for the rest of the year. They're gonna want to get their hands on whoever caused it."

"Fine," Coburn said. "I'll file a report on it."

"You're gonna have to do more'n that," Jeffries warned him. "Things could get ugly. Them Injuns need buffalo for just about ever'thing in their lives. If they think they ain't gonna be able to get more, they'll turn nasty. A report won't do nobody any good."

"Don't you go giving me advice or telling me what to do!" Coburn snapped. "You step outta your place with me, and you'll find yourself in deep trouble. Anyhow, their beef issue is due pretty quick, so them redskins aint' gonna starve to death."

Coburn had no use for the black man. Jeffries didn't conduct himself or even speak like the blacks the agent was used to in his home state. Rather than shuffle like a slave with a hang-dog look in front of white men, Jeffries carried on as his environment and upbringing had dictated. He was independent, and his method of speaking was not the subservient monosyllabic manner of a field hand. The scout had spent most of his childhood and all of his manhood among white men and Indians.

When Jeffries came into the store the first time, Coburn had refused to serve him. Jeffries, having no other source of shopping for necessities, complained to Major Matt Devlin. The fort commander informed the agent that Jeffries was under contract to the United States

Government as a scout and interpreter, and had a right and need to make purchases at the agency store. Afraid making trouble might bring in competition if the army authorized a sutler at Fort Buffalo, Coburn gave in. But he made Jeffries fetch the things he needed off the shelf.

The first time he made up a bill for the black man, he almost doubled the price and was sorely surprised when Jeffries proved his ability to not only read and write, but to work arithmetic as well. It was another skill the scout had acquired growing up with the trader.

"I'm taking War Heart over to Fort Buffalo," Jeffries said.

"You ain't taking him nowhere!" Coburn yelled. "This here is agency business, and I'm the official agent!"

Jeffries said nothing more. He packed his purchases into a cloth bag he'd brought with him and walked out of the store, motioning War Heart to follow him.

The two mounted up without comment to each other and rode the short distance over to Fort Buffalo's headquarters. The other Kiwotas, patient and willing to let the matter take its course, followed without comment.

The sight of the hunting party riding into the middle of the garrison caused some preliminary alarm among the dragoons. But when they noted Jeffries and the fact that the Indians were not arrayed for war, the soldiers relaxed. Those who were able stopped their tasks to watch what was going on.

Jeffries took War Heart into the building to a desk manned by the acting sergeant major. The noncommissioned officer, a pipe-smoking veteran named Edgar O'Rourke who had spent considerable time in the field with Jeffries, gave him a warm greeting.

"How've you been, Fred?" O'Rourke said. "I think

this is the first time I've seen you since that December blizzard."

"Things may not be so good right now, Edgar," Jeffries said. "We may have some trouble with hunters on treaty land. Is Major Devlin in?"

"That he is," O'Rourke said with a serious expression on his face. "Wait a minute." He went to the commander's office door and knocked on it. The sergeant stuck his head inside and exchanged a few inaudible words. Then he came back. "The major says to go in now."

Jeffries and War Heart went into Devlin's office. The Indian found the interior of the building stifling and confining. He wanted to get the business over with as soon as possible.

Jeffries quickly related to the major what had happened. When he finished, he sighed and said, "I was hoping for a quiet summer."

"Damn it!" Devlin said. He looked at War Heart. "I'm upset about this, too. Don't worry, I am going to take immediate action and run those sons of bitches off the Buffalo Steppes."

Jeffries said to War Heart. "Looks Ahead's heart is hot with anger. He will take soldiers and find the hunters and make them leave the treaty land."

"Tell Looks Ahead that our hearts are hot as well," War Heart said. "The buffalo are wasted except for their horns and bones. But we need more than cups and ladles and digging tools and sled runners. We need meat to eat and hides to make robes and lodges and leggings. If we find the white hunters, we will kill them because they have made bad medicine for the People. If it happens again, our young men will be angry and do what they want."

Jeffries didn't bother with a direct translation. He summed up the situation, saying, "Major, the Kiwotas are gonna raise some hell if them hunters ain't stopped. You and I both know that can spill over and the young warriors is gonna ride off the reservation and kill more'n buffalo hunters."

"Do you think War Heart can keep the tribe calmed down, Jeffries?" Devlin asked.

"For a while, maybe," Jeffries said. "I can help some, too. But when this hunting party goes back without news of a kill and tells what they found, the Kiwotas is gonna start grumbling. I'll have a talk with Running Wolf, too. That's the one hothead we got to fret about. He'll prob'ly cool down this time, but remember it'll go just so far."

"Thank God the beef issue is due almost any day," Devlin said. "But I'm still worried." He stood up and went over to take his cap off the rack in the corner. "Tell War Heart I'll be personally taking the patrol out to find those trespassers. I'm asking him to delay any hunting for at least a couple of days."

Jeffries nodded to War Heart. "Looks Ahead is going to lead some soldiers out and find those whites. He wants you to not seek buffalo for two suns."

War Heart smiled. "I will do that because the white hunters will be caught by Looks Ahead. Now my anger cools. The young men will not act crazy."

Jeffries went to the door and opened it. "Major, War Heart figures you can handle the situation, so that's gonna help things." Then he added, "This time."

Devlin walked past them, motioning them to follow. When he reached Sergeant O'Rourke's desk, he said, "My compliments to Captain Teasedale. Have him assemble B Company for an immediate patrol of three days' duration."

O'Rourke quickly got to his feet. "We ain't back to Injun fighting, are we, sir?"

"If things don't go right, we sure as hell will be," Devlin said. He left the building to get himself ready for the field as Jeffries and War Heart joined the waiting Indians.

Chapter 5

Ned Wheatfall took the jug of whiskey and tipped it up. He treated himself to three deep swallows before lowering it and wiping his mouth.

"I'll tell you something, boys," he said to the numerous men sitting around the scattered campfires within the circle of wagons. "There ain't nothing that tastes better'n free whiskey."

A burly fellow called Red-Eye Morgan growled, "Liquor's fine, but how's come we couldn't get no women to come along on this here job, Ned?"

"We cain't have ever'thing, can we?" Wheatfall remarked.

"There's plenty o' damn women who'd work a crew like this," Red-Eye said. "It'd make it easier for a long summer's stay."

"You'll get some chances at squaws," Wheatfall said. "Anyhow, y'all'd end up fighting over some ugly ol' whore after you been out here awhile."

"Only us romantic ones, Ned," Red-Eye said. "Some of us got tender feelings toward women. We kinda work up an affection of one in particular now and then. Why, hell! We don't even beat 'em up more'n once a week or so."

Wheatfall gave the jug to a man named Pockets Dugan. "Pass this around, Pockets."

Pockets was generous with himself as he drank his turn at the jug before passing it to another man. "We shoulda skinned them carcasses. The more we take, the more extry cash money we can end up with. That's what I say. All we took was enough meat to eat."

"We ain't out here for hides," Wheatfall said angrily. "I ain't a-gonna keep reminding you o' that! If we get a chance to skin a few, we'll do it. If I figger it ain't convenient, then we won't." His gray eyes flashed under the heavy brows making his gaunt features almost demonic. "The pay you fellers is getting is to rile Injuns. I told you that when you signed on. So just fergit about lugging a lotta buffalo outta here whether it be the insides or the outsides of 'em."

"There ain't nobody complaining 'cept Pockets," Red-Eye Morgan assured him.

"I ain't bellyaching!" Pockets Dugan retorted. "I was just wondering, that's all. A feller can wonder about something now and again, can't he?"

"Sure!" Wheatfall said. "As long as he keeps it to himself. Now, I don't want to hear nothing else about it."

Pockets got to his feet. "You been showing a big mouth lately, Wheatfall. And I'm growing weary of it. A feller's got a right to speak his mind."

"Not in my crew, he ain't!" Wheatfall said. The gang leader, skinny as a rail, sized up the other man. Although the potential challenger was much larger, Wheatfall felt no fear. "You got some muscles on your ass, Pockets, but I'm the fastest knife man on either side o' the Mississippi River. You want to bring this to a head?"

Pockets Dugan glared at him. He knew he could pick up Wheatfall and break him like a dried tree branch. But he would have to kill him, because Ned Wheatfall would get the knife into him someday for it."

Wheatfall sneered. "Well?"

Pockets calmed down and showed a lopsided grin. "Hell, I'm making good money anyhow. I ain't got no complaints." He sat down and went back to stirring the pot on his fire to show the situation was over as far as he was concerned.

Wheatfall surveyed the crowd for any more potential trouble before squatting down to tend to his pot of boiling stew. It had taken him several long months to round up that crew of frontier rabble-rousers. Most had been living rustic, but comfortable lives in hunting camps and outlying settlements, getting along by living off the land. Others, who had wandered into civilization, had been worse off. Because of their lack of marketable skills or trades, they could not earn decent livings. This situation forced them to settle into the roughest parts of towns and cities, outcasts from normal society where they never could fit in. Wheatfall had located half of these in local jails and lockups awaiting trial for various offenses involving disturbing the peace.

But his persistence, and Senator Osmond Torrance's money, had resulted in the organization of a crowd of some of the roughest men who ever sallied out from civilization and society's demands of decorum to seek their fortunes in the wild, unsettled lands of the West.

Red-Eye Morgan joined Wheatfall at his fire. He sat down and pulled a flaming splinter of wood out to light his pipe. "How long you reckon we'll be out here, Ned?"

"All summer," Wheatfall answered. "That's something else y'all been told."

"I know," Red-Eye said. He gestured at the others. "There's more'n fifty of us in this outfit, Ned. Somebody's paying out a lot o' money to keep us all here all that time."

"What're you leading up to?" Wheatfall asked.

"I ain't stupid," Red-Eye said. "There's got to be one hell of a good reason fer taking on all that expense."

Wheatfall stared into the fire. "Now, don't you start getting nosey, Red-Eye. It ain't healthy."

"Hell, Ned, I ain't nosey," Red-Eye said. "I just figger that if there's a chance for more work, I'd like to stay on. Get my drift?"

"Sure," Wheatfall said. "I'll keep that in mind, but let me tell you something. I don't know the full story myself, and I don't figger to until the right time—if ever."

Their conversation was interrupted when a scuffle broke out between a couple of the hunters. It was one of those quick, violent episodes that frequently occurred between that sort of men. After exchanging some punches and kicks, they had gone to their knives and now moved warily around in a circle, making feints at each other.

Ned Wheatfall knew that both would end up badly hurt if not dead. One way or the other it meant the loss of two men. He strode over and spoke loudly, "I'll have no damn knife fighting! Both o' you pull back."

The combatants still went on with their testing, their eyes glaring at each other in anticipation of an attack.

Wheatfall pulled his own knife. "I'm telling you to stop and step back and put them blades away. I mean it!"

One of them, a short, bandy-legged little man named Dan Lilly, did as he was told. He slipped his knife into its scabbard. The other fighter suddenly lunged at him, slashing out with a downward movement of his arm.

Wheatfall reacted quickly, flipping his own knife

which turned only once before sinking up to the hilt in the man's neck.

The victim gurgled in frightened surprise, grabbing at the thing that was now lodged so deep in his neck that it stuck through his throat, blocking off the air he tried to breathe into his heaving lungs. He whirled and stumbled, falling to his knees in weakness as his strength drained away with the pumping of his lifeblood that soaked his shirtfront down to the waist. Finally, in desperation, he gestured to the watching crowd for some kind of help.

He never got any.

Ned walked over to what was now a corpse and withdrew his knife. "Y'all know there ain't gonna be nothing but fistfighting tolerated in this outfit. Anybody that pulls a gun or a knife on anybody else is dead. Understand?"

"He started it, Ned!" Dan Lilly exclaimed, defending himself.

"I ain't faulting you, Dan," Wheatfall assured him. "What the hell was the ruckus about anyhow?"

"He took one o' my blankets," Lilly said. "He was the only one who coulda done it."

Pockets Dugan said, "Are you talking about the red one with the black stripe?"

"That's the one," Lilly said, kicking the corpse. "This son of a bitch stole it from me."

"No, he didn't, you dumb bastard," Pockets said. "You traded it to me for that Sioux medicine pouch, remember?"

Lilly thought a moment, then slowly grinned. "Oh, yeah! That's right. I forgot."

The crowd broke out into loud laughter at what they considered the humor in the situation. Lilly took some ribbing, and his face reddened in embarrassment.

"Hey!" The shout came from the edge of the camp

from a man named Early Denmore, who had gone out to relieve himself. "Looky yonder! Soldiers!"

All the hunters gave their full attention to the prairie outside their camp. Quick glances around showed they were completely surrounded by a large number of blue-clad horse dragoons still about a hundred yards away. The troops, with carbines at the ready, slowly approached.

"Y'all keep your mouths shut!" Wheatfall cautioned them. "Pockets, you and Dan drag that dead son of a bitch outta sight afore they ride in here. Hide him under one o' the wagons and pile some stuff on him. I don't want to have to explain nothing to no damn army officer."

When the soldiers arrived, most stayed on the other side of the wagons. But two officers, with ten men following, came in through the opening between two wagons.

"Who is in charge here?" Major Matt Devlin, in the lead, asked.

Ned Wheatfall walked up. "That'd be me, Major. Howdy do to you."

"What's your name, mister?" Devlin asked.

"Ned Wheatfall," he answered. "What's yours?"

The hunters all laughed.

Devlin's expression was one of cold anger. "You and these friends of yours are on Indian Land. Are you aware of that?"

"By God!" Wheatfall said, feigning surprise. "I didn't see no signs when we come in here to do some buffalo hunting."

"I'm ordering you out of here immediately," Devlin said.

"That don't make no sense," Wheatfall protested.

"I'm not interested in explaining things to you," Devlin said. "I'm ordering you out of here."

"Well, Major, I was in the army myself," Wheatfall said. "Five years and didn't get no bobtail discharge neither. I ended up a sergeant. But I ain't a soldier no more, so I got no inclination to take shit off some officer."

"If you served in the army, you know how much authority I have in a situation like this," Devlin said. "I am going to tell you again, get the hell off this reservation. That means you have to get on the east side of the Des Lacs River."

"What if we want to go north?" Wheatfall asked. "Or south or west?"

"You will go east," Devlin said in a cold, angry voice. "That's the shortest distance to the reservation boundary."

"We'd like to finish our grub," Wheatfall said. He pointed to some uncooked buffalo meat on the tailgate of one of the wagons. "We should have her et up in three or four days."

Devlin motioned to Captain Paul Teasedale. "Put your men to work, Paul."

"Yes, sir," Teasedale said. He gestured to his senior noncommissioned officer. "You know what to do, Sergeant Kennedy."

"Yes, sir!" the dragoon answered. "Get to it, lads! Don't waste no time!"

The soldiers immediately dismounted and began kicking over pots of food. A couple took the meat and threw it on the nearest fire. Pockets Dugan made a move toward the soldiers, but Devlin pulled his revolver and aimed it at the man.

"Stand fast, mister!"

Pockets stopped and instinctively raised his hands. "I ain't gonna do nothing."

Devlin rode closer to Wheatfall. "I'll not bother the food in your wagons unless I have more trouble from you or your men. Now, as I said before, you are to vacate this area immediately. That means now, goddamn you!"

"Yes, sir," Wheatfall said. He walked over to his own gear and began loading it onto a wagon. Senator Torrance had told him what to do in case of confrontation with the army. "Let's go, boys!" he hollered. "The major's right. We got to get out of here."

"And you'll not return!" Devlin snapped.

Wheatfall said nothing. His men, also remaining silent, quickly went about the chore of packing up.

"Hold it!" Devlin said. The corpse under the wagon had become exposed. "Who is that?"

"One of the fellers took sick and died," Wheatfall said. "We'll leave him here."

Devlin rode over and saw the gaping wound in the dead man's neck. "He's been murdered."

Wheatfall looked at the body and feigned surprise at the injury. Then, knowing he couldn't get away with a lie, the gang leader grinned. "Well, it was a fair fight. We got lots o' witnesses."

"Bury him," Devlin ordered.

"We ain't got any shovels," Wheatfall protested.

"Then, you'll dig a grave with your bare hands," Devlin said.

Wheatfall snapped his fingers. "Oh, yeah! I just remembered. We got some shovels in that wagon over there."

"Get to work," Devlin said.

"Are you gonna say some words over our poor departed brother?" Wheatfall asked.

"Just put that piece of shit into the ground," Devlin said. "Now!"

"You're a cold man, Major," Wheatfall said.

He quickly picked out a couple of men, and the grave digging began. Within a short time, the corpse was buried and the hunters went back to packing up. The experienced frontiersmen had their camp completely broken down and ready to move within a quarter of an hour. Drivers got up into the wagon seats while the remainder of the men mounted up.

"Move out!" Wheatfall yelled.

Major Matt Devlin and Captain Paul Teasedale watched the group slowly move away toward the east.

"Send a section to escort them, Paul," Devlin said. "Have the men follow them until they're on the other side of the Des Lacs River."

"Yes, sir," Teasedale said.

He set the order into motion, and a couple dozen dragoons headed out under the command of Sergeant Kennedy.

The rest of the troops fell back into column formation to begin the return to Fort Buffalo. The orange and white guidon of Company B whipped in the breeze as the dragoons cantered across the prairie. Equipment slapped in time to the pounding of the horses' hooves in the formation of blue and yellow. The martial scene seemed out of place in the stark beauty of the untamed prairie country.

They arrived at the garrison in time to dismount and properly restore their horses to the post stables before falling in for retreat formation which would mark the end of the duty day. Since Devlin and Teasedale were not properly attired for the ceremony, Captain Bernie Blanchard of A Company took charge. After the final bugle call and firing of the post's small cannon, Devlin went directly back to his quarters.

His wife, Beth, was waiting for him, and she didn't have good news. "Freddie got into trouble yesterday," she announced in a terse voice.

"I don't know who's worse," Devlin said. "Illegal

buffalo hunters or my oldest son." He sighed. "What did he do?"

"Private Kubelsky brought him home yesterday," Beth said. "I've kept him in the house ever since."

"Just tell me what he did this time," Devlin said testily.

"The commissary sergeant caught him stealing hardtack crackers and jam from the storeroom," Beth said.

"Now, why would he do that?" Devlin asked.

"I did not discuss the matter with him," Beth said.

"How many children were with him in this mischief?" Devlin inquired.

"Apparently he didn't see fit to bring any of the other kids in on this particular prank," Beth said.

"Where are our darling offspring?" Devlin asked.

"Mattie and Tommy are out playing," Beth answered. "Freddie is back in the children's room."

"How much hardtack and jam did he take?" Devlin asked.

"Not very much," Beth said. "Private Kubelsky said the sergeant only reported it because you had issued orders stating you wanted to know about any misbehavior that involved the boy."

Devlin hung his cap and pistol-and-saber belt on the rack in the corner of the living room. He strode through the house and stepped into the children's bedroom.

Twelve-year-old Freddie Devlin, who had heard his father's entrance, stood waiting for the worst. "Hello, Papa."

Devlin was not the type of army officer or father to waste time. "Whatever made you want to steal hardtack crackers and jam from the commissary?"

"I got 'em for my friend, sir," Freddie answered.

"What friend?" Devlin asked. "Who would want hardtack crackers to begin with?"

"His name is Swift Rabbit, and he gimme something to eat; so I had to go and get him something," Freddie said.

"An Indian boy?" Devlin asked.

"Yes, sir," Freddie said. "I asked Mama for something, but she tole me to leave her alone. It's her fault!"

"It is not your mother's fault!" Devlin shouted. He calmed down. "I'm not so sure I want you hanging around with those Indian children. They have lice."

"I don't think so, Papa," Freddie said. "They don't scratch their heads much."

"That's not important now," Devlin said.

"Sergeant Dawson's kids have got lice," Freddie said.

"I don't know a thing about the sergeant's family, but I am certain those Indians have lice," Devlin said. "What did what's-his-name give you to eat?"

"His name is Swift Rabbit," Freddie said. "He calls me Fox."

"Never mind," Devlin said. "What did he give you to eat?"

"Dog meat," Freddie said.

Devlin swallowed. "You ate a dog?"

"Not a whole one," Freddie answered. "Just part of a hind leg. I never ate a dog before. I've petted 'em and played with 'em, but I don't think I ever ate one. So after Swift Rabbit gimme some, I had to get him something to eat. Mama wouldn't give me nothing, so I had to get something, so I knew where there was that hardtack in the commissary and I found some jam and I only took a jar and that seemed a pretty fair swap for dog. Nobody even seen me take the stuff."

"Oh, you're very mistaken about that, young man," Devlin said. "The commissary sergeant saw you run off with the stuff and told Private Kubelsky."

65

"There was lots o' jam in the commissary, and hardtack, too," Freddie said.

"That doesn't matter," Devlin said. "The food in there is for the soldiers. It didn't belong to you. You stole it, Freddie."

"No, I didn't! I swapped it for dog!" Freddie insisted.

"If you take something that doesn't belong to you, it is stealing," Devlin said. "I don't care if you swap it for dog meat or keep it. We whip soldiers for stealing."

"I get whipped for just about ever'thing I do," Freddie said, unimpressed.

"I think that the next time there is a flogging, I am going to let you watch," Devlin said. "Then you'll know what a real whipping is." He undid his belt and pulled it from the loops in his trousers.

Freddie, knowing the routine from plenty of experience, turned around to receive his just due. Devlin laid on three good ones, pleased to note that the boy did not utter a sound.

"Now what do you say?" Devlin asked as he replaced the belt.

"I'm sorry, Papa," Freddie said, rubbing his behind.

Before either could speak again, a hard knocking at the front door could be heard.

"You stay in your room, boy," Devlin said. "And no supper for you tonight."

The major walked through the house and reached the living room in time to see his wife standing at the open front door with the commissary sergeant.

"What can I do for you, Sergeant Harrigan?" Devlin asked. "If it's about that hardtack and jam, I've already been informed and have punished my son."

"It ain't about that, sir," Harrigan said. "It's about

the issue o' beef that come in while you was out on patrol."

"It arrived, did it not?" Devlin asked.

"Yes, sir, and right on time," Harrigan said. "The problem is that it is short."

"Short?" Devlin asked with a groan. "How short, Sergeant?"

"By half, sir," the sergeant said. "There ain't but a hundred head. Between that and them slaughtered buffalo, them Kiwotas is gonna be real upset."

Devlin fetched his cap and pistol-and-sword belt. "This is going to be one hell of a summer," he said under his breath.

Beth asked, "Shall I wait supper, Matt?"

"No," he answered. "Go find Mattie and Tommy and get them in the house. I'm going to pass the word that everyone at Fort Buffalo is confined to the post."

"Is it that bad?" Beth asked with a worried expression.

"Yes, and bound to get worse," Devlin said, walking out of the house to join Sergeant Harrigan for a quick walk over to the agency.

Chapter 6

When Devlin arrived at the agency he found a large group of agitated Indians milling around in front of the place. Because no warrior, not even War Heart, had seen fit to step forward as a speaker, the Kiwotas seemed confused and uncertain of themselves. Dealing with whites had always been confusing. An honest Indian never knew if he was being lied to, swindled, or being spoken to in a genuine, truthful manner.

But, in spite of this lack of cohesiveness and full knowledge of the situation, their anger was intense, even if not directed, and that irritation was punctuated with numerous shouts and gestures at the agency building.

The major pushed his way through the crowd which quickly quieted down when his presence was noted. Even though the man they called Looks Ahead had been a bitter enemy, there was respect and some trust for him among certain members of the tribe.

War Heart and the army officer momentarily exchanged glances, but neither spoke. Devlin turned his attention to the building. He saw that the door was closed. He tried to open it, but the heavy portal was locked. The major pounded on it.

"Get the hell away from here you Injun son of a

bitches!" Wheeler Coburn yelled in a shrill voice from within the shelter of the building. "I'll have the goddamned army kill ever' one o' you! Go away!"

"Coburn!" Devlin hollered. "It's me. Major Devlin."

"It's about goddamn time!" The sound of the bar being removed could be heard. He pulled the heavy door open and peeked out. "Where's the troops?"

"Never mind about the troops," Devlin said, pushing his way inside.

"You mean you come over here all by your lonesome?" Coburn asked in a nervous voice.

"Let's take a look at what's going on before we call out any of my dragoons," Devlin said.

Coburn quickly closed the door and replaced the bar. "Them Injuns is madder'n hell about the beef issue. It ain't my fault!"

"I heard only half the cattle showed up," Devlin said. He noticed a group of men sitting in a dark corner of the agency store. "Who are they?"

"Them's the drovers that brung the herd over from Minnesota," Coburn said.

"What happened to the rest of the cattle?" Devlin angrily demanded to know.

One of the men got up and walked over. "Don't you go yelling at me, soldier-boy," he growled.

"You call me soldier-boy one more time and I'll take you outside and feed you to those Indians," Devlin said. "Answer me, damn your eyes! Where are the rest of those cattle?"

The man involuntarily stepped back from the officer's rage. "Hang on now, mister. I'm as upset as you are. We picked up that herd at Fort Snelling and signed fer a hunnerd head. That's all they was, and that's all I got." He fumbled in his pockets and produced the receipt, handing it to Devlin. "The first thing

I know when I deliver 'em is that there's a tribe o' crazy redskins want me and my boys' scalps."

Devlin examined the document, then returned it. "You're right. All Fort Snelling issued was a hundred beeves."

"I sent for Jeffries," Coburn said.

"I'll bet you'll be glad to have him around for a change, won't you?" Devlin asked.

"He's the onliest one that can speak to them goddamned Injuns," Coburn said sullenly.

Devlin nodded. "Well, we'll need him, that's for sure." He turned to the drover chief. "What's your name?"

"Connors," he answered. "Who're you, mister?"

"I'm Major Devlin, Mr. Connors," the army officer replied. "You, like us, have found yourself in a most unpleasant situation in which none of us have the blame. Somebody made a mistake and sent only half the cattle needed."

"Oh, shit!" Connors said. "If'n I'd knowed that, I wouldn't have even come over here. I never liked dealing with that Injun Bureau! They ain't dependable all that much, and the money I'm making ain't worth my ass."

A knock at the door sounded. "It's me Jeffries. You better let me in."

Devlin opened the door, allowing the scout to enter. "Only half the cattle arrived for the spring issue."

"That's what the Kiwotas told me," Jeffries said. "They ain't much on counting, but it's easy enough for 'em to tell that they're being shorted bad."

"I'm going to file a report," Coburn said.

"That should help a lot," Devlin said sarcastically.

Jeffries continued. "Between this and those slaughtered buffalo, things could go real bad for the tribe. I don't blame 'em for being madder'n hell."

"Let's go out and talk to them," Devlin said.

"Good idea," Jeffries said.

"Are you two crazy?" Coburn demanded to know. "Them Injuns'll scalp you and burn you at the stake! You better go get some soldiers damn quick."

"A show of force is the last thing we need right now," Devlin said. "Come on, Mr. Jeffries. You, too, Coburn."

"I ain't going out there!" Coburn exclaimed.

"I don't blame you none," Connors said. He went back and joined his men in the dark corner.

Devlin didn't want to waste any more time. He and Jeffries undid the door and stepped outside.

"Listen to me!" the major yelled.

"Looks Ahead would speak to you," Jeffries translated. "Listen to what he has to say."

War Heart, Running Wolf, and White Elk stood in the front. They gave no commands, but when they quieted down and gave their full attention to the white man and the black man standing in front of them, the other Indians did likewise.

Speaking through Jeffries, Devlin said, "You have all seen that not all the cattle have arrived. You grow angry, and I do not blame you. But, I say this to you, the rest will be here soon. I do not know why, but the Great White Father did not send them all at once. Perhaps he had trouble finding as many as he wanted. But he sent what he had so you could at least have a few. When he finds the rest he will send them to you."

War Heart responded, saying, "We must have all the cattle or we will know hunger. It is folly to know hunger in the summer. But the white men killed many buffalo and scared other herds away. All we have are these cows brought to us. These are not enough. We must have the others to get by until more buffalo come onto Kiwota land." He scowled and looked directly into Devlin's face. "Looks Ahead, we agreed not to leave the reservation. But the men of the People will not let their families starve."

"I will see to this problem," Devlin said. He knew that even if any of the warriors left the Buffalo Steppes with only hunting on their minds, other trouble could easily develop if they made contact with whites. "It will take a while."

Running Wolf sneered, "How long is that to be, Looks Ahead?"

"I will be as fast as I can," Devlin promised.

"When I see the first hungry child, I will leave this cursed reservation and take what I want where I want when I want anyway that I want," Running Wolf said. "I have said this now."

"All the young men will be angry," War Heart said. He did not make the statement as a threat, only as a fact.

"You have promised to stay on the reservation," Devlin reminded him.

"You have promised to give us enough cattle to eat and to keep whites off Kiwota land," War Heart replied, also making a reminder.

"We have no reason to be angry with each other," Devlin said. "Do you not see that I come alone? I did not bring soldiers. There is no reason to fight. Enough cattle will be given to you."

"We will take what is here," War Heart said. "These will not last long before they are eaten. I do not think it is a good idea to keep talking about this."

He abruptly walked away toward the cattle, taking the other Kiwotas with him. Wheeler Coburn emerged from the trading post with the drovers behind him.

"Well, that calmed 'em down," Coburn said.

Connors gestured to his men to get back to their horses. "Mount up, boys, we're gonna skeddadle outta here afore our hair is hanging on some lodgepole." He nodded to Devlin. "I'll tell you something, Major. There ain't no cattle of any kind back at Snelling. I don't know how'n hell you're gonna get any more for these Injuns."

"All I can do is try," Devlin said.

Connors shrugged. "Well, goodbye and good luck. You army folks and that Injun Bureau can take your jobs and send 'em to hell as far as I'm concerned. You ain't gonna see me or my boys around here no more."

Jeffries watched the drovers make a hasty exit. He shook his head, "I hope you got some kinda plan, Major."

"I'll have to dispatch a rider back to Fort Snelling with a message," Devlin said. "Meanwhile, I'm going to have to put our garrison on alert. You and your wife might want to stay at Fort Buffalo for a spell. We have an empty house on soapsuds row."

"I'll take your advice and come in," Jeffries said. "But no thanks on that empty house. It wouldn't be as comfortable as our soddie, anyhow. Me and the woman can set up a tepee since it's summer."

"What about me?" Coburn asked.

"You're right next to the fort," Devlin pointed out.

"I'd rather be right *in* the fort," Coburn said.

"There's no walls around the garrison, Coburn," Devlin said. "You're probably as well off here as there."

"I'd feel better over at Fort Buffalo," Coburn insisted.

"In that case, you're welcome to that house I told Jeffries about," Devlin said.

"I ain't living down there with them soldiers," Coburn said. "Ain't you got nothing on officers' row?"

"Sorry," Devlin said. "Filled up."

Coburn sighed. "I'll take my chance for a few weeks, anyhow. Maybe the rest o' them cattle will show up."

The sound of the Kiwotas and the half herd leaving the agency interrupted the three men. They watched as the sullen Indians drove the beef issue toward the present site of their village.

"It will be dark in another hour," Devlin said. "I have a lot to tend to." He bid the other two a goodbye and walked back toward the garrison area.

Jeffries mounted up and rode off to gather up his wife and a few belongings. Coburn reluctantly returned to the agency trading store, but he once again barred the door.

When Devlin arrived at headquarters he set the soldiers in the building to work. The duty bugler was given orders to sound Officers Call. The charge of quarters, a bored corporal glad to have something to do rather than just sit around until the next day's duty began, was sent to fetch Acting Sergeant Major O'Rourke. The sergeant of the guard responded to orders to turn the guard out for a quick inspection, and all garrison prisoners were ordered released and returned to their companies.

By the time Devlin settled down at his desk with a hot pot of coffee on the stove brewed by Private Tommy Kubelsky, the other officers—two captains and four lieutenants—presented themselves in response to Officers Call. Kubelsky made sure everyone had a cup of his famous strong brew. When Sergeant O'Rourke reported in, he was told to waste no time in arranging for a dispatch rider to head for Fort Snelling without delay.

Devlin personally penned a report on the situation with the beef issue and requested either additional troops or the other half of the cattle. He had just completed the missive when the dispatch rider reported for duty.

"Take this and go like hell for Snelling," Devlin said. "There's a full moon to help you across the open prairie. When you've crossed the Des Lacs River, you can pick up on Stensland Trail down to Olson Road. From that point on, it will be easy riding to the fort."

"Yes, sir," the dragoon said cheerfully. "I've done it a coupla times before in the daylight, so I don't reckon I'll have any trouble on a bright night."

"This is damned urgent, soldier," Devlin said. "When you report into headquarters, I want you to repeat that to the first officer you see. I don't care if it's the departmental commander himself!"

"Yes, sir!" the rider replied. "This is damned urgent, says the major. That's what I'll tell him, sir."

"Right," Devlin said. He put the message in a brown envelope and sealed it. After writing the word URGENT across the front and signing his name, he handed it over. "Go like hell."

"Yes, sir!"

After the dragoon left, Devlin gave his attention to his officers. He explained the shortage of the beef issue and how, along with the slaughter of the buffalo herd, the Kiwotas faced some difficult times in the coming weeks.

He finished his summation by saying, "Gentlemen, we could very well be on the brink of another war with the Kiwotas."

Captain Blanchard, the Louisianian, shrugged. "Then, we'll whip them again."

"Yes, we will," Devlin said. "Any future conflict with the tribe is going to mean they'll range out farther than ever before. That means more innocent settlers being killed than in the past. I am hoping to work out this situation to avoid any kind of bloodshed."

"Do you have any idea of what happened to those cattle?" Captain Paul Teasedale asked.

"I'm at a complete loss," Devlin said. "The drover who brought them over from Fort Snelling said that he picked up all they had over there. He said there were no more. He even had a receipt to substantiate his statement. I can just hope that the commissary officer did not receive the full issue himself, and will have the remainder shortly."

Blanchard shook his head. "Well, if he doesn't—" He let the statement hang.

"Right," Devlin said. "I want this post to go on a full alert. That means fifty percent of all men to be under arms and ready for action twenty-four hours a day. It will be rough on the men, but I'm sure they will appreciate the situation once it is explained to them."

"Are carbines and pistols to be kept loaded?" Lieutenant Standish, a young subaltern in A Company, wanted to know.

"Most assuredly," Devlin asked.

"What about mounts, sir?" another lieutenant asked.

"They must be kept in good shape and well-fed at all times," Devlin replied. "It may be necessary to go to the field for a prolonged period. The animals belonging to men under arms on duty will be saddled and ready for immediate action."

Sergeant O'Rourke, at the back of the crowd, raised his hand. "What about the families, sir?"

"Everyone is confined to the interior of the post," Devlin told him. "I don't even want the women to go over to the agency trading post for shopping except in groups and with a proper escort under arms."

"I'll pass the word, sir," O'Rourke said.

"That's it, gentlemen," Devlin said. "Call your

noncommissioned officers together and set things in motion immediately. You're dismissed." He stood up. "If anyone needs me, I'll be in my quarters having supper. Between my eldest son's antics and shortage of beef issues to the Indians, I'm not getting much time to eat."

Devlin took their salutes, then followed them from the building. As the officers headed for their companies, he walked rapidly to his house. He also had to let Beth know what was going on. As the commanding officer's wife, she had responsibilities of her own where the other wives and their children were concerned.

When Devlin arrived home, Beth greeted him and took him into the dining room. As the post commander and his family, only they enjoyed that extra room in their larger quarters. Mary Harrigan, the oldest daughter of the commissary sergeant, worked part-time as a maid and helper in the Devlin house. She served the major his supper and listened intently as Devlin explained the situation to Beth.

"I'll see that the other ladies hear about it," Beth said. "I'm sure Mary will help me."

"Yes, ma'am," the girl of fifteen replied. "I'll let 'em know down on soapsuds row what's going on. We've been through this before, including a couple of actual attacks. Remember?"

"That's right," Devlin said. "I keep forgetting that many of the soldier's wives and children are also veterans." He remembered Freddie, in his room without his supper. "Mary, fetch Freddie for me, will you?"

Mary laughed. "Y'know, my pa thinks it's funny about him taking that hardtack and jam."

"Freddie doesn't," Devlin said.

When Freddie came out of his room, he stood by the table. "Yes, sir?"

"Do you think you've learned your lesson about taking things that don't belong to you?" Devlin asked.

"Oh, yes, Papa," Freddie said.

"Then, sit down and have some supper with me," Devlin said.

"Yes, Papa!"

Mary served the younger Devlin as Beth joined them to have a cup of coffee. Meanwhile, a flurry of activity swept through the barracks and soapsuds row as irritated sergeants and corporals put the fifty percent duty and guard rosters into effect.

Over at the Kiwota village, the people sat in silence, mulling over their bad luck. The only hope they had was that Looks Ahead would bring the rest of the cattle, and that another herd of buffalo would come onto the reservation.

If that didn't happen, a few warriors, like Running wolf, knew exactly what they would do about it.

Chapter 7

An uneasy, demanding routine fell over Fort Buffalo. The troops, spending as much time on duty as off, became sullen and lethargic. They responded to bugle calls and the orders of the officers and noncommissioned officers in a slow, resentful manner.

The activity in the garrison was a constant twenty-four-hour cycle. The monotony, increased by the lack of decent recreational activities, complicated what had been a standing problem in the underpaid, overworked frontier army.

Because of the good weather, a half-dozen dragoons were able to desert during the second week following Major Matt Devlin's orders for full alert. This even included a sergeant from B Company. In spite of the the extra security, they escaped easily, leaving at night and reaching safety on the east side of the Des Lacs River by dawn. From that point on, they continued toward civilization, where they could return to their former lives and melt back into the civilian population. Unable to spare troops to chase after the deserters, Devlin could only hope that no more men snuck away from his command.

When a reply finally came back from Devlin's dispatch to Fort Snelling, it wasn't what he expected or wanted. The rider, rather than carrying a message explaining the shortage of the beef issue and a promise to remedy it, returned in the company of a major from the department commander's staff. An escort of a dozen troopers from another dragoon regiment rode with them.

The major, a stout fellow on detached duty from the infantry, was named Harold Pendergrass. He was a blustering, sullen officer who was obviously unhappy with having to leave Minnesota and visit the wilds of the Buffalo Steppes. The nature of his business with Matt Devlin did not serve to improve his disposition.

Trouble started immediately after Pendergrass's introduction to Major Devlin. Pendergrass refused to be quartered in the tent set up for visitors. He insisted on having regular officers' quarters during his week's stay at Fort Buffalo. That meant that young Lieutenant Emil Standish of A Company, as the subaltern with the least seniority, had to move out of his quarters and stay in the tent. Pendergrass was the type of officer with long years of service who would insist on every privilege and right due him by his rank. He did, however, permit the lieutenant to leave the bulk of his possessions behind.

The situation didn't improve much the next day when Pendergrass had a meeting with Devlin in his office. The visitor came straight to the point:

"A rather serious situation has arisen concerning you, Major Devlin," Pendergrass said as he settled down in front of Devlin's desk.

"In the light of the mood of the Kiwota tribe, I hope it concerns those missing beef cattle," Devlin said.

"No," Pendergrass replied, shaking his head. "A member of the senate, the Right Honorable Osmond Torrance, has lodged a complaint against you concerning one of his constituents. It is a situation the departmental commander is taking very seriously."

Devlin frowned in irritation. "What in the hell are you talking about, Pendergrass?"

Pendergrass's eyes flashed. "Your date of rank, sir!"

Devlin answered, "August of fifty-one."

"Mine is December of forty-nine," Pendergrass said. "Have you any brevets?"

"I do not," Devlin replied.

"Then, I outrank you," Pendergrass said. "As a senior officer, I protest your addressing me by my last name alone. I must insist that my rank be included when you speak to me."

"As you wish, Major Pendergrass," Devlin said. "In which case I will insist on the same courtesy as a matter of protocol. Now! Please get on with what you have to say about this complaint."

Pendergrass, who had a leather dispatch pouch with him, opened it up and fished out a document. "According to this, you conducted yourself in a—" he unfolded the paper and refreshed his memory—"most insulting and arrogant manner in dealing with a certain Mr. Ned Wheatfall."

"Wheatfall?" Devlin asked. "The buffalo hunter?"

"He is not a buffalo hunter, Major," Pendergrass said. "He is an employee of the U.S. Government working for the Indian Bureau. As a matter of fact, he has been appointed as an assistant to the Buffalo Reservation agent Mr. Wheeler Coburn.'

"He said nothing of that when I found him out on the prairie," Devlin said.

"He insisted that he did," Pendergrass said. "In fact, Mr. Wheatfall was very emphatic in asserting that he told you he was the recently appointed assistant agent at the Buffalo Steppes Reservation. Naturally, as

I said before, the departmental commander is very upset about this. It reflects badly on the army."

Devlin was so angry that he leaped to his feet. "That son of a bitch and his men slaughtered approximately a thousand buffalo out on land given to the Kiwota Indians per a bona fide, legal treaty. Their presence in the area was illegal, unlawful, immoral, and dangerous when it comes to maintaining peace in this area. To further make their presence undesirable, one of their number had even been murdered by another of the group."

"Did you investigate the crime, Major Devlin?" Pendergrass inquired.

"That would have been useless among that pack of liars," Devlin said. "Furthermore, when I ordered Wheatfall and his men off the reservation, he obeyed me in a sullen, hesitant manner that not only insulted me, but also the United States Army. And, I say again! He *did not* identify himself as an employee of the Indian Bureau!"

"That does not make sense, Major Devlin," Pendergrass said. "Why would he keep such important information to himself under those circumstances?"

"Do I sense a doubting tone in your voice, Major Pendergrass?" Devlin asked, sitting back down. "Are you suggesting I am a liar?"

"I would not use that strong a term," Pendergrass said. "I respect you as a fellow officer, Major Devlin. Perhaps you missed or even forgot him identifying himself in the heat of the moment."

"I am neither stupid nor deaf," Devlin said. "On the other hand, why would an assistant Indian agent have fifty men with him?"

"It was an organized excursion, put together by Mr. Wheatfall at the request of Senator Torrance," Pendergrass answered.

"Those men out there were the worst sort of riffraff on the frontier," Devlin said. "I cannot believe they are friends and acquaintances of a United States senator who had them entertained with a hunting trip out west."

"I will not argue about this," Pendergrass said. "The departmental commander wants you to apologize to Mr. Wheatfall when he arrives here."

"Here?" Devlin asked. "That fellow Wheatfall is coming *here* to Fort Buffalo?"

"Well, to the Buffalo Steppes Agency, of course. Where else would he situate himself?" Pendergrass said. "You'll have to make that a public apology by order of the departmental commander."

"What!" Devlin exclaimed.

"That is a direct, legal order to you from a superior officer who is your commander in the Department of the Dakotas," Pendergrass added. "He feels so strongly about this that he dispatched me personally to deliver the order and witness it being carried out."

Devlin knew he could not refuse, short of resigning his commission in the army. "I shall obey, of course."

"The army does not need trouble with any members of the senate," Pendergrass said. "Remember, they represent the American people and provide the funding so necessary for military operations. There is another matter involving policy. The department commander has sent a written order to you. One moment please." Another search of the pouch ensued. "Here it is, Major Devlin."

Devlin took the order and read it. "So, I am not supposed to take any action at the Buffalo Steppes Reservation without direct authority from Mr. Wheeler Coburn, the chief agent, or his assistant, Mr. Ned Wheatfall."

"I'm glad you understand, Major," Pendergrass said.

Devlin seethed for a moment more, than asked, "What about the issue of the shortage of the cattle?"

"We have investigated the matter," Pendergrass said. "The Indian Bureau informed us that the correct amount of cattle were shipped. That would be a total of—" He went to the pouch again, fishing around for another document. When he found it, the major checked the information. "one hundred head per the treaty signed last fall."

"The treaty says *two* hundred head," Devlin said. "I know that for a fact because I was there at the pow-wow and I helped establish that number based on the population of the Kiwota tribe."

"I believe we'll have to let Mr. Wheeler Coburn follow up on that particular situation," Pendergrass said. "I must point out it is not army business."

"It will damned well be army business if the Kiwotas go on the warpath again," Devlin said.

"I agree a hundred percent on that one, Major," Pendergrass said.

"As it is, I am keeping a full alert in effect on this post," Devlin said. "Fifty percent of the men are under arms at any time in each twenty-four-hour period."

"I shall make a note of that in my report," Pendergrass said. "It will reflect favorably on you, Major. I may have sounded harsh in delivering these messages and orders, but your reputation as an able field officer is well-appreciated back at Fort Snelling."

"You're submitting a formal report on this?" Devlin asked. "A written one?"

"You would be surprised if I didn't, wouldn't you?" Pendergrass asked.

"I suppose," Devlin conceded. He sighed, asking, "Is there any other business?"

"We received information regarding the escape of six deserters from Fort Buffalo," Pendergrass asked. "The departmental commander wants a further report on what you are doing to prevent such occurrences in the future."

"Major Pendergrass," Devlin said, holding on to his temper. "There is not one goddamned single thing I can do. That senate we are so mighty eager to please might help if they saw fit to raise the pay of soldiers and noncommissioned officers, improved their food, saw to it that the clothing and equipment issued them were serviceable and of decent quality, and perhaps showed consideration in pensions to disabled or sick men who have served long and faithfully. I have a private in my command who is crippled up from rheumatism but will get no monetary compensation in spite of the fact he acquired the disease from long spells of unpleasant duty in the cold and wet of the frontier."

Pendergrass shrugged. "You are right, Major. We have the same problem in the infantry. But—"

"I know," Devlin said. "I shall, of course, submit a report as to what I am personally doing to keep down the desertion rate."

"That is all you can do," Pendergrass said.

"Is there anything else?" Devlin asked.

"Until Mr. Wheatfall arrives, I think not," Pendergrass said.

Devlin gritted his teeth as he tended to his social responsibilities as post commander. "May I tender an invitation to you to dine with Mrs. Devlin and me in our quarters this evening at eight o'clock?"

"I would be delighted, thank you," Major Pendergrass said. He replaced all the papers in his dispatch pouch, and stood up. "Now I believe I shall retire for a hot bath and a bit of a rest. That's quite a trip out here from Fort Snelling."

"Yes, it is," Devlin said. "Good afternoon, Major Pendergrass."

"Good afternoon, Major Devlin."

Major Matt Devlin stayed in a bad mood for the rest of the day. That evening, when Pendergrass came for dinner, he was barely cordial for a while. But Beth, an experienced army wife and hostess, sensed the animosity between the two. She wisely kept the conversation informal and even humorous. After a while Devlin's mood lightened as he came to know Pendergrass on a different level. Before the evening was over, he realized the other army officer was only doing his job. The final toast of the evening was a sincerely cordial one between the two.

Things got even better in the next couple of days. Pendergrass made a quick inspection of Fort Buffalo and wrote a splendid report, complimenting the commanding officer and all personnel for a good job done under difficult and even potentially threatening circumstances. That evening, he and Devlin were on a first-name basis and got drunk together in the unfortunate Lieutenant Standish's quarters. That young officer spent another drafty, sober night in the visitors' tent.

The next day, Major Matt Devlin, in a better mood, went about his duties feeling fresh, enthusiastic, and even a bit optimistic.

Then Ned Wheatfall arrived.

Devlin remembered his orders to apologize. That was one thing he wanted to get over with as soon as possible. Assembling all his officers and calling on Major Harold Pendergrass, Devlin went over to the agency store and found Wheeler Coburn behind the counter.

"What brings y'all over here?" Coburn asked.

"Did you file a report on the beef shortage?" Devlin asked.

"I sure did, Major," Coburn said. "That just worries me to death."

Devlin decided not to hesitate. "Do me a favor and fetch your new assistant agent, will you? I need to speak to him. I belive his name is Wheatfall, is it not?"

"With pleasure, Major Devlin," Coburn said, grinning. "With pleasure!"

When Wheatfall came out of the back room, he was positively beaming. "Why, looky here now!" he crowed. "If it ain't my old friend Major—er, what was that name again—soldier-boy?"

Devlin clenched his teeth, speaking in a strained voice. "I am Major Matthew Devlin, commanding officer of Fort Buffalo."

"So y'are, yes, so y'are!" Wheatfall said. "What can I do fer you—soldier-boy?"

Pendergrass stepped forward. "Disrespect on your part will not be tolerated, Mr. Wheatfall. There is no army regulation that requires an officer to stand and take insults."

Wheatfall backed down, knowing he had wandered into a sensitive and dangerous area. "Why, that's just my little joke. I didn't mean to rile nobody. If I did, I'm right sorry. Why, I served under the colors myself and was honorably discharged in the rank o' sergeant. And that's a fact."

"It sure is," Coburn said, backing him up.

"Listen to me, Wheatfall," Devlin said. "I am apologizing in public to you for making you leave the Buffalo Steppes Reservation."

Wheatfall chuckled. "Now, ain't that neighborly? I'm right glad to see you've changed your ways, Major."

Pendergrass's own temper started to boil. "Major

Devlin was ordered to render an apology by the departmental commander. He has obeyed that order."

Now Wheatfall knew he had not really beaten the army officer. "Well, we'll try to get along anyhow, won't we? Especially since I'm the agent here now."

"Assistant agent," Coburn pointed out. He regarded all the army officers with some amusement. "Do y'all understand you ain't to take no action out there on the reservation without my say-so?"

"We do, Mr. Coburn," Devlin said. "Good day."

The two agents remained silent until the group of army men had left the store.

"They sure didn't stay any longer'n they had to, did they?" Wheatfall remarked.

Coburn pulled a cigar from his vest. "I think we got 'em where we want 'em."

"Yeah," Wheatfall agreed. "As long as the senator can put on the pressure, we'll be able to run things out here exactly like he wants 'em." He poked the other in the belly. "Get one thing straight, Wheeler. I ain't your assistant. You understand?"

"We got to act like you are, don't we?" Coburn said. "How else are you gonna be able to move free around here."

"I just wish them boys o' mine had the same privilege," Wheatfall said. "It'd made our job easier."

"Don't worry," Coburn said. "The senator is right in the middle of this. Things will keep getting better and easier for us."

Wheatfall chuckled. "That's fer sure!"

Coburn leaned against the counter as he languidly puffed on his cigar. "After all, Senator Torrance done a good job with the Injun Bureau in cutting the cattle herd for the Kiwotas."

"He's a powerful man," Wheatfall said.

"I wonder what the senator really wants out here?" Coburn mused.

"He wants a damn Injun war," Wheatfall said.

"So he can get the Buffalo Steppes for hisself?" Coburn wondered. "It don't make sense. There's plenty o' prairie country all around if he wanted it. Hell, there's millions o' acres just for the taking."

"I reckon we'll just have to wait and see," Wheatfall said.

"I'll tell you one thing, Ned," Coburn remarked. "I'm powerful glad them boys o' yours is out here. I was mighty worried about them Injuns, I don't mind telling you."

"When they get riled, they won't bother us this close to the fort, anyhow," Wheatfall pointed out. "They'll head out to other parts o' the country to take scalps."

"The sooner things start, the better as far as I'm concerned," Coburn said.

"Don't worry about it," Wheatfall assured him. "In about two days, them Injuns is gonna be ready to forget all about that damn treaty."

Chapter 8

White Elk and the two braves with him, Lone Cougar and Spotted Calf, allowed their horses to meander across the open prairie as they carefully studied the ground for sign of buffalo. With no idea where the nearest herd might be, the Indians saw no sense in keeping their mounts traveling in any particular direction. The only attention the Indians gave the animals was to keep them moving when they stopped to graze on the sweet, fresh grass.

The three were one of several teams of trackers acting on suggestions by War Heart to find out if any more scattered bison had wandered onto the reservation. The remainder of the beef cattle had been slaughtered and consumed a week previously. The hides, when treated as the Indians had learned to do the skins of buffalo, did not turn out well. The cow skins ended up stiff and leathery, of no use except to make shields. No Kiwota would huddle comfortably under one of those when the next Moons of Cold Hunger came upon the prairie.

White Elk and his companions could find no sign of buffalo. They wandered farther west to Greasy Flats which marked the edge of the reservation in that direction. White Elk, a tracker with a strong instinct for the job, suddenly felt the presence of the animals or at least of a trail.

"Ah! My medicine tells me there is a herd nearby!" White Elk exclaimed.

Long Cougar laughed. "Is it your medicine or do you smell buffalo shit?"

Spotted Calf smiled. "My belly and the bellies of those in my lodge care not if it is medicine or stench. Which way is the herd?"

White Elk pointed the direction in which he wished to go and pushed on with Lone Cougar and Spotted Calf following. They rode out onto the flats, able to see for great distances in the area where only the barest rise of ground existed.

Lone Cougar pushed himself up and stood on his horse. He peered around in all directions. "I see nothing of buffalo," he complained.

"There is something," White Elk insisted. "I can feel it. Even if it is nothing more than tracks, we can follow them. If we find the herd, we can turn it toward the reservation and drive it where we can kill many animals without breaking the treaty."

The trio of warriors continued on their quest. After a short time they discovered some tracks and dung. Spotted Calf slid from his horse's back and studied the droppings.

"Ah!" he exclaimed happily. "They came by here two suns ago."

"Yes," White Elk agreed. "The main herd must be farther that way. These are the marks of young bulls who have yet to mate. The old bulls keep them away."

Lone Cougar laughed. "Like an old man with young wives who are wanted by men of their own age."

"Come!" White Elk said. "You make your jokes later. Now let us find this herd and turn it east. Then one of us will go to the village and bring other men to make the kills."

"I will go," Spotted Calf volunteered.

"Wait until we find them," White Elk said. "If we can drive them closer to the village, it will make an easier kill."

The warriors picked up the pace a bit until they found the tracks of a medium-sized herd. There would be enough meat to feed the People for a short while and relieve the hunger that had begun to set in from the shortage of beef and the slaughter of the large herd.

"Hold!" White Elk said. "More tracks. Look! White men's horses, see?"

Spotted Calf pointed to the ground. "They are turning the herd to the west." He looked around. "I think the white men came from the south and found the buffalo. Look at the tracks now. The buffalo started to run."

"The white men drove them away from the reservation so we could not find them," Lone Cougar complained. "I thought Looks Ahead told those hunters to go away."

"Maybe they will slaughter the herd and leave them to rot like they did before," White Elk said. "If they do it off the reservation, we can do nothing."

"I think that Running Wolf will then look for those whites and kill them," Lone Cougar said.

"I will help him!" Spotted Calf said.

"And I!" vowed White Elk. "But let us see if the buffalo got away and maybe turned back toward the east. Come!"

More riding and tracking showed no dead buffalo, but the Kiwotas reached a place where the marks of the shod horses indicated they had turned in another direction.

"The buffalo kept going away from the reservation,

so the white men knew they had done what they wanted to," White Elk said. "At least they did not kill the buffalo. That means we might find them again some day."

"The whites have still done us harm," Spotted Calf reminded his companions. "The People will once again feel hunger. It is not right or proper during the Moons of Warm Weather."

"The whites are on the reservation. Let us follow these hoofprints and find them," Lone Cougar said. "They are not many. If we use stealth, we can kill them."

"I agree," White Elk said. "I will watch the ground. You two look around as we ride so nobody will sneak up on us."

The sun went a quarter of its journey across the sky to the west as the tracking continued. By that time, the trail had veered slightly to the east out of the Greasy Flats and back onto the Buffalo Steppes. Scattered copses of trees became more numerous until there were enough of them to stop the east wind's gusty wanderings across the reservation. The trail the Kiwota warriors followed meandered in and out of the formations of sporadic growth of elms, cottonwoods, and spruce.

"I think these whites did as we have been doing," White Elk surmised. "They were a small group out hunting buffalo."

"Not hunting buffalo," Spotted Calf corrected him. "They searched for buffalo to run off so we would not have them."

"Let us find those dung-eaters and kill them!" Lone Cougar exclaimed. "They have caused misery for our women and children."

White Elk pressed on with his two companions. Suddenly smoke and bright flashes appeared in one of the tree lines. A split second later, the whine of bullets cut the air around them.

The Kiwotas whirled and rode in an oblique direction to seek shelter in another wild orchard. But fire came from there, too. Spotted Calf grunted and slipped to the ground. He managed to get back to his feet as Lone Courage rode toward him. But the young Kiwota collapsed to sprawl in the prairie's deep grass before help could arrive.

White Elk's horse took a hit and stumbled. He slipped from the animal's back, staying on his feet. He quickly knelt and fired in the direction of the attack. Then he went to his bow and arrows, sending three of the projectiles flying toward the targets. Two fell short, and one entered the trees.

The heavy firing continued, and Lone Cougar took several hits simultaneously. He went limp and fell from his horse. The way he hit the ground showed White Elk he was already dead. Now White Elk could see numerous white men coming at him from three different directions. He and his friends had stumbled into a cleverly concealed camp that was scattered between the different stands of trees.

White Elk sent arrows flying as he turned from group to group. He made no strikes, and his efforts came to a halt when a bullet shattered his skull. Collapsing to the dark earth, he joined his companions in death as the two unhurt Indian horses galloped off.

Coming across the open space, walking cautiously, the attackers approached to inspect the three corpses. Pockets Dugan was the first to arrive. He went to each Indian and bashed in their skulls with the butt of his Hawkens rifle.

"I ain't a-going to put up with no possum playing," he said. "I seen redskins lay still 'til it suits 'em to jump up and fight again."

Red-Eye Morgan, Dan Lilly, and Earling Denmore joined him. One of the others finished off White Elk's injured horse with a shot in the head.

"Poor ol' thing," he said in sincere sympathy.

"I'll tell you one thing about Injuns," Pockets remarked. "They can be real dumb bastards sometimes, can't they?"

"These three thought they was tracking no more'n a half dozen of us," Red-Eye said. "They damn sure didn't know we'd have our camp scattered and hid in these trees like this neither."

The remainder of the gang gathered up the Indians' firearms and ammunition. They checked for other belongings that might prove useful, taking what they wanted. Red-Eye Morgan took out his hatchet and started chopping at the corpses, leaving gaping wounds. He slashed the legs so bad that a slight tug would separate them.

Dan Lilly chuckled. "Do you believe the same as them Injuns that a mangled dead man is going to the afterlife as a cripple?"

"Shit no!" Red-Eye replied. He had been left in charge by Ned Wheatfall. "I always do this for the misery it gives their pals and squaws on account o' they think the dead'uns is gonna be stumbling through the Happy Hunting Ground for eternity like this. They got the belief that they'll have to depend on the charity of others in the afterlife or whatever they call it."

"Anybody want scalps?" Pockets Dugan asked. "It's gonna be first come, first served."

"Hurry up at it if you do," Red-Eye said. "And don't get real comfortable when we get back in the trees. We're gonna have to leave early to be south o' Bear Gap by late tomorrow like Wheatfall wants."

After the scalps were taken by a couple of the hunters, they all went back to their various camps. The

Indian corpses, mutilated and robbed, lay in undignified positions from the rough handling they'd received.

A couple of hours later, when the sun set and the evening breeze came up a bit, the darkness settled in over the remains of White Elk, Lone Cougar, and Spotted Calf.

No animals came near the dead men that night. The strong smell of humans coming from the three closely located bivouacs made the wolves, coyotes, and even the bears wary. When first light came the following morning, a heavy dew covered the bodies still lying in the same positions. By the time the sun was high enough to evaporate the moisture, Red-Eye Morgan and the rest of Wheatfall's men had broken camp and were cantering south across the prairie, skirting the Buffalo Steppes as they headed for Bear Gap.

The insects, having no fear of humans, were the first to descend on the remains. Buzzing blow-flies landed on the gaping wounds, sticking their proboscises through the congealed blood to reach the still-liquid stuff farther down. They swarmed over the bodies, across the open eyes, and into the mouths of the dead Kiwotas.

A crippled coyote, his kill-limiting injury making him desperately bold, wandered in closer. The smell from the camps was still strong, but he had not eaten in three days. The famished animal bit into White Elk's belly, pulling away flesh to expose the organs. The wild canine was able to take one mouthful of intestine and bite into the belly cavity for another before the arrow slapped into its shoulder. The animal yelped and tried to get at whatever had attacked it, stumbling on injured legs.

A second arrow from Running Wolf's bow put the animal out of its misery.

The group of a half-dozen Kiwotas had picked up

the dead men's trails late the previous evening. Curious about the buffalo tracks, Running Wolf had decided to see where White Elk, Lone Cougar, and Spotted Calf had gone.

Running Wolf dismounted and squatted beside the body of his dead friend White Elk. He felt a long stab of pain and grief as he thought of the brave warrior going blind and crippled through the afterlife. Tears welled up in his eyes and flowed down his cheeks with the awful remorse that racked his body.

Other warriors, sent on to investigate the various stands of trees, now rode up and looked at the mutilated corpses with numb misery. None uttered a word. They remained silent, turning their eyes to Running Wolf, waiting for his reaction.

Running Wolf wiped at his eyes and stood up. "Now I know what the white men want," the warrior said. "They will use this treaty to kill us a few at a time. When all the men are gone, they will let our women and children starve. Then they will cut up this ground like they did on the other side of the river on the east to grow crops."

"Will we fight Looks Ahead again?" one of the other men asked.

"We will fight them all!" Running Wolf shouted. He vaulted back onto his horse. "Let us go back to the village. I would speak with War Heart."

There were no more thoughts of finding buffalo as the group of Kiwotas rode cross the expanse of the prairie. Angry and desperate, they galloped on as fear for their families and their tribe grew with each stride of their war horses.

It took the greater part of the day to make the return journey. By the time they reached the village and splashed across the river to the lodges, the afternoon sun sat poised for its dive to the west. Running Wolf sent two of the men, Little Dog and Bear Claw, to announce the deaths of White Elk and his two companions. He then went directly to War Heart's tepee and found him sitting in front, watching his wives tend to their chores.

Running Wolf dismounted. "White Elk is dead. So are Lone Cougar and Spotted Calf. They were killed by whites in the trees near Greasy Flats."

War Heart's eyes opened wide. "How can this be?"

"It was done by white men who then cut them up. Now they will go to the Spirit World blind and crippled," Running Wolf said. "There is no medicine strong enough to mend their souls. Others will have to feed them."

"You saw this?" War Heart asked. He did not weep openly; but his voice quaked, and tears eased down his cheeks.

"I saw their corpses and the tracks of the white hunters," Running Wolf said. "The treaty is a trick to make us stop fighting so they can kill the warriors and starve our families."

"I will speak to Looks Ahead," War Heart said.

"What for?" Running Wolf demanded to know. "He will not get us the beef cattle we need. He said he made the hunters leave the reservation. But they have come back and even killed three of our men. All Looks Ahead does is lie. He used to be an honorable warrior and fighter. Now he hides behind lies because I think his medicine has grown weak."

"He is a strong warrior," War Heart said.

"Ah! Then, why did he quit fighting us and make a treaty?" Running Wolf asked. "I know. It was because his medicine will not work against us anymore."

"I think his medicine is still strong," War Heart said.

"You led us before when we fought Looks Ahead

98

and his soldiers," Running Wolf said. "We always fought him here on the People's land. I will fight him differently and take the angry warriors who will follow me."

"How will you do that?" War Heart asked.

"I will leave the reservation and go far and wide across the flat country and kill whites," Running Wolf said. "Looks Ahead will have to take his soldiers and ride far to find me. It will be different."

War Heart, consumed by grief and misgivings, hung his head and said nothing.

"I will kill white soldiers, too," Running Wolf said. "After they are all dead, we will go back to the way it was before they came here."

"You cannot kill all the white soldiers," War Heart said. "They are too many. Don't you know? The White Father has so many soldiers that he sends them here to be killed. He does not care."

"I will make strong medicine for myself," Running Wolf said. "I know I can do that because I am so angry and ready to fight. This fills me with sacred strength and valor. I fight for the People! I cannot fail." He scowled at War Heart. "You have failed!"

"I will speak to Looks Ahead about the white hunters," War Heart said. "He will kill them for us."

"He will not," Running Wolf argued. "He wants all the People to die like the other whites."

"I will speak to Looks Ahead," War Heart said.

"You are a woman, and he is your husband," Running Wolf sneered. "Will you fight with us?"

"No," War Heart replied. "It is not good for the People to make war now."

"We cannot find buffalo, and we have no cattle to eat," Running Wolf said. "Would you scratch at the ground like the white man for your food? We are meat eaters! The only growing things we eat are what the women and girls gather in the forests. Would you live on berries?"

War Heart signaled his decision to speak no more by staring ahead.

"Ah!" Running Wolf said. "Go to your husband! I will take Kiwota warriors and go to war!"

Chapter 9

Bear Claw peered through the thick brush from his vantage point at the apex of the rise. Although the cover of vegetation was only waist-high, the warrior was well-concealed in its midst. He wasn't alone. The rest of the war party, crouched and ready, were located in the brush several running paces toward the rear. They also kept an eager vigilance. They could see a wide section of the open prairie spread out before them, but, like Bear Claw, the Indians were not admiring the view.

A small cloud of dust on the horizon had caught Bear Claw's attention while out on a scout for the war party. He'd recognized the floating dirt's wispy makeup as being the type kicked up by the rolling boxes of the whites, and had wasted no time riding back to the main group led by Running Wolf to inform them of what he'd seen.

Excited at the prospect of a fight and booty, the other twenty warriors had followed the pair back to a place that offered the best opportunity to spring a successful ambush.

Now, spread out in a single line, the warriors waited for the wagons to continue their slow approach to their position. Running Wolf licked his lips in anticipation.

"See?" he whispered loud enough for all to hear.

"The whites continue this way without knowing we are here. We will not have much longer to wait."

"But we do not want anybody to get excited and rush out, giving us away," Bear Claw cautioned him.

The remark angered Running Wolf. "Do you think only War Heart can be a good leader? Everyone will obey me."

"I hope this is so," Bear Claw said, going back to his observation.

This would be the first chance of making a raid for the Kiwota men, all painted and arrayed for war, since beginning this latest excursion. Although War Heart and most of the other men refused to join them, this group of young fighters had eagerly followed Running Wolf to seek adventure.

They had ridden south off the Buffalo Steppes Reservation, ready to attack whatever targets of opportunity they could find. The prospect of a wagon train excited them all. Since Running Wolf led the war party, the others decided his war medicine was indeed strong if they could find victims this fast.

By darting their eyes about and coming back to the object of their attention for short glances, rather than staring at the line of approaching wagons, the warriors were able to clearly see their intended victims. They quickly determined that three wagons made up the train. Some time later, when the vehicles were closer, the Kiwotas could tell that there were not many people in the party. After a few more minutes, it was easy to determine that women and children numbered among the travelers.

A bit more time passed; then Running Wolf judged the time was right. "Come!" he said.

He got to his feet and trotted back to the place where a young boy named Red Cub minded the horses. Within seconds, the warriors had leaped on the backs of their mounts and galloped up over the top of the rise and down across the descending terrain toward the wagons.

The white men did as the Kiwotas expected. They fired hastily and early in their panic. The Indians, not wishing to waste precious ammunition, didn't bother with their own firearms. Instead, they loosed arrows, carelessly aimed because of the excitement, that arched high in the air and fell around the vehicles, sticking into the ground.

The men driving the wagons kicked the teams into a wild gallop. Running Wolf, knowing there was really no place for them to go, was glad they didn't take up a defensive position. These were not experienced frontiersmen or Indian fighters. Now it would be easier to overwhelm them one at a time as they spread out in their frantic run for nonexistent safety.

"Get the front rolling box!" the young war chief yelled at his companions.

In a matter of minutes the war party rode on both sides of the wagon. The frightened expressions of the man and woman on the seat could easily be seen by the Indians. The woman tried to reload the man's musket, but the jarring ride made it impossible for her to properly pour powder down the bore.

"Get the long-eared horses!" Running Bear hollered.

The range was short and the warriors skilled, so the two mules pulling the wagon were quickly assaulted by numerous arrows that pained and slowed them. The man stood up and whipped at them, yelling in frightened rage as the animals began to stop running. They struggled in their traces and kicked in an instinctive effort to fight back.

Running Wolf, Bear Claw, and another warrior called Charging Bull put their bows to work. Of the three arrows sent streaking across the short space, two found their target. One went through the man's side, and another entered his neck, sending him falling back into the wagon. The woman began to scream hysterically as they came to a stop.

The second wagon, unscathed, came on. The two men there were full of fight and ready to take on the warriors. Although they hadn't been able to reload their long guns, they both had revolvers. When their vehicle reached the other, they stopped and began to fire at the attackers.

Two Kiwotas, one named Waits-All-Day and the other Snake, were the closest. Bullets whistled around their heads. Snake made no attempt to defend himself. Instead, whooping in defiance, he charged forward, sweeping past the startled occupants of the wagon. He came so close that he was able to slap one of the white men.

"Look at me and what I have done!" he shouted, turning his horse. "I have counted coup this day, brothers! I would claim this as a battle honor!"

Waits-All-Day was more practical. As Running Wolf and Charging Bull joined him, he sent arrows at the men. Within moments the whites were pierced by nearly a dozen apiece, and they died almost instantly. One slumped to the wagon bed, and the other pitched over the side to land on the ground.

The people in the third wagon, a man and a woman, came to a stop. The man did not offer any resistance. Instead, with the woman clinging to him, he spoke aloud to the Indians, holding up a strange, rectangular object the Kiwotas did not recognize. His voice grew louder as he realized the Indians did not understand him.

"Let us kill him," Running Wolf said.

"I will help you," Bear Claw said.

They both shot arrows at the man, but one missed and hit the woman in the chest, causing her to sink to her knees. The man died, falling on top of her. When the two Indians leaped onto the wagon and pulled the corpse away, they found the woman had also been killed.

"Your arrow hit her!" Running Wolf exclaimed in anger.

"There are two more women," Bear Claw reminded him. "That is plenty. Let us go back to the other rolling boxes."

Running Wolf leaped back aboard his horse and rode up to the vehicle and jumped onto the driver's box. He pulled the dead man up and threw him down to land on the other. Stepping inside, under the canvas cover, he found a wide-eyed, hysterical woman and two children huddled in the corner. Whooping, he grabbed each and pushed them out the back, where the other Kiwotas quickly surrounded them.

Two more Kiwotas dragged a struggling, screaming woman from the front wagon. Within moments, the warriors stripped them and pushed them to the ground. The raping was done in turns as the men who had finished with the women began to loot the wagons. They were enraged when the one thing they sought was not among the white people's possessions.

"No whiskey!" Charging Bull bellowed in anger.

"Look, brothers," Bear Claw said. He had opened a box that was full of sheets of paper bound by black leather.

"What are those?" Waits-All-Day asked.

"Nothing!" Bear Claw said, tossing them aside. "The man in the other rolling box held one up and shook it at Running Wolf and me like it was strong medicine. There are the marks white men use to make words all over these things."

"Then, search for other things we can use," Running Wolf said. Though it was unusual in a case like this, he was glad they hadn't found any whiskey. He didn't like to see what the fiery liquor did to Indians.

The looting went on. Most of the items they found would have been useful if the village were closer. Barrels of flour, beans, and other staples were in abundance for a long stay in the wilderness. But the containers were too bulky and heavy for transport other than by travois. These were broken open and scattered by kicking them around until they were well-mixed with the prairie dirt on which they'd been thrown.

Personal clothing of the whites was examined as it was pulled from the containers in the wagons. The Indians had no interest in any of this except the men's hats. Waits-All-Day caused a stir when he put on a woman's bonnet and leaped around, yelping in a falsetto voice while the others laughed at his antics. Running Wolf made sure all the guns, powder, ball and other accoutrements of the weaponry were collected. He also gathered up mirrors, combs, brushes, and other things the wives of the raiders might like to have.

Bear Claw climbed up into the back of the second wagon to join the war chief. "We have finished with the women. Nobody wants to do it again. What about you?"

"Once is enough for me," Running Wolf said. "Now the children have yet to be dealt with."

The war chief leaped out of the vehicle and walked over to where a boy and girl huddled together. Running Wolf was fascinated by the blond color of their hair and especially the clear blue of the little girl's eyes. He guessed her to be five summers of age and the boy, obviously her brother, about six or seven. He reached out and touched the girl.

The boy yelled and charged the warrior, pummeling

him with his small fists. Running Wolf laughed and pushed him away numerous times as the boy continued to charge.

"That one has heart," Waits-All-Day remarked. "He protects his sister."

Running Wolf nodded his agreement. "He is too brave to kill. We will let the children live. If their luck or medicine is strong, they will be found. If not, these little ones will perish on the prairie like orphaned coyote pups."

"What about the women?" Waits-All-Day said. "Since everyone took their turn, nobody wants them anymore. Even Red Cub took his pleasure. I think it is his first time with a woman."

"My first was a Cheyenne captive," Running Wolf said. He thought a moment. "If we do not want the women, kill them. Then set the following boxes on fire and throw the dead whites on it."

The naked, violated women were clubbed to death with musket butts. After the mules were cut loose, the wagons were pushed together and put ablaze. After the flames were going well, the dead were picked up and thrown in the fire. The two children, now huddled together, were silent through the ordeal. The mules, unconcerned and glad to be rid of the routine of pulling the wagons, began to peacefully graze off to one side of the scene of horror.

"What about the long-earred horses?" Red Cub asked. As the group's horse handler, they would be his responsibility.

"Never mind them," Charging bull said. "They are no good for war."

"Let us go!" Running Wolf announced.

The warriors leaped aboard their horses and rode off, leaving the attack site behind as they continued their southward trek, going farther and farther from the Buffalo Steppes.

Running Wolf had no particular destination in mind. He simply wanted to put distance between the scene of the attack and his war party in case a dragoon patrol might come into the area. In spite of his bravado in speaking to War Heart about Looks Ahead's medicine fading away, he didn't want to take any chances. Better to be out of reach if the army officer suddenly experienced a return of all his powers.

The war party traversed the empty prairie until the sun began to prepare itself for evening. They found a secure place where a small creek flowed through a long stand of trees, and the Kiwotas decided to spend the night there. Red Cub and a couple of the younger warriors went out to find some game. It didn't take long before they returned to camp with some fat rabbits. There was plenty to give everyone more than enough to eat.

The evening passed pleasantly for the warriors. Snake recounted his glory in counting coup on the white man shooting from the wagon. All agreed that what he had done was a brave deed and he had a right to make up a song about it. Red Cub took some good-natured teasing about having his first woman. He smiled shyly and said it hadn't been such a wonderful thing as he had imagined.

"Wait until you get under robes with a beautiful girl who wants you," Running Wolf said. "She will not be like the whining, wiggling white women."

"Ha!" Charging Bull laughed. "She will make you a prisoner by clamping her legs around you and tell you to thrust faster and deeper."

Red Cub, who felt an attraction to a certain girl in the tribe, smiled to himself as he imagined himself wrapped up with her on a cold winter's night in a warm lodge.

The Kiwotas, as was their custom, did not bother to organize a guard when darkness settled in. If someone was concerned enough, he would sit up and keep an eye on things. If not, then all would peacefully snooze the night away. In the case of that particular war party, all were tired after the day's excitement, and all rolled up in their blankets to go to sleep after making sure the horses were secure.

The next day began in the same informal, relaxed manner. The first men awake stirred up the coals and reheated the meat left over from the previous evening's meal. Then, by twos and threes, the others joined them for a leisurely breakfast and preparation for the day. The sun was a quarter of the way off the eastern horizon when they finally broke camp and once again headed south behind Running Wolf.

It seemed the remainder of the morning was going to be without incident. Then, just before the sun was at its zenith in the sky, careless whites once again gave themselves away to the alertness of the Indians.

This time it was noise. The loud voices of boisterous men could be faintly heard from the southwest. Slowing down in order to be able to hear better, Running Wolf led the war party toward the source of the sounds. The search led them back toward the same creek where they'd spent the night, a long body of water that meandered for miles through the prairie. At that point, it began to widen until it was almost the size of a small river.

Running Wolf, once again with Bear Claw as a partner, left the others and went forward to see what the situation offered them. The Kiwota scouts were able to find some trees along the river that offered them plenty of cover when they finally found the exact spot where the whites were located.

This time there were no rolling boxes. Five riders with packhorses had stopped to make a camp and cook food for a midday meal. They were all in a good mood, laughing and talking. One of them took a drink from a bottle and passed it to the others.

"Whiskey!" Bear Claw happily exclaimed.

"The whites are drunk," Running Wolf said. "Bah!" He spat and stood up. Slowly and deliberately he set an arrow in place on his bow. Drawing back the string, he took aim and let the missile fly. It went completely through the neck of the nearest man, continuing on across the creek to land in the prairie grass.

The victim's sudden, gurgling scream shocked his companions. He staggered around holding his neck, and blood gushed from the wound like water from an underground spring. His shirt quickly took on a wet, scarlet color as he weakened and fell awkwardly to the ground.

Now Bear Claw shot another. This time the arrow went through an arm, pinning the limb to the target's body. Bellowing in pain and rage, the man pulled his holster and began to fire in the wrong direction.

The noise brought the other Kiwotas. They quickly caught on to the game. While the drunken whites staggered around their camp in sodden bewilderment, the Indians meticulously picked them off one by one. The last fellow, quite portly, looked like a porcupine from the eight arrows that had entered his fat body. He finally became so weak that he sat down. Unable to raise his pistol, he watched the approaching Indians through half-closed eyes.

Running Wolf walked up to the corpulent individual. He removed the man's hat and set it on his own head. Then, pulling his tomahawk from the belt around his waist, the Indian raised it high and lowered it with full force on top of the wounded fellow's head. The skull split open in a spray of blood and brains.

They found another who was still alive. He was dragged over to the campfire and thrown on. The sudden pain and shock sobered him up, and he screamed in a loud, shrill voice as he was repeatedly kicked and pushed back into the flames. Finally, in utter desperation, he picked out one of his tormentors and charged. It was Snake, and the victim grasped him tightly around the neck and pushed him toward the flames.

Laughing, the other Kiwotas stepped back and watched. The white man was large and muscular, much heavier than Snake, and he managed to throw the Indian onto the blaze several times.

Snake was angry, embarrassed, and in pain. He pulled his knife and, wildly yelling, sliced the man until the badly bleeding sufferer finally keeled over and quickly died.

Now all the whites lay dead and immobile. Running Wolf suddenly remembered White Elk, Lone Cougar and Spotted Calf. Their mutilated bodies guaranteed an eternity of suffering in the Spirit World. Snarling, he set about working on the fresh corpses to make sure all would be crippled and blind when their spirits left the earth. When he finished, he raised his bloody knife and tomahawk to the sky and yelled out his battle cry.

It was good to be at war.

Chapter 10

The return of a patrol after weeks out in the wilderness was an exciting event on any frontier army post. Tensions eased in the garrison as emotions ran the gamut from grateful relief to outright joy when all members of the mission returned safely from an outing that offered every opportunity for contact with hostile Indians.

Even men from other companies, who barely knew the troopers who had gone to the field, came to watch them ride back into the garrison area and give them a friendly greeting. It was their way of showing comradeship to fellow soldiers while demonstrating that the regiment was truly their home. Another, very serious consideration in isolated garrisons facing threats of Indian attacks was the relief that the number of soldiers at the post had not diminished.

The patrol led by Lieutenant Emil Standish of A Company received its share of the usual greetings and attention along with the accompaniment of shouting children and barking dogs when it returned to Fort Buffalo. As the people who first met the homecomers noticed the patrol's unusual situation, they quickly hollered out for any stragglers to hurry and join the early spectators.

The reason for this particularly attentive crowd was the fact that the first two dragoons in the column each held a small, blond-haired youngster in front of him on his government-issue Grimsley saddle.

As the young lieutenant led his detachment past officers' row, he noted the wives standing there gaping at the sight. He was more concerned about the children than the attention he received. As he came alongside Mrs. Beth Devlin, Standish leaned down to speak to her.

"Ma'am, we could use some help from the ladies," the patrol leader said in an urgent voice. "We have come upon a most unusual and vexing situation."

"So I see, Lieutenant Standish," Beth replied, looking at the disheveled children. "Poor dears!" She motioned to her friend Mrs. Dora Teasedale, wife of Captain Paul Teasedale, who commanded B Company. "I don't know what in the world is going on, but I would certainly appreciate your help. We must take those children and tend to them."

"Of course!" Mrs. Teasedale said.

The pair of dragoons were glad to turn their small charges over to the officers' wives. The children, with no expressions on their little faces, allowed themselves to be handed down to the two ladies, showing neither distress nor happiness.

"Thank you most kindly, Mrs. Devlin," Lieutenant Standish said. "You, too, Mrs. Teasedale."

The women, tightly holding on to the little boy and girl, hurried away with several other ladies following after them.

The patrol continued through the post until reaching Company A's orderly room. At that point, Lieutenant Standish turned the unit over to his senior sergeant and, wasting no time, went directly to post headquarters where Major Matt Devlin would be waiting for him.

After turning his horse over to the duty orderly, the young lieutenant presented himself to the adjutant and was immediately ushered into Devlin's office.

"Sir!" Standish said, saluting. "Lieutenant Standish of A Company reporting to the post commander after completion of patrol duties."

"Stand at ease, Lieutenant Standish," Matt said, returning the salute. "I've already received word that you've returned with two lost children."

"Two orphans to be absolutely correct, sir," Standish said. "Your wife and Mrs. Teasedale have been kind enough to take charge of them."

"What are the circumstances that have brought them to our care?" Devlin asked.

"We found three burned-out wagons and the charred remains of several adults at a location approximately twenty miles to the south of Bear Gap," Standish explained. "We're not quite sure how many were killed because of the condition of the corpses. The children had been left alive by the raiding party for some strange reason. The hostiles were Kiwotas, Major. Of that, there is no doubt. The location and a couple of broken arrows plainly point to that tribe."

"War Heart has been at the agency several times during the past week, so I know he's not been up to any mischief," Devlin said. "If I were forced to make a guess as to who led the war party, I would say Running Wolf. I knew that shortage of rations was going to create problems. Not to mention those damned buffalo hunters out there."

"I agree, sir," Standish said. "I gave the site a vigorous investigation. The wagons carried some school books that had been scattered around the scene. No doubt the Indians could not figure out what they were for." He reached in his tunic and pulled out a copy of the Bible. "I found this, too, sir. If you look on the inside, you'll see by the inscription it was a gift to someone in the Mission of Indian Reform."

Devlin took the Bible and looked at it. "I'm familiar with the organization. They are an influential group that feels the answer to the Indians' spiritual and physical salvation is to be turned to civilized ways."

Standish showed a slight, sardonic smile. "I guess those particular Kiwotas had no desire to be transformed into farmers or merchants."

"None of the plains tribes do," Devlin said. "I am not an expert on anthropology, but it seems to me that trying to turn nomadic hunters and warriors into a sedentary society is a lost cause from the beginning."

"It would be necessary to destroy their spiritual beliefs and customs," Standish remarked. He was well aware of Indian religion and their great trust in the strong medicine of the supernatural.

"I am certain that religious conversion is part of the program," Devlin said. He laid the Bible down on his desk. "Continue with your report, Lieutenant."

"Because of the children's exhausted condition, I detailed a couple of men to stay with them while I immediately mounted a pursuit of the hostiles, but I'm afraid they had a lead of at least three days, sir," Standish said. "We followed the hostiles' trail in a southerly direction until reaching a point on Deacon Creek where we discovered another outrage. The bodies of five white men, recently murdered, were scattered within a short area along the watercourse. They were badly mutilated, of course, and whatever animals or other possessions they might have had were taken. At that point, I had already gone beyond the bounds of normal patrolling and returned to retrieve my men and the children.

As stated, as I rode into the garrison area I turned the little ones over to the ladies."

"Well done, Lieutenant Standish," Devlin said. "You're dismissed to put the report into writing. Triplicate, if you please, for forwarding to departmental headquarters at Fort Snelling. Also, any sketch maps you could make to accompany it would be greatly appreciated."

"Yes, sir," the lieutenant said. He saluted, executed an about-face, and marched from the office.

A few moments later, after straightening up the last figures on an ordnance report, Devlin picked up his cap and left his office. He went directly to his quarters where he knew Bess would have the children. He found a half dozen of the other officers' wives in the parlor when he entered.

"Oh, hello, Major Devlin," the wife of one of B Company's subalterns greeted him. "Mrs. Devlin is in the kitchen with Mrs. Blanchard and Mrs. Teasedale. They're giving those poor children baths."

Devlin went through the house and stepped into the kitchen. The little boy, his face showing no emotion, stared blankly from where he sat in a tub of warm water. Beth and Rose Blanchard gently sponged the lad. Meanwhile, Dora Teasedale sat in a chair nearly, holding the little girl who had been wrapped in a warm blanket.

"Have they said anything?" Devlin asked, looking at the children.

"Not a word from either of them," Beth said, looking up from her work. "The poor little things have been terrorized to muteness. They didn't even have a desire to eat, and I know they must be half-starved."

Devlin, his fatherly instincts brought strongly to the surface by the plight of the orphans, walked up to the little girl and knelt down, showing a gentle smile.

"Hello, sweetie," he said in a mellow voice. "My name is Matt. What's yours?"

The child looked in his direction, still showing no sign of being aware of his presence. Then she raised her blue eyes and focused them on the army officer's face. For a moment she did nothing. Then, very slowly, her features drew up into a frown, and she began to cry softly. Her weeping grew in intensity until she shook violently.

Devlin took the girl in his arms and pressed her to him. "There, there, little sweetie. Not to worry, hear? Everything is all right now."

Next the boy broke down, his crying louder as heavy sobs racked his little body. Beth pulled him from the bath and began to dry him.

"Thank the good Lord!" she said. "They're coming back."

"Maybe we can get some hot food into them now," Dora Teasedale said.

Devlin handed the girl back to her. He looked at his wife. "I'll be gone for a bit. I have some business to take care of."

He left the house, walking through the parlor as the younger women went to the kitchen to see what they could do. Devlin went directly to the stables and, rather than wait for the sergeant to detail a man to the job, saddled his own horse for a ride over to the agency.

He found Wheeler Coburn and Ned Wheatfall sitting at a table behind the trading store counter. The pair were engaged in a game of two-handed poker, playing five-card draw for cigars.

"Coburn!" Devlin snapped. "Are you aware some of the Kiwota warriors have left the reservation?"

"Have they?" Coburn asked, studying his cards. He pulled out a couple and laid them down. "Gimme two."

"Two it is," Wheatfall said. He dealt the cards, then glanced at the dragoon officer. "Ain't the army supposed to ride herd on them damn Injuns?"

"We are supposed to be informed when any members of the tribe are absent without authorization," Devlin said. "They hit a small wagon train and killed an unknown number of adults. For some reason, they left two children unharmed at the site."

Wheatfall gave himself a card. "That don't' sound like redskins," he mused. "They gener'ly bash the young 'uns against a tree or something if'n they don't want 'em." He gave Coburn a close scrutiny. "I'll bet a cigar."

"Raise you one," Coburn said with a grin.

Devlin jumped over the counter and walked up to the table, giving it a kick that sent cards and tobacco flying. "When I'm here on official business, you son of bitches will give me all your attention!"

Wheatfall leaped to his feet. "I've had about enough o' your pushy ways, Major! You been warned about how you act around us!"

"That's right, by God! You ain't got no right to call me and Ned son of a bitches!" Coburn said angrily. "I'll be making a report on this. You can be sure it'll go to somebody who'll do something about it, too."

Devlin, mad as hell, snarled. "I'm not sure I remember who your patron is, Coburn. A Senator Torrance, is it not? I know all you Indian Bureau types owe your jobs to some wag in Congress. Tell me about your boy. Did you buy some votes for him? Shine his shoes? Or maybe you got some names off tombstones to put down as votes during a difficult election."

"Never you mind, Devlin!" Coburn snapped. "The Right Honorable Senator Osmond Torrance is gonna make plenty o' trouble for you."

"Yeah!" Wheatfall said. "Especially when he finds out you can't protect folks from renegade Injuns."

"You do what you feel you must do," Devlin said. "In the meantime, I'm going to try to sort this thing out and put an end to this latest foray on the warpath before more blood is spilled."

"You ain't supposed to do nothing without my authority or request," Coburn reminded the army officer.

"I swear I just heard you ask for help in this matter," Devlin replied. He went back outside and mounted up, then he turned the horse directly for Fred Jeffries' cabin, riding at a brisk canter as he crossed the flat country of the Buffalo Steppes.

Jeffries, who had returned to his soddie, was outside chopping wood when the army officer rode up. He laid down his ax, knowing that serious business was afoot when the post commander appeared at his place.

"Howdy, Major," Jeffries said.

"How do you do, Mr. Jeffries," Devlin replied. "A patrol has returned with the word that some of the young warriors on the reservation have taken off to do some raiding."

"I ain't surprised," Jeffries said. "The Kiwotas have been real uneasy this past week. I got turned away when I went over to see if there was any buffalo meat for trade. I think there's been some trouble out on the steppes they been keeping to themselves."

"Something is going on, no doubt," Devlin said. "I think we'll find Running Wolf at the bottom of all this."

"He's the one all right," Jeffries agreed.

Devlin said, "I'm going to need an interpreter."

"You want to talk to 'em, huh?" Jeffries said. "Hang on while I saddle up. It won't take long."

Within a few minutes, both men rode toward the

Kiwota village. It took them almost a half hour to reach the camp, and upon arrival, the pair wasted no time in ferreting out War Heart's lodge.

Devlin recognized the designs decorating the chief's tepee. Like his war paint, the Kiwota battle leader had white stripes painted all around the living quarters. There was no conventional or customary reason for War Heart to choose that pattern except that it had come to him in a dream.

War Heart, already hearing of their arrival, waited for the pair to ride up. He gave a casual greeting as they dismounted. Devlin wasted no time in speaking through Jeffries.

"Some of your young men have left the reservation," Devlin said.

"All the People are hungry and angry, Looks Ahead," War Heart said.

"I know the beef rations were short, and I am trying to take care of that," Devlin replied. "I think you can find enough buffalo to help you through these hard times until the rest of the cattle arrive."

"There are no buffalo on the reservation," War Heart replied. "The white hunters have run them off. They killed our friends who tried to make them stop."

Jeffries, knowing most of the warriors personally, asked, "Who was killed by these white hunters?"

"White Elk, Lone Cougar, and Spotted Calf," War Heart said. "My heart is heavy because White elk was my best friend. They were cut so they would be crippled and blind in the Spirit World. It is wrong."

Jeffries took Devlin aside to translate his conversation with War Heart.

"We got bad troubles here, Major. Them white hunters killed three Kiwota braves," the scout said. "One of 'em was War Heart's best friend. They was mutilated, too. That makes it double bad 'cause these folks believe your spirit is in the same shape as your corpse."

Devlin was silent for several moments. Now he was certain of the suspicions he'd had all along. Ned Wheatfall's sudden appointment to the Indian Bureau as assistant agent had not meant his gang of buffalo hunters were gone. They were still under his control and making mischief out on the steppes by keeping the herds turned away from the area and murdering Kiwotas.

"War Heart," Devlin said through Jeffries. "My heart is heavy, too. A few of your young men have killed some white people. Those dead ones did no harm to you or the Kiwota tribe. They were innocent and not on the reservation. The Great White Father will be angry with his Kiwota children. The warriors who did this must be punished."

"We are not his children," War Heart said. "We are warriors and hunters and have sired our own children."

"I did not mean it that way," Devlin said. "I meant that he has kind thoughts of the Kiwotas."

"Then, tell him to get off our land and keep his children away," War Heart said. "Tell him to tear up the treaty and stay away from us. We will stay away from all white people."

"I cannot tell him anything; I am his son," Devlin said. "But the young men who ran off and killed whites did wrong and must be punished."

"I will not punish them," War Heart said. "It is not for me to do."

"You must turn them over to me to be punished," Devlin insisted.

"I will never do that, Looks Ahead," War Heart vowed. "I would rather die myself than to betray any of the People. Your Great Father of the whites is powerful, but he is as weak as a newborn baby when he tries to rule over my heart."

"Who led the war party?" Devlin asked. "Running Wolf?"

From that moment on, War Heart would not speak. He stared beyond the two men who tried to talk to him. Finally, Devlin gave up and signaled to Jeffries that they must leave.

As they walked to their horses, Jeffries asked, "What're you gonna do, Major?"

"The first thing is to track down those Kiwota raiders and capture them," Devlin said.

"That'll delay getting that beef ration problem took care of," Jeffries pointed out.

"That can't be helped," Devlin said. "Can you be ready to move out at first light in the morning?"

"Are we going to war, Major?" Jeffries asked.

"There is no getting out of it," Devlin said grimly as he swung up into his saddle.

Chapter 11

A few days later another emotional crowd gathered at Fort Buffalo's western gate.

This time, however, there was no jocosity as had been demonstrated when Lieutenant Emil Standish led his patrol back into the safety of the garrison. The troops assembled and mounted on this particular day were not returning from a mission. These were going out into the wild country. This time the operation was more than just routine patrolling or reconnaissance. This detachment would actively seek combat with hostile Indians. Their only mission was to find, destroy, or capture the renegade Kiwota war party led by Running Wolf.

Major Matt Devlin decided to personally lead the operation. Unfortunately he could detail no more than twenty dragoons on this patrol. To take more men away from Fort Buffalo would seriously weaken the garrison. Although this would not afford him a numerical superiority over the hostiles, he had no choice. The possibility that War Heart might suddenly decide to attack Fort Buffalo was something that could not be ignored. Even under strict military discipline, married men would hesitate to leave their families behind if the post was weakly defended.

The major stood with his wife and their three children as the patrol was formed up under the less-than-gentle leadership of Sergeant Theodore Dawson. Devlin looked down at his offspring, giving young Freddie extra attention.

"I want you kids to be especially good while I'm gone," he warned them.

"Yes, Papa," eight-year-old Mattie responded. "I'm always good. But Freddie and Bobby are bad sometimes."

"You do your share of misbehaving, too, young lady," Devlin said. "I want a promise from each of you."

"I promise, Papa!" Mattie said.

"Me, too," Bobby said.

Devlin looked at Freddie. "Well?"

"I'll do my best, Pa," he said.

"That's not good enough," Devlin said in a stern voice.

"Pa!" Freddie pleaded. "I don't want to lie or make a promise I can't keep. All I can say is that I'll do my best to be good."

"I suppose that's better than nothing," Devlin conceded. "But not much." He looked over to see that the patrol was formed up. He smiled at Beth. "We'll get back as quickly as we possibly can." They had already said their goodbyes the previous night. A public showing of affection between the commanding officer and his wife would not be considered in the best taste.

"Take care, Matt," she said.

"I shall," he said, as he subtly pushed his hand toward her and she gently laid her own on it. A look of affection cast into each other's eyes took the place of a kiss.

"I'll pray for you, Matt," Beth said with a faint smile.

"Goodbye," he said. He gave each boy a rub on the head and bent over to lighty kiss Mattie's face. Then he went straight to his horse.

Devlin left Captain Bernie Blanchard to command the post during his absence while he took half of Company A with him. Three packhorses carrying enough rations for up to six weeks gave grim evidence that the job was not going to be quick or easy. It was to Lieutenant Standish's credit that he volunteered to return to the field after enjoying the comforts of the garrison life for only a short time since his last patrol. But he knew exactly where to start the hunt for the war party.

The people seeing the detachment off waved goodbye on that cloudy, early morning as Devlin and the contract scout Fred Jeffries, with Standish behind them, led the column out onto the prairie.

The detachment turned southwest after skirting the agency building and headed for the last place Running Wolf and his men had been spotted on Deacon Creek. The trail would be terribly cold and stale, but it was the only place they had to start.

Devlin's manner of conducting an active campaign consisted of more than simply traveling from one point to another. The veteran officer's philosophy of war included the opinion that active and aggressive action made things happen his way. The Kiwotas may have thought this medicine allowed him to peer into the future, but Devlin was the sort of leader who simply made things happen by aggressive action and tempting fate.

He sent flankers and scouts ahead and around the column in wide sweeps just in case Running Wolf and his men had decided to return or were hoping to lay an ambush for any unwary troops heading their way. These teams of dragoons found nothing but empty prairie, but all had to agree it was no waste of time. The activity kept the Kiwota war party from springing any deadly surprises.

The first day went well as the line of horse soldiers and their scout plodded across the wide expanse of the Dakota wild country. They rode onto Greasy Flats, continuing to the south until that first evening when they reached the northern limits of Bear Gap, a low stretch of country measuring some five miles between distinctive rises in the terrain on both east and west. Since the skies had begun to cloud up, Devlin headed for the higher country to make the first camp of the patrol.

The senior sergeant of the detachment, a dour old soldier named Dawson, was the type of noncommissioned officer who knew his duties and performed them without any reminder from anyone. He immediately set up a guard roster, assigned sleeping places, and saw to it that the men made their horses comfortable before seeing to their own well-being.

"The army can enlist any tramp off the streets to take yer places," he growled at the men. "But good horses is hard to come by. So rub 'em down, feed 'em, and give 'em a good-night kiss."

The men obeyed the order to the letter, except for the kisses. Each individual trooper knew his life depended on a rested, nourished mount if any nasty or dangerous situation came up. For that reason, and to avoid trouble with Sergeant Dawson, not a dragoon sought out his own camping area until his horse was taken care of and safely placed in the picket line.

Since Devlin would not allow the luxury of tents, the men's sleeping arrangements consisted of a pair of dragoons forming into a team. Each man, in spite of the warm weather, carried two blankets and had his winter overcoat on the pommel of the saddle. For sleeping, they spread out one blanket on the ground and used their saddles for pillows. Next they laid down their overcoats and added the two horse blankets to the crude bed. They used the remaining blanket to cover themselves. That way, even if the night produced a heavy dew or rain, they had dry blankets to put on the horses' backs the next morning. This protected the horses' sensitive hides and also ensured that no dragoon would be forced to walk while having to lead a horse suffering from a sore back.

Most of the experienced troopers had ways of keeping any heavy rain off them. Bits of canvas, rubberized covers, and even blankets tightly woven then shrunk to the point that no moisture could penetrate the material were kept handy if needed.

Devlin, Jeffries, and Standish settled down together. Because of their own privately purchased camping gear, the three did not have to combine blankets in order to fix up a comfortable place to spend the night. This was particularly true in Jeffries' case, whose Cheyenne wife saw to it that he was well-equipped for spending time out on the prairie.

With the first guards posted through Dawson's persistent efforts and the rest of the detachment settled in, the two officers and scout sipped coffee and gnawed on the salt pork furnished by Commissary Sergeant Harrigan.

"I got to tell you," Jeffries said. "I didn't see no sign o' them Kiwotas. If they passed through here, they didn't leave a track or a hank o' hair or nothing."

"I just hope they haven't gone so far south that we won't be able to find them," Standish said.

"You're right," Devlin agreed. "If they mate up with any Comanches, they might try raiding down in Texas."

"Or Mexico," Jeffries added.

Devlin finished his coffee and poured another cupful for himself. "They might go pretty far south, but eventually they'll swing back up this way toward the Buffalo Steppes. This is their natural home, and they won't stay away for long."

"There's something I want to point out, Major Devlin," Jeffries said. "I been able to learn that there's a bit more'n twenty warriors in that party. That means there's a coupla more of them than us."

"That's right, sir," Standish agreed. "I was able to determine that when I followed their trail to Deacon Creek. Since we're the hunters and they're the hunted, the advantage is going to be theirs all the way."

Devlin nodded, then grinned. "But our hearts are pure and we're in the right. Doesn't that give us an advantage?"

Jeffries didn't appreciate the humor. "They think they're hearts is pure and they're in the right, so I reckon we won't have much advantage in that department, will we?"

"I suppose not," Devlin admitted.

"We'll just have to fight like hell," Standish surmised. "Like always." He winked at his commanding officer. "Of course that is always combined with your vigorous and fiendishly clever field tactics."

Fred Jeffries tipped his head back and emitted a laugh so loud that the outlying pickets turned to look in his direction. "Them Injuns do call you 'Looks Ahead,' Major. Have you got any big medicine you been keeping to yourself?"

Devlin shrugged. "To fight an Indian and beat him, one must think like an Indian. That's all I try to do."

"You done good so far," Jeffries complimented. "But that was back on the Buffalo Steppes. Out here, things is gonna be more wide open. Another thing to consider is that Sioux or Comanche or Kiowa warriors might decide to join up to have some fun with them Kiwotas."

Standish gave the scout a serious look. "What are the possibilities of that?"

"A hell of a lot more'n I like to think about," Jeffries admitted.

Just then they were interrupted by Sergeant Theodore Dawson's appearance. He saluted Devlin, reporting, "First relief is posted, sir. I got the packhorses along with the rations and extry ammunition set between the two picket lines o' mounts."

"Good idea, Sergeant," Devlin said. "If any raiding hostiles come in, they'll want those items even more than scalps."

"Yes, sir," Dawson said. "The camp is laid out, and ever'body is quartered proper. I'm settled in with Corp'ral Dientz over yonder. Corp'ral Baily and Corp'ral Monroe is 'twixt us and the mounts. We'll all be close if you need something."

"Thank you, Sergeant," Devlin said. "You're dismissed."

But Dawson didn't make an immediate withdrawal. He stood there awkwardly a moment, then said, "Begging the major's pardon."

"Anything else, Sergeant Dawson?" Devlin asked.

"Well, sir, the lads want you to know that they been through a hell of a lot with you in the past," Dawson said. "They asked me to tell you that they're right happy to be out in the field under your command again, sir."

Devlin felt pleased. "Thank the men for me, Sergeant. Please tell them that I feel confident having such good troops under my command."

"That I will, sir!" Dawson saluted and made an about-face to march off to where the dragoons had settled down with their blankets.

Standish gave his commander a most respectful glance. "Damn! I hope that when I'm up in a rank I have the unswerving loyalty and confidence of my men."

"Win battles and keep casualties light," Devlin advised him. He sighed and pulled a cigar from the inner pocket of his jacket. "So far I've been lucky." He bit the end off the tightly rolled tobacco. "I'd appreciate it if you would make a round of the guard posts at least once in the night."

"Yes, sir," Standish said.

Jeffries also fished out a stogie. "So, Major, you consider yourself a lucky officer, do you?"

"Most certainly," Devlin replied. "I hope good fortune continues to hold up for me."

"The best luck you might be able to have out here could prove none too good," Jeffries observed. "Just getting back with our hair in place might be considered a real accomplishment."

Standish, who didn't smoke, watched his campfire companions light up. He frowned at the scout. "You don't seem particularly optimistic about our chances, Mr. Jeffries."

"I ain't," Jeffries said in a frank voice. "We're heading out into the wilds o' the prairie where about ever' tribe o' Injuns we're bound to run into is gonna want to pick a fight with us. That don't exactly lighten my mood none, Lieutenant."

"Then, why are you here?" Standish wanted to know.

"Same reason you are," Jeffries said. "Same reason Major Devlin is. Same reason all them dragoons is. I signed up for the job."

Devlin chuckled. "Also a bit of insanity does help, right?"

The other two laughed, then turned this attention to

the last of the coffee that boiled away on the fire. When the brew was finished, the evening's dusk had begun to settle in. The camp went into its night routine with the posting of the second relief of the guard. The dragoons of the first watch then fed themselves and prepared to settle in and grab what sleep they could until the roster came around once more to put them back on sentry duty.

An hour later a bright moon came into the sky, giving a brilliance to the primitive scene. But eventually heavy clouds eased in from the south and cast darkness on the camp. A light, intermittent rain began. The sprinkles lasted until an hour or so before dawn. When Sergeant Dawson began waking the troops to begin the new day, he found them slumbering under wet blankets. Each pair of sleeping dragoons enjoyed a damp warmth brought on by their combined body heat.

Fires were quickly started to heat the coffee so necessary on a cool morning in the field. Hardtack crackers and jam were produced by a few hearty individuals while others broiled hunks of salt pork on sticks.

"It's times like this that I miss Tommy Kubelsky," Devlin said. "That is one soldier who can brew up excellent coffee in the field."

"Too bad he got so crippled up with the rheumatiz," Jeffries said. "I recollect enjoying his cooking back before he got so bad he couldn't take to active campaigning no more."

"He's just a poor old soldier," Devlin said. "He can't read or write. If he was discharged back to civil life, I'm afraid he wouldn't last long out there before too much drink and too little nourishment would do him in."

Lieutenant Emil Standish rolled up his blankets. "I made a tour of the guard posts last night, sir."

"I know," Devlin said. "I was awake when you got

up. Since you didn't make a report, I assume everything was in order."

"Yes, sir," Standish said. "There's never much trouble about sleeping sentries when the chance for hostiles to spring out of the dark is always looming."

"I had one eye open myself," Jeffries said.

Within twenty minutes Sergeant Dawson had the troops and their horses packed, saddled, and ready to move. The noncommissioned officer presented himself with a snappy salute, saying, "The patrol is ready to get going, sir."

"Very well, Sergeant," Devlin said. He, Jeffries, and Standish were also prepared to resume the mission. "Let's get back to work."

The small column swung up into their saddles with a shouted "For'd, yo!" from Major Matt Devlin. The march to the southwest took up where it had left off the previous evening.

Jeffries wasted no time in ranging far to the front to check things out as the body of dragoons followed after him through the waving sea of prairie grass. Flankers were positioned by Sergeant Dawson as the men settled in for another day of traveling across Dakota Territory's trackless wild country.

Lieutenant Standish, riding directly beside Devlin, asked, "How much farther south will we be going, sir?"

"Not much more than another couple of days," Devlin answered. "That's Pawnee country down there, and they are mortal enemies of the Kiwotas. I don't think even Running Wolf thinks he can take that bunch on with only twenty or so warriors."

"This group of ours should tempt him, though," Standish remarked.

"Of that, I am absolutely sure," Devlin said. He glanced at the lieutenant. "We're heading for a fight."

"It's too bad we can't choose the time or place," Standish said.

Devlin replied, "One thing to never forget, Lieutenant Standish. An Indian enemy would never allow that luxury."

The dragoons, lulled by the boredom of the journey, yet buoyed up by the expectation of a violent, bloody encounter, pressed on.

Chapter 12

It was mid-afternoon when Fred Jeffries appeared on a rise some three hundred yards to the front of the patrol. He had been gone for almost two hours on an advanced scouting mission in which he had ranged far ahead of the dragoon column.

He hadn't gone on a solo reconnaissance simply to be alone for a while. Many times a man alone could discover prey—human or animal—that might evade discovery if warned by the disturbance created by numerous pursuers.

Since the scout was in no hurry as he rode toward them, none of the dragoons were alarmed by his unexpected return to the column. A feeling of disappointment swept through the detachment, however. The sooner they found Running Wolf and his band, the sooner they would return to enjoy what they could of Fort Buffalo's questionable comforts.

When Jeffries reached Major Matt Devlin, he reined in. "I found the place where Lieutenant Standish and his patrol buried them dead men."

"Good work, Mr. Jeffries," Devlin complimented him. "That will save us a lot of time in having to find a spot to begin serious tracking of the hostiles."

"Five graves, correct?" Standish asked.

"That's what I counted," Jeffries said. "Them poor jaspers sure picked a bad place to set up camp. That was the lowest laying country in the area. Ever'where else was higher, so nearly anybody coulda looked down on that place. Even a small herd o' nervous buffalo coulda snuck up on 'em."

"Let's press on over there," Devlin said. "The trail left by the Kiwotas is old and cold, but we know for sure that Running Wolf and his band passed through there. At least we can pick up which direction they headed, even if the tracks eventually disappear.

"That'll take some looking around," Jeffries remarked. "But don't worry, Major. I'll be able to figger it out."

"Then, let's go," Devlin said.

The patrol moved forward, reaching the place where they could look down on the scene where the five white men had been killed. The patrol leader signaled a halt as he surveyed the area.

"You're right, Mr. Jeffries," Devlin said. "Those men did pick an extremely poor place to set up a bivouac."

"If it had rained, they'd have been flooded out," Standish observed.

"They was prob'ly all from back east and plumb inexperienced, that's all," Jeffries said. "A feller has to be out here awhile to start thinking in terms of finding the most comfortable spots to sleep or to avoid trouble."

The view from their vantage point offered an immense amount of the prairie country for visual inspection. It was easy to determine that no other human beings—neither friendly whites nor hostile Indians—were nearby. This was the spot that victims should have picked for their camp. It would have been impossible to launch a surprise attack on them.

"This was a good place for Running Wolf and his friends to launch their assault," Devlin remarked.

"Those unfortunate men were struck with dozens of arrows each," Standish recalled. "I imagine the Indians sat up here and leisurely shot downhill at their victims."

Devlin shook his head. "It's a shame. You would think the poor devils could have fought back or at least made an attempt to escape."

"They were probably too drunk," Standish surmised. "The area was filled with scattered whiskey bottles. I'm pretty sure the Indians didn't drink it all."

"Well, that's two mistakes, then," Devlin observed. "Besides camping in a bad place, they were also intoxicated."

Jeffries grinned. "I learned a long time ago that there was always a time and place to drink. For them boys on that day, things was definitely all wrong for enjoying liquor."

"Let's get on down there and see if we can pick up any information on which way Running Wolf and his warriors went," Devlin said.

"I recall that the trail seemed to lead off to the south," Standish said. "But because I had to return to the site of the wagon massacre to retrieve those children, I didn't have time to make certain of that."

"We'll let Mr. Jeffries determine which way to go," Devlin said.

"I'm much obliged for your confidence, Major," Jeffries said.

"You've sure earned it," Devlin said.

"We might be able to figure out if they changed direction later on since there's been no real bad storms or nothing to wash away tracks," Jeffries explained.

When they reached the site of the killings, the troopers could easily see the relatively fresh patches of dirt that revealed the locations of the graves where the five white drunks had been buried.

Jeffries dismounted. "I'll ask y'all to not walk around as of yet. I want to see what kind o' sign I might find."

Sergeant Dawson barked at his dragoons, "Sit fast to saddle!"

Jeffries walked all around the area, nearly bent double as he searched for some evidence that would give an indication of which way Running Wolf and his cohorts had gone. The best thing he could find was scuffed dirt and a few stones that had been kicked away as if struck by horses' hooves. That was enough for the skilled frontiersman. He mounted up and rode out, following the faint trail as best he could. He went a little more than a mile before he turned back and rejoined Devlin and the rest of the dragoons.

"They headed south like the lieutenant figgered, Major Devlin," Jeffries announced. "But we still ain't got much to go on, but I'm sure they didn't turn off to the east or west. It was straight toward Kansas Territory all the way."

"Are you sure they would go in that direction?" Devlin asked. "That's Pawnee country down there."

"I'm positive, Major," Jeffries assured him.

"That's good enough for me," Devlin said. "Then, it's to the south we'll travel."

Young Lieutenant Standish was not so sure. "The Kiowtas and Pawnees have been fighting and looting each other for eons, sir. Such a move would seem dangerous on Running Wolf's part."

"That is exactly why he did it," Devlin stated.

Jeffries agreed. "Running Wolf is still perty young. He's got to make his reputation as a war chief, so he's prob'ly hoping he can find a few wandering Pawnees or at least a small camp of that tribe. It'd be quite an honor for him and his pards if'n they showed up back home with Pawnee scalps and trophies."

Devlin was thoughtful. "The whole idea might turn sour for him, too. What if a large group of Pawnees finds that small Kiwota war party?"

"That's part o' the fun for 'em, Major," Jeffries said. "If there wasn't no danger involved, Running Wolf wouldn't do it 'cause he couldn't win no honors."

"Then, let's proceed to the south, Mr. Jeffries," Devlin said.

"Here we go," Jeffries said, once again heading out to scout ahead.

"Columns of twos!" Devlin commanded his men. "For'd, at a trot, yo!"

Once again the dragoon patrol moved across the prairie to close the distance between themselves and their clever, dangerous quarry. Sergeant Dawson sent out flankers as usual, but this time he also picked a couple of the veteran soldiers to act as rear guard. Those men would occasionally leave the detachment to make sure no one was closing in from the opposite direction.

They pressed on across the vastness of the open range country, crossing over the invisible boundary that divided the Dakota Territory from Kansas Territory. The sun, though far from the intensity it would reach in mid-summer, was warm enough to affect both men and animals. However, since there was plenty of water in the area in the form of creeks and ponds, no one experienced any discomfort from thirst.

Devlin glanced to the southeast. "Fort Leavenworth is about seventy-five miles in that direction."

"Yes, sir," Standish said. "I wouldn't mind being stationed there. As far as I'm concerned it's the perfect post. The place is too far west to have any idiotic pomp and ceremony, yet close enough to the east to be able to boast of quite a few comforts and conveniences."

"Not at all like our poor old Fort Buffalo, hey?" Devlin remarked with a grin. "But wouldn't you like all the luxuries of an eastern garrison sometime in your career?"

"I would never be able fit in normal garrison society, sir," Standish said. "I've been out on the frontier since leaving West Point three years ago."

"That's true of most of us, Lieutenant," Devlin said. "My poor family hasn't been in comfortable quarters even once during all my years of service. I don't think the army wants any of us brought back to civilization either. We would be like embarrassing country cousins."

"You want to know something, sir?" Standish asked. "I take a great deal of pride in that."

"Me, too, Lieutenant Standish," Devlin said.

Standish suddenly pointed ahead. "Look, sir! Here comes Mr. Jeffries, and he's riding hell-for-leather and waving his arms."

Devlin wasted no time. "Detachment! Form as skirmishers left and right, at a trot, yo!"

The two lines of the patrol split up, half going to the right of the officers and half to the left to form one rank facing outward. As Sergeant Dawson joined Devlin and Standish, the patrol's three corporals saw to it that their men were correctly aligned.

Jeffries cam on, riding hard, closing the distance between himself and the dragoons as fast as he could.

"Detachment, halt!" Devlin commanded.

The patrol, now with carbines drawn and ready, reined in as one man. Sergeant Dawson took a quick moment to make sure everything was proper, then turned his attention back to the approaching scout.

Jeffries' horse almost stumbled from the violent way

its rider brought the wild gallop to a halt. The scout, breathing hard, spoke directly to Devlin, saying, "Pawnee—war party—close by."

"How many?" Devlin asked.

"Wait—" Jeffries took a deep breath. Wait—"

"I shall wait if it pleases you, Mr. Jeffries," Devlin said. Aside from respecting Jeffries' ability as a scout and tracker, he also had such faith in the man's ability to accurately judge situations that he followed, without question, whatever advice the scout gave. "But I would appreciate it if you could recover yourself as quickly as possible."

Jeffries took a drink from his canteen, then another breath. "Now I can talk," he said. "There's a Pawnee war party a coupla miles to the south. They got about forty, maybe fifty warriors. But they ain't gonna give us no trouble. They're looking for Kiwotas."

"I see," Devlin said. "Evidently our old friend Running Wolf and his friends managed to do some mischief against their old enemies, hey?"

"That's right, Major Devlin," Jeffries said. "They stole some women and horses and killed three Pawnee men. That's how come that war party is looking for them. I know the leader from when I was a boy traveling through here with my boss. The feller's name is Sees-the-River, and he's hopping mad."

"Did you tell this Sees-the-River about this patrol?" Devlin asked.

"Just a little," Jeffries said. "Since he ain't upset at us, he wants to have a pow wow. He thought it was a good thing that we both was after the same Kiwota war party."

"Do you think I should speak with him?" Devlin asked.

"It'd be a good idea, sir," Jeffries said. "But I figger it's best if'n just you and me went. Some o' them

Pawnee might get upset if they see these dragoons. There's some old scores they might want to settle, y'know what I mean, Major?"

"Indeed I do," Devlin said. He turned to his second in command. "Take over until my return, Lieutenant Standish."

"Yes, sir!" the lieutenant replied.

"Lead on, Mr. Jeffries," Devlin told the scout.

Jeffries turned his horse and took off at a canter with the army officer close behind him. They went easily across the rolling country for a couple of miles before spotting the Pawnees. Jeffries didn't hesitate a bit as he led Devlin to the meeting with the war chief called Sees-the-River.

Devlin experienced a stab of nervousness as he noted that all the warriors were mounted, painted, and obviously spoiling for a fight. But Jeffries' calm demeanor eased most of the anxiety he felt.

One of the Pawnees rode forward. He was a large, muscular man with only a strip of hair left on his shaven head. Painted in a black, white, and blue pattern, his bronze-colored face had a savage, yet aristocratic look about it.

"Hello to you again, Fred Jeffries," the Indian said in English.

Jeffries replied in the Pawnee language, then added, "This is Soldier Chief Devlin. The Kiwotas fear his war making and call him Looks Ahead."

"Hello to you, Looks Ahead," the Pawnee said. "I am called Sees-the-River."

"Hello to you," Devlin said. "My friend Jeffries tells me you search for a Kiwota war party."

"Yes!" Sees-the-River exclaimed. "The son of bitches bastards killed three men of my tribe and took away women and horses. We find the women yesterday all dead and used. The horses are with the Kiwotas."

"Do you know which direction they went?" Devlin asked.

Sees-the-River pointed to the northwest. "That way to visit their Sioux friends, I think. They are other son of a bitches bastards that we hate. It will be hard for us to go there and kill them. The Sioux will kill us. Can you go there? If you go there and see the Kiwotas, kill them. Do this, and I will call you my brother, Looks Ahead!"

"I would be happy to be your brother, and if that is the direction they went, I most certainly shall fight with them to kill or capture all the war party," Devlin said. "I, too, am angry at them. They killed some white men and white women. I want to catch them and punish them."

Sees-the-River looked past the major and scout. "Where are your soldiers, Looks Ahead?"

"They are waiting for me back a ways," Devlin answered. "All are ready for a good fight."

"Do you have many?" Sees-the-River asked in unabashed curiosity.

Devlin smiled. "I have plenty." He didn't want to tempt the Pawnees into testing his detachment's strength. "Together, we can make the Kiwotas run for their lives."

"I like that idea, Looks Ahead," Sees-the-River said.

Jeffries spoke directly to Devlin. "That gives me an idea, Major. If them Pawnee head to the northwest as far as they go, they might turn the Kiwotas back eastward before they can find the Sioux."

"I understand," Devlin said. "And if we go straight north, we might intercept them."

"That's the plan, but we might not either," Jeffries said. "There's always a chance they'll slip through or meet up with the Sioux and settle in for the rest o' the summer."

"It's worth a chance, though," Devlin said. "As a matter of fact, it's the best we can do right now."

Jeffries looked back at Sees-the-River and spoke to him in the Pawnee tongue. Then he finished in English, saying, "What do you think of that idea?"

"I think it is good," Sees-the-River said. He immediately swung his horse around and rode back to where the rest of the Pawnee warriors waited a short distance away. After only a few short moments, shouts arose from the group, and they all galloped off toward the northwest.

"It doesn't take them long to go into action, does it?" Devlin remarked with a grin.

"They're boiling mad, Major," Jeffries said.

The pair wheeled their own horses around and galloped back to the detachment. They found the dragoons still drawn up for battle. Devlin wasted no time in reforming them back into a double column, then moving northward.

"Let's slant a little to the east, Major," Jeffries advised. "That'll give the Pawnees some running room to stampede Running Wolf and his band in the direction we want 'em to go."

"Lead on, Mr. Jeffries!" Devlin said.

As they cantered across the prairie, Devlin informed both Lieutenant Standish and Sergeant Dawson of the plan to allow the Pawnees to flush the Kiwotas before they had time to join up with any of their Sioux friends.

Jeffries stayed close enough to keep in sight, yet far enough ahead of the patrol to be able to give ample warning if the situation turned nasty. They continued to travel, the anticipation of a potential fight keeping everyone keyed up and alert.

"Sir!" Standish shouted. "Jeffries has just signaled."

Devlin glanced up to see the scout making a rapid return. Jeffries came to a dust-billowing halt. "It's the Kiwotas, Major!" he shouted. "Just over the rise. The Pawnees have got 'em heading south."

"Form as skirmishers left and right, at a trot, yo!" Devlin commanded.

The patrol quickly and efficiently performed the maneuver, aligning themselves for the coming fight as they continued forward in the battle formation.

"Draw pistols!" the major ordered.

With revolvers held in their right hands, the dragoons moved toward the rise. When they topped the high ground, they could see the Kiwota war party a couple hundred yards ahead.

Wishing he had a bugler, Devlin took a deep breath and bellowed, "Charge!"

CHAPTER 13

After the war party's glorious start, Running Wolf's luck had turned completely bad.

The initial successes of hitting the small wagon train, killing the white men and pillaging their belongings, and then scoring in blood and coups on the traditional enemy, the Pawnees, made the young Kiwota war leader begin to think he was invincible and fated to attain the greatness of War Heart.

During the victories, his medicine seemed to grow within him, making his blood course faster through his veins. With each triumph the young warrior could feel the strength of his muscles and spirit grow beneath his copper-colored skin.

After the killing and rape of the Pawnees, Running Wolf's plan was to take the stolen horses north until he made contact with one of the Sioux villages that summered on the Platte River. Surely, with such booty, he would be able to recruit some young Sioux warriors into his band for future forays against both white and Indian enemies for even more additional glory.

Such accomplishments would add greatly not only to the strength of his war making, but would even further increase the strength of his personal medicine. With such supernatural power, he might even drive the whites off the People's ancestral land, and eastward across the river they called the Des Lacs. His strength and prowess would be so great that even Looks Ahead would fear him.

But the sudden appearance of numerous Pawnees put an end to all that. Running Wolf had made a valiant attempt to attack the traditional enemies, but they were far too many. He was forced to head farther toward the northwest to close in on the Sioux villages where the men of those clans would be more than happy to ruthlessly deal with any intruders. But the strong band of Pawnees had forced the Kiwotas to the east, finally making it impossible to reach the safety of the Sioux nation.

The final disgrace was when several of the enemy warriors managed to separate the stolen horse herd from the Kiwotas and regain possession. Then, under hot pursuit, Running Wolf and his young warriors galloped madly for their lives, forced to leave their booty behind.

Finally, the Pawnees inexplicably broke off the chase, leaving the Kiwotas alone in the vast country. Running Wolf knew it would be impossible to head west to join the Sioux. The Pawnees would undoubtedly be waiting to renew the fight. Since he and his friends were low on ammunition and arrows, and their horses were close to being worn out, they decided to return to the Buffalo Steppes and sneak back on the reservation. Perhaps the remainder of the beef issue had arrived or the men in the village had managed to find some buffalo. After a good rest and feed to replenish their strength, they could try their luck again on the warpath. If Running Wolf talked and cajoled enough, perhaps he would be able to gather even more warriors for another foray.

But even with potential glory in the future, Running Wolf's mood was black. His dream of glory to be won on this warpath was dashed, and the ignoble route and loss of the horse herd forced on him by the Pawnees would take away whatever other honors he had earned in the previous attacks. He had even heard some grumbling among the warriors about how much better they would have done had War Heart been the band's leader.

"Soldiers!" someone shouted.

Running Wolf looked toward the rear and could see a sight he dreaded. A line of dragoons, with pistols drawn, charged straight at the war party. He recognized Looks Ahead in the center of the soldiers and realized that the army officer's medicine was as strong as ever.

Normally the warriors would have sent some arrows flying at the troopers, but they were too short of the missiles to waste any. At that point, whatever cohesiveness and leadership Running Wolf had enjoyed with his friends in the past dissolved like snow in sunlight.

The Kiwotas, like other Indians under similar circumstances, acted independently with no thought to any coordinated effort at defense.

Waits-All-Day and Snake split off from the group, turning due north. They had no plan. Snake had noted his friend's movement and decided to follow him. There was no cover available in the open grassland as they fled. Their only hope was to outlast any pursuers.

But Lieutenant Emil Standish and the two dragoons with him had horses that were relatively fresh and well-nourished from frequent feedings of oats brought along on the patrol. After receiving a signal from Major Devlin to pursue the pair of absconding Kiwotas, the three army men, still holding on to their pistols, gave determined chase to the fugitives.

The run went on for another ten minutes before

Waits-All-Day turned in his saddle and aimed an arrow at Standish. The young lieutenant, one of the best pistol shots in the regiment, aimed as best he could on the bounding horse and squeezed the trigger.

Waits-All-Day's jaw flew off; then a second bullet went through his shoulder, hit a bone and ricocheted through flesh and muscle deep into his body. As the warrior cartwheeled from the saddle, Snake made a ninety-degree turn that brought him within a few scant yards of the dragoon on the right. The soldier had only to shoot once at such a close range to blast the warrior off his horse.

Standish and his men immediately turned back toward the main chase that still ranged crazily across the prairie. The lieutenant kept the pace hot, but watched for any more opportunities should any of the warriors try another break for freedom on their own.

The dragoons, all veterans, kept their firing to the minimum. All knew the difficulty of hitting moving targets while bouncing in the saddle, so none fired unless there was a good chance of sending a bullet into one of the Kiwotas. The Indians, on the other hand, found it impossible to turn and shoot or loose arrows over their shoulders. Angry and frustrated, they continued riding. All they could do was hope for the best and wait to see what would eventually happen.

Suddenly, on the left of the skirmish line, several troopers closed in enough to do damage. A series of detonating pistols sent several bullets streaking into the close-packed Kiwotas. Three more slipped from their horses to bounce and roll in the dusty prairie grass.

The warrior Charging Bull kept glancing around him. He noted Waits-All-Day and Snake when they cut loose, but decided not to follow them. He also saw the three soldiers gallop after his friends. He didn't know their fate, but the three warriors so recently cut down were near enough for him to see them die. He fully realized that the number of men in the war band seemed to be dwindling fast.

Charging Bull decided to tempt fate by making his own break for safety. He made a quick turn and headed south. Five more of the young Kiwotas, indecisive and undisciplined, followed after him.

Major Devlin gestured to Sergeant Dawson to follow. The noncommissioned officer, quickly summing up the situation, motioned to Corporal Dientz and his squad to ride with him. They left the formation and chased after the half-dozen escaping warriors.

The chase did not go far before the Indians reached a small copse of trees. They went straight into it and dismounted. One of the number was the boy Red Cub. He knew his duties and quickly gathered up the horses, keeping them under control while the other five Kiwotas prepared to carry on the fight.

The dragoons dismounted and had their own animals taken care of by quickly hobbling them and leaving them under the care of a private. Dawson and Dientz led the rest of the troops toward the trees. They moved in short rushes, taking advantage of the concealment offered by the tall prairie grass.

"Corp'ral Dientz," Dawson hollered. "Send two men around to each side o' that grove. Have 'em cover the rear. I don't want them son of a bitches sneaking away in that direction."

Dientz, a German immigrant who had served as a conscript in the Prussian army, quickly obeyed.

"Right, lads!" Dawson yelled at the other dragoons. "As skirmishers, move for'd and fire at will!"

The horse troopers, now fighting as infantry, advanced with their carbines at the ready. For the first few paces, they caught no sight of the elusive Indians.

Then some arrows flew from the trees, landing a few yards behind the soldiers.

"Ha!" Dawson crowed. "The bastards ain't got our range, lads. Move out on the double and let's finish 'em off."

The dragoons cheered and charged forward.

While the detached unit moved toward the trees, the chase of the remainder of the Kiwotas thundered on across the wide Dakota prairie.

Devlin, for his part, kept the pressure on the main body of Kiwotas, who now numbered a dozen. With the determined soldiers riding hard after them, it would be only a matter of time before the battle was settled.

Devlin now closed in on a warrior. The Indian slashed out at him with his war club, forcing the army officer to pull back a bit. Once more, by kicking his horse's flanks, Devlin moved in to make contact. He raised his pistol and pulled the trigger, but the weapon misfired.

Bear Claw, the band's scout, had no intention of giving up the fight. Once more he made a wild swing with the club. He hissed in anger when he missed again, then decided to count coup by slapping Looks Ahead.

But Devlin was in no mood to play at war.

The officer took his useless pistol and struck at the Indian. When Bear Claw made another attempt to touch the army officer, he received a hard knock on the head. Blood spurted from the gash in his forehead. The second blow smacked him on the temple so hard that he was knocked unconscious. The warrior tumbled over the back of his horse and landed on top of his head. His neck broke and he died instantaneously.

Devlin kicked his horse into a faster pace to regain his position in the dragoon formation. He was pleased to note that Lieutenant Standish and the two dragoons had now also caught up with the detachment. The major wanted to keep the pressure on the Indians to avoid any nasty situations where they might be able to make a last stand behind cover.

Running Wolf had not paid much attention to what had been going on. The young war leader had scarcely glanced back at the pursuers, but his mind had been occupied with more than a blind desire for escape.

War Heart had been a warrior the young Running Wolf had admired since boyhood. Countless forays against whites, Pawness, Cheyenne, and other enemies as well as many hunting expeditions to feed the People had been successfully led by the old master. It had been the deep respect of the tribe that led them to follow War Heart along the path of peace by agreeing to the treaty. Even if the buffalo were killed or run off by the white hunters, and the promised beef issue never materialized, the Kiwotas felt that War Heart could solve whatever problem came up.

Now, deep in Running Wolf's heart, he knew he had made a bad mistake. His leadership had not produced great victories. The killing of the people in the wagons had been no difficult fight, filling the bodies of drunken white men with arrows had produced no glory, and the sudden raid on a small Pawnee camp had not resulted in any deeds that would be talked about around tribal council fires. And now the final stages of his war expedition were reaching a humiliating end, being chased first by Pawnees, then by soldiers as his warriors were killed off one by one.

Running Wolf decided the time and circumstances had arrived for him to become a real war chief.

The first thing he did was raise his arm and wave it to attract the attention of the ten warriors who still galloped in the main pack. Although he didn't exactly know what he was going to do, he turned toward the north and began riding in a wide circle.

The other Kiwotas, for lack of anything better, followed after him. Their formation spread out a bit, making them more difficult targets. As a result, the soldiers lost some of the tightness in their skirmish line in spite of all their fighting and drill experience on horseback.

Running Wolf turned back in the opposite direction, then quickly reversed himself again, this time going into a tighter turn. He took the revolver he'd gotten in the first raid and held it in his right hand. Once more he forced his horse toward the inside, slowing down a bit, maneuvering the soldiers into a position where they were not situated to the exact rear of the war party.

Some more turning maneuvers followed until Running Wolf was able to get clear views of the soldiers who tried to match the direction in which he led his warriors. At one point, several dragoons were forced close together as they wheeled violently to keep up.

Running Wolf aimed into the mass of bluecoats and squeezed the trigger several times.

One soldier slumped in the saddle and pulled out of the chase. Two more unceremoniously fell from the backs of their horses and slammed into the ground.

Back in the formation of dragoons, Major Matt Devlin was doing his own planning. When he saw the three casualties, he knew it was time to act. Shouting and signaling, he turned the troopers into the opposite direction, keeping the turn as tight as Running Wolf had done.

The result of the action was the two groups exchanged positions, which brought the Indians within the gunsights of the soldiers. Skills in fire-and-maneuver were something in which the army clearly outmatched the Indians.

The dragoons, working under orders to fire at will, wasted no time in blasting into the now exposed Kiwotas.

The effect was catastrophic for the warriors. A half dozen were blasted from their horses almost simultaneously. The second volley took another four, leaving a lone survivor—Running Wolf.

The young war chief's position in front had saved him from injury, but he took no pleasure or comfort in the fact. He straightened out his run and galloped down into a gentle dip in the ground, coming out onto a rise in the terrain. After crossing that, he dropped down into another low spot. He suddenly brought his horse to a stop and leaped off. A slap on its flank sent the animal running on.

Running Wolf turned to face the oncoming soldiers. Like all Kiwota warriors, he had composed his own death song many years previously, before he was old enough to be a warrior. He had sung it many times for practice, but now knew this would be the actual and final time to recite the words. Standing alone on that prairie, he faced his enemies. Somehow, he also felt it was the end of the Kiwotas as he knew them, and that the tribe's way of life would die with him. Running Wolf, unafraid, took a deep breath and sang in a firm, clear voice:

"It is better to die a young warrior than an old man.
My spirit will fly away happy knowing this."

The Kiwota warrior repeated the chant as the dragoons came over the rise, heading straight for him. He slipped one of his three remaining arrows onto the bow string and let it fly. It flew between Jeffries and Standish, causing them to swerve and slow down.

Running Wolf continued to sing:

"It is better to die a young warrior than an old man.
Even my enemies will honor me as they kill me this day."

The dragoons swept past him, a bullet striking Running Wolf in the shoulder. He staggered, but kept to his feet. In spite of the pain, he fired another arrow. This one dug into the back of a soldier, who yelled in painful anger before leaning forward and slipping to the ground.

"It is better to die a young warrior than an old man.
Only the earth is supposed to last forever."

Another bullet hit him, this time striking with such force that it knocked the young warrior to the ground. It was a fatal shot, and he knew that blood flowed freely inside of him. But he did not want to be in the dirt because an enemy had knocked him there. Running Wolf forced himself back to his feet.

"It is better to die a young warrior than an old man.
I will see other dead warriors who went before me."

Running Wolf purposely fell to the ground of his own accord rather than being knocked there by an enemy. He lay on his stomach, knowing he was dying.
The warrior tried to sing another verse; but the blood

came up in his mouth, and all he could do was vomit. So he chanted the words in his mind, closed his eyes, and went to his god.

Chapter 14

When Major Matt Devlin's patrol returned to Fort Buffalo, they had only one prisoner out of the more than twenty warriors they had fought in the bloody battle on the prairie. This was a particularly galling defeat for the Kiwota warriors. Of all the future war stories that would be told in the tribe, the one about those who had followed Running Wolf on the ill-fated adventure would be the most melancholy and have the least glory.

It would be but a short time before the mourning songs began for those unfortunate Kiwotas who had been left by the dragoons sprawled dead across the prairie on the west side of Greasy Flats. Devlin had already seen to it that War Heart was notified of the location of the corpses.

The one Kiwota survivor was the adolescent boy Red Cub. As they rode into the confines of the garrison, he sat defiant and unrepentant aboard a horse with his hands tied behind his back. He had a broken nose and black eye along with the abrasions from the beating that Sergeant Dawson had administered during his capture. He wore the injuries as proudly as he would a war bonnet.

The soldiers' wives, however, gave him scant attention. They peered frantically at the column, looking for husbands, then displayed smiles of relief, for all the dragoons killed had been bachelors. Their bodies, wrapped in blue army blankets, were draped across their horses, which brought up the rear of the formation.

Sergeant Major O'Rourke waited for Devlin to ride up; then he rushed to the post commander giving him a sharp salute.

"Sir!" he said. "You'll have to get over to headquarters as soon as possible. There're visitors there, and I don't mind telling you that me and the quartermaster sergeant have been having a devil of a time billeting them."

Devlin motioned the patrol to pass him by as he pulled his horse aside and dismounted. "What visitors are you talking about, Sergeant?"

"There's no less than a U.S. senator visiting our darling post," O'Rourke said. "And he's got a secretary with him along with a feller from the Mission of Indian Reform. There's a hell of a lot going on, sir. Cap'n Blanchard is about to go stark crazy from all the fuss and bother that's happening around here."

"Did any more beef cattle show up to issue to the Kiwotas?" Devlin asked.

O'Rourke shook his head. "Nary a single, solitary cow, sir."

"Thank you, Sergeant," Devlin said. "Meanwhile, I'll need you to see to our dead. We'll hold services and burial tomorrow."

"I'll organize a detail and honor guard now, sir," the sergeant major said.

With that sad duty taken care of, Devlin mounted up and rode in the direction of post headquarters. He could see Beth and the children waving at him. He gave them a smile to let them know he had returned unscathed, then continued on until he reached his destination.

The duty orderly took his horse as the major bounded up the steps to the porch. He went straight past the adjutant and into his office, where he found Captain Bernie Blanchard sitting at the desk.

"I'm really glad to see you, Major," Blanchard said, standing up. He walked around the desk and gestured. "Welcome home and please take over. I sent Sergeant Major O'Rourke to intercept you. I assume he did so."

"Yes," Devlin said. "Now, what's all this about a senator?" He tossed his hat toward the rack in the corner. "Sergeant Major O'Rourke said you were pretty upset."

"Senator Osmond Torrance has descended upon us," Blanchard explained. "His secretary came with him as did a Mr. Gilbert Paxton from the Mission of Indian Reform. And to make things complete, they were accompanied by your old friend Major Pendergrass from Fort Snelling."

Devlin, tired as hell anyway, sank to the chair and leaned forward to cradle his head in his hands. "Oh, goddamn it!"

"There's more," Blanchard said in an ominous tone.

Devlin looked up at him. "Well, hell, give me both barrels, Bernie. Don't just leave me here slowly bleeding to death."

"Do you remember the assistant agent at the reservation?" Blanchard asked. "That tall, skinny, dark fellow who came onto the reservation with buffalo hunters?"

"Of course. You're talking about my old antagonist Wheatfall, are you not?" Devlin said.

"Well, he is now *Colonel* Wheatfall of the territorial

militia," Blanchard said. "Appointed by the governor through the influence of the honorable senator himself." Then he added, "Wheatfall is even in uniform."

Now Devlin stood up. "I don't believe it!"

"There's still a bit more," Blanchard said. "All those hunters of his are also in the militia, having been legally enlisted for a period of ninety days."

Devlin sat down again. After a couple of deep breaths, he said, "Listen up now, Bernie. I want you to organize a meeting here in this office for this evening. I want the senator, Wheatfall, Major Pendergrass, and that fellow from the Mission of Indian Reform to attend the session. I'm going to straighten things out around here or ruin my career once and for all. At this point, I think those are the only two options open for me."

"I'd say you're right. I'll see that some liquor is made available," Blanchard said. "It might help loosen things up a bit for you. Sometimes people tend to get careless and reveal more than they should when they're drunk."

"Good idea," Devlin said, agreeing. "I must admit that I don't have the slightest idea as to what's going on around here. But, meanwhile, I'm going home to take a nice hot bath and have something to eat. Then I'll change into a clean uniform and be back here by seven o'clock. Can you have things ready by then?"

"I'll work with Sergeant Major O'Rourke," Blanchard said. "Don't worry a bit. This place will be set up in a proper manner for an official meeting between the post commander and visiting dignitaries."

"Thank you, Bernie," Devlin said. "Now, please excuse me."

The major left the fort's main building and went directly back to his quarters. He found Beth waiting with the children for a proper greeting after his return from the field. The children, excited to see their father but anxious to get back outside and play, exchanged hugs with their father—except for Freddie, who insisted on a handshake—then bounded out of the house.

With the place to themselves, Devlin kissed his wife, long and deep, as they embraced tightly. "I missed you terribly," he said.

"I was worried," Beth said. "But there's nothing unusual in that. Thank God you've returned safely to me once again."

They broke the embrace, and he said, "It was not a pleasant experience out there. It was one of the worst I've been through, and I've seen a lot."

"I see you had to do some fighting," she said. "I'm always sorry to learn that dragoons have lost their lives, but at least the families were spared this time."

"Yes," Devlin said. "It wasn't the same for the Indians. I've sent Fred Jeffries over to the Kiwota village to give them the news. There'll be a period of mourning and anger, but I had no choice. Right now, I need something to eat and a bath. Then I'm going to attend a meeting with that senator and the rest of those busybodies who came with him."

"I already have your good uniform laid out," Beth said. "The one with the gold epaulets." Her experience as a military wife gave her a special insight which allowed her to stay on top of the major's needs. "Meantime, I'll get your supper while you put some water on the stove."

"Isn't Mary Harrigan here to keep house and cook?" Devlin asked.

Beth looked at him and smiled. "I sent her home."

Devlin grinned back. "Good idea!"

Both turned to their chores. By the time Beth set down a plate of elk steak, corn, gravy, quartermaster bread, and coffee on the table, Devlin had a couple pails of water heating. The bathtub sat in the corner of the kitchen.

"What has become of those children young Lieutenant Standish rescued?" Devlin asked.

"They are being claimed by the couple from the Mission of Indian Reform," Beth answered.

"Couple? I heard there was a man," Devlin said.

"He brought his wife, a very charming but rather naive lady," Beth said. She changed the subject. "Now tell me about this patrol."

Beth sat across from her husband at the table, listening to him tell of what had happened during the mission to the field. He ate heartily as he gave a sketchy account of the fighting and how of the twenty-two Kiwotas who had followed Running Wolf on the warpath, only the boy Red Cub had survived. The youngster was safely stashed away in the post guard house until a pow wow could be arranged with his tribe.

"I hope War Heart keeps himself and his tribe under control," Beth said.

"That is also my most fervent prayer," Devlin said.

"They've still plenty of warriors left even after suffering this loss. So they could cause plenty of grief and death if they decide to seek vengeance."

He finished the meal and turned his attention to washing several weeks of patrol dirt off himself. After filling the tub and stripping, he stepped into the hot water and sank down to soak and scrub. Beth brought him his razor and soap cup to tend to shaving. She knelt down and held the mirror as he scraped away the accumulation of beard, leaving his face smooth and clean.

With the cleaning up completed, Devlin toweled off and went into the bedroom. Beth went to the doors to make sure they were locked, then joined him.

"The children won't be able to get in without knocking," she said.

Devlin smiled, taking her in his arms for another kiss. When they parted, she took off her own clothes, and they went to the bed. The couple renewed their love in a slow, leisurely way that pleasured them both. Then Beth dressed while her husband dozed off for a short nap before going back to headquarters.

Captain Bernie Blanchard and Sergeant Major Edgar O'Rourke had not been wasting their time while their commanding officer ate, bathed, and made love. With help from a detail of men from Company A, they had Devlin's office changed into a meeting hall complete with a long table with chairs down each side. Then one chair was set at each end for Devlin and the guest of honor, Senator Torrance. Along the side of the room stood another table, this one ladened with different sorts of liquor, water pitchers, and a couple pots of hot coffee. There were no suitable snacks available at Fort Buffalo, where the only place to shop was the agency store run by Wheeler Coburn.

Major Devlin made sure he arrived a few minutes early so that he could be there to properly greet his guests. Captains Bernie Blanchard and Paul Teasedale along with the other officers also made themselves available for the occasion.

At a few minutes after eight the first guests arrived—Wheeler Coburn and the senator's secretary, Harvey Puffer. Coburn, arrogant as hell, wasted no time in introducing the man to Devlin.

The next two were Major Harold Pendergrass of Fort Snelling and Mr. Gilbert Paxton of the Mission of Indian Reform. After Devlin and Pendergrass renewed their acquaintance, the post commander turned to Paxton.

"I have been expecting someone from your group to

collect the two children from the massacre," Devlin said.

"Actually, while I am here to retrieve the children, I will be attending to additional chores. I have been given the responsibility of establishing a mission school in this vicinity. So, as you can see, this is going to be more than a temporary visit," Paxton said. "I have been charged with turning the Kiwota tribe toward civilization."

"You are planning on taming them, sir?" Devlin asked.

"That is not exactly the expression I would use," Paxton said. "But I suppose, in a way, it is true."

"Well, good luck to you, Mr. Paxton," Devlin said. "Please treat yourself to some of our liquid refreshments."

"Thank you, Major," Paxton said. While the other three immediately fixed themselves stiff drinks, Paxton poured himself a cup of coffee.

Colonel Ned Wheatfall, wearing a uniform fresh out of a military warehouse, next presented himself. He offered his hand to Devlin, saying, "Looks like you and me're in the same business now, Major."

Devlin did not take Wheatfall's hand. "I think not, Mr. Wheatfall."

"Colonel Wheatfall, that is," the other reminded him. "Now let me think. As I recall from my days in the army, don't a colonel outrank a major?"

"Go get yourself a drink," Devlin said tersely. "I suggest that at the first opportunity, you look into the proper protocol between officers of the regular army and those of the militia."

"No need, I already know," Wheatfall said. "But I thank you kindly for the offer of a drink." Grinning, he went over to the table to pour a glassful of rye whiskey.

Finally, making a grand entrance with the young lieutenant assigned him as an aide, Senator Osmond Torrance stepped into the room. "Good evening, gentlemen," he said as a way of announcing his presence. The officer who accompanied him withdrew, happy to have the politician in someone else's care for a while.

Bernie Blanchard once more made the introductions. "Senator Torrance, may I present the post commander, Major Matthew Devlin?" He turned to the army officer. "Sir, I have the honor of introducing the Honorable Senator Osmond Torrance."

Devlin shook hands with the office holder. "My pleasure, sir."

"Oh, the pleasure is mine alone, Major," Torrance said with a wide grin. "I've heard many favorable things about you, sir. Why, just today, they've informed me that you scored quite a victory against the Indians out there on the prairie."

"Thank you, Senator," Devlin said. Not giving a damn what the politician thought of him, he turned and addressed the other six men. "Gentlemen, may I ask you to grab a drink and seat yourselves at the table? An orderly will be made available to serve you while I conduct this business meeting."

"We're going to have business meeting?" Torrance asked. "Why, bless my soul! I thought we were simply going to enjoy each other's company."

Devlin smiled and shook his head, saying, "Business meeting."

Everyone sat down, instinctively leaving the seats at the ends for Devlin and Torrance. Even Wheatfall, as a militia colonel, made no effort to dominate the affair.

"Orderly!" Devlin barked.

Immediately a white-jacketed dragoon appeared. He carried a tray on which he had placed several liquor bottles. The soldier went to each of Devlin's guests, making sure their glasses were filled. Only Paxton refused his offer of the alcohol. After tending to the chore, the trooper positioned himself to one side of the room to keep his eye on things, ready to leave no glass unattended for long.

Devlin smiled down at the senator. "Let's talk about territorial militias, shall we?"

Wheatfall looked at the senator. "I reckon the major is surprised to see me in uniform."

"I am presuming you arranged the appointment," Devlin said.

"Why, Major Devlin, whatever made you think that?" Torrance asked. "Though I must admit that in a discussion I had with the territorial governor, the subject of hostilities with the Kiwotas did come up." He took a small sip of liquor. Obviously, like Devlin, he was not going to get drunk. "I believe I stated that the regular army out here could use a little help from a legally appointed militia."

"If I felt the need for reinforcements, I would have requested some from departmental headquarters at Fort Snelling," Devlin said.

Torrance smiled. "I don't believe any additional troops are available." He turned to Pendergrass. "Is that not correct, Major?"

"Probably not," Pendergrass admitted. "But in the case of an emergency—"

The senator interrupted. "But there was an emergency. I was informed that a number of Kiwota warriors had not only left the reservation, but had committed murder, robbery, and rapine during a wild spree of raiding." He swung his glance back to Devlin. "Could you corroborate that, sir?"

Devlin only nodded. "That band was destroyed except for a young boy who had gone along with them as an auxiliary."

"At any rate, I was concerned," Torrance said. "You army people do a wonderful job, and I mean that most sincerely. My admiration and respect for you and your colleagues know no bounds, Major. But you are not many, and the few that you are seem to be scattered across the width and breadth of the wild country. Naturally, I am pleased to be instrumental in affording you at least a few reinforcements."

Devlin said nothing. He decided to let the senator have his say.

The politician continued, "Of course, I don't wish to see our Indian brothers massacred, so I saw to it that the Mission of Indian Reform was brought out here to bring our Kiwota brothers into the bosom of civilization. Thus, we are honored with Mr. Paxton's presence on the Buffalo Steppes Reservation."

"I would have preferred the missing cattle from the Kiwota's ration issue had been sent instead," Devlin said. He nodded to Paxton. "No disrespect to you, sir."

"Perfectly understandable," Paxton said graciously.

"Couldn't you have seen to that, Senator?" Devlin asked. "That would have been much more helpful than bringing in militia and reformers."

"Alas!" Torrance exclaimed. "I am unable to interfere or influence the actions of the Indian Bureau. If I could, Major Devlin, rest assured I would see to it that all the cattle due our Indian friends would be sent. And on time!"

"I would appreciate an effort on your part in that area," Devlin remarked.

Wheatfall, already a bit tipsy, laughed. "Don't you worry none, Major. Me and my boys is gonna see to it that them redskins mind their manners, or else!"

"I must insist that all military activities be coordinated through me," Devlin said sternly. "I am the post commander here at Fort Buffalo."

"Why, when we're on the reservation we sure will," Wheatfall said. "But off'n it, while we're out there in the Dakota Territory, I'm the commander. I answer to the senator."

Torrance raised a finger. "I believe you answer to the territorial governor, not me, Colonel."

Wheatfall laughed. "Oh, yeah! That's right."

Torrance smiled. "When Colonel Wheatfall is on territorial lands, he serves the governor. After all, that is the duty of militia. Unless under federal authority, they do not serve the U.S. Government."

Devlin retained his poker-faced expression. But his thoughts boiled through an angry brain. A gang of legalized killers was now loose in the guise of militia, a misguided do-gooder reformer would soon be adding to the problem, and there was no certainty that the Indian Bureau would honor the agreement to provide the hungry Indians with their rations.

The major turned his thoughts to wondering what possible interest Senator Osmond Torrance had in that area of the Dakotas. There was some reason the son of a bitch was doing everything possible to kick up trouble.

Devlin picked up the glass of whiskey in front of him, and downed it in a few gulps.

To hell with it.

He would get drunk. Only God knew how much blood was going to be spilled on the Buffalo Steppes before the arrival of the first snows.

Chapter 15

Another short, but important meeting took place the next afternoon at Fort Buffalo. This session, however, was more clandestine, and no subterfuge was involved. The two participants knew exactly what they wanted to accomplish and shared that aim. For that reason, they spoke frankly with each other without innuendos or guarded remarks.

Senator Osmond Torrance and Colonel Ned Wheatfall got together in the politician's quarters in officers' row. The two talked while Harvey Puffer stood by the open window to make sure no one came close enough to hear the conversation. It was too warm outside to close up the building in which the two were situated. If a passerby appeared, the diminutive secretary would clear his throat as a signal. Torrance and Wheatfall then stopped talking and waited until Puffer nodded his head to indicate it was all clear.

"An army post is a hard place to find privacy," Wheatfall remarked after the fifth interruption. "It don't take long to find out ever' secret in a regiment." He chuckled, adding, "O'course that means which sergeant is diddling which other sergeant's ol' lady. Haw!"

Although Wheatfall had taken on a snootful during

the session with Major Devlin, he showed no ill effects. In fact, he did some more serious drinking from the senator's private stock as they sat around the table in the politician's quarters.

Torrance smiled. "A military community is one in which most pretenses are ripped away once you get past the pomp and ceremony."

Wheatfall took two quick swallows of bourbon, then wiped his mouth. "I been meaning to ask you, Senator. How're you doing on keeping that beef ration cut?"

"There will be no problem, Ned," Torrance assured him. "My contacts in the Indian Bureau are most cooperative if the right amount of influence and money is spread about. For that reason, I can personally guarantee that hunger is going to drive those Indians to even more desperate measures."

"I don't think they'll go on the warpath again," Wheatfall said. "At least not for a while, since ol' Devlin went out there and wiped out the last bunch. They got a lotta fear and respect for that feller, so they ain't gonna tangle with him afore they think about it first."

"We don't need any more killings to justify taking action against the Kiwotas," Torrance informed him. "The reason I had you and your men legally set up as territorial militia was to give you the opportunity to strike against any Indian hunting parties that wander off the reservation."

"Which is what they'll have to do to find buffalo," Wheatfall said.

"The fact that they've already raided outside this area provides us with an inarguable license to attack them," Torrance explained. "You can defend your actions by claiming they started the trouble. Therefore, all you have to do is wait for the right opportunity, then begin annihilating that tribe."

"I ain't got enough men to take on the whole tribe at once," Wheatfall said. "But I won't have to. They'll be broke down into small groups when they head out to find buffalo. Me and the boys can pretty much knock 'em off little by little." He became thoughtful for a few moments. "Come to think of it, even if we find a group of 'em *on* the reservation, we can still attack 'em. Like you said, all we got to do is say that they went at us first."

"An excellent observation, Ned," Torrance said. "I'll leave those situations up to you."

"I'll see to it, don't worry none," Wheatfall promised. "I can take any situations that arise one at a time."

"I want the job done by the end of summer if at all possible," Torrance said.

Wheatfall shook his head. "Can't be done, Senator. I'm sorry as hell, but things ain't gonna move quite that fast around here. Particularly on account o' that Paxton feller."

Torrance nodded. "You're right, of course. But do your best, Ned."

"You can count on me for that," Wheatfall said. "Most of the job will be did before the first snowfall." He narrowed his eyes and looked into Torrance's face. "What's the rush, anyhow?"

"That's not for you to worry about, Ned," Torrance said. "All you have to do is succeed."

"I'll drink to that," Wheatfall said. "Here's to success and happy hunting. And Injun killing, too!"

Torrance smiled, raising his own glass. "An appropriate toast, Colonel Wheatfall."

Senator Osmond Torrance stayed around Fort Buffalo for only three more days. He conducted some informal and hasty investigations into conditions at the post, using Major Harold Pendergrass as a guide and adviser. Then he suddenly abandoned any more inquiries and announced his departure. After packing up, he and Harvey Puffer left for Fort Snelling to begin the trip back to civilization.

Meanwhile, Gilbert Paxton and his wife Rachel, quickly settled in an area between Fort Buffalo and the agency store. Besides a large amount of supplies, they had also brought with them a handyman and assistant named George Fenwick, a milk cow, some chickens, and a few pigs. It was obvious to everyone that they had come to settle in for a long, serious stay on the Buffalo Steppes.

Although the Paxtons were childless, they quickly took the two rescued children into their own care. This was because the orphans' parents had also been members of the Mission of Indian Reform.

The little ones' names were Oren and Naomi Duncan, and they were seven and five years of age respectively. After getting over the shock of the terrible experience of seeing their parents and the other adults in the wagon train murdered and violated, they were inconsolable and almost hysterical at times, suffering from nightmares that brought them awake, shrieking in the middle of the night.

Then, just as suddenly, they began to ease back to normalcy as if forgetting the horrors of the event. By the time they moved in with the Paxtons, they seemed perfectly ordinary children.

The one thing the Mission of Indian Reform had supplied the Paxtons that far outstripped that of the Indian agency or even the army was generous funding. Through the monies allotted by their organization, the couple was able to hire soldier-craftsmen to aid George the handyman in working for them during off-duty hours. Through these laborers, the Paxton compound soon consisted of a well-made house, a school, a small dormitory complete with wooden bed frames built three tiers high, a small corral for the cow and pigs, and a respectable chicken yard complete with a roost.

When all that was completed, Mr. and Mrs. Paxton were ready to go to work. The first order of business was for the husband to make a call on Fred Jeffries in his quarters.

He rode his mule over to the scout's place. As he rode up, he could see Jeffries sitting in front idly whittling on a stick while his Cheyenne wife tended to chores in the yard. Paxton and Jeffries had met briefly after the patrol's return a few weeks previously.

Paxton dismounted. "Good day to you, Mr. Jeffries."

"Howdy," Jeffries replied. He was curious as to why the visitor had come calling. He continued his casual knife work and waited for Paxton to speak.

Paxton nodded politely to the woman Moon Deer. "Good day to you, Miz Jeffries."

Moon Deer, not acknowledging the visitor's presence, kept to her work of laying out strips of elk meat on a handmade rack to dry.

Paxton decided this was not a place to waste time on convention or ceremony. "I was wondering, Mr. Jeffries, if you would be interested in employment with the Mission of Indian Reform."

"I'm already a contract scout for the U.S. of A. Army," Jeffries replied.

"I assure you that working for us will not interfere with your employment by the military," Paxton said. "We only require you part-time and are willing to pay you fifty dollars a month for your services."

Jeffries gave the man a narrow-eyed look. "What kinda services, Mr. Paxton? I noticed you got a cow and pigs and chicken. I ain't much on looking after livestock."

"Oh, nothing like that, I assure you," Paxton said. "I need you to act as a translator to begin with. Your services in that line will be necessary so I might tell the Kiwotas about the school my wife and I have set up. We want to urge their children to attend."

Jeffries rubbed his chin and frowned. "Just what in hell are you gonna teach them Injun kids?"

"Well, the English language to begin with," Paxton said. "Along with that would be reading and writing as well as lessons in simple arithmetic. That's the school work. In addition, we shall teach the boys how to farm and tend animals. Such skills as sewing, cooking, and housekeeping would be imparted to the girls by Mrs. Paxton."

"Them Injun girls already know how to sew and cook," Jeffries said. "They also know how to butcher, skin, take care o' the camp, and other things."

"We'll transfer those skills into more civilized methods so they'll be able to live in regular houses and adapt themselves to civilized lives," Paxton said.

Jeffries stopped whittling. "Are you trying to tell me you're planning on turning them Kiwota boys into farmers and herders? Is that what y'all are out here for?" Jeffries asked.

"Certainly," Paxton answered.

"They're more inclined to hunt and fight," Jeffries informed him. "It's right natural for 'em. You got to remember, Mr. Paxton, that them Kiwotas has been follering their own ways for a god-awful amount o' time."

"That will be changed, sir, through education and enlightenment," Paxton said. "It is the purpose of the Mission of Indian Reform to turn those Indian children into a new generation of civilized beings who will find happiness and fulfillment in the white man's world."

Jeffries chuckled. "Hell! That's more'n I ever did." Then he added, "Outside o' the army and the frontier, that is."

"I believe in equality for all, sir," Paxton said in a firm voice. "If I didn't, I would not be a follower and practitioner of the philosophy of the Mission of Indian Reform. Nor would I be offering you a position."

"I appreciate that, Mr. Paxton," Jeffries said. "I really do. But I don't see how in hell you're gonna get them Kiwotas to send their kids to your school."

"The children will live there and have plenty to eat," Paxton said. "Their health will also be looked after."

Jeffries was thoughtful. "That might induce 'em during these hard times when the buffalo is scarce and the beef rations ain't been what they're supposed to be."

"We also will have them forced to comply with our demands," Paxton added. "This is being worked out right now in Washington City. But we really would prefer to use persuasion. Attitudes are most important in a situation like this."

"I'm glad to hear that," Jeffries said. "But I can tell you here and now that having their boys changed into dirt farmers ain't gonna be took kindly to by them warriors."

"No matter what, I fully intend to carry out that plan," Paxton said. "Now, sir, do you accept employment with me or not?"

"I do, Mr. Paxton," Jeffries said. "But I advise you to wait about a week before going over there. The Injuns is still upset about them warriors that was killed. It's been damn near a month now, so a few more days should cool things down even more."

"Very well, Mr. Jeffries," Paxton said. "I shall follow your counsel with great appreciation." He went to his mule and mounted up. "We'll go to the village a week from today."

"That'll be fine, Mr. Paxton," Jeffries said. "A good day to you, sir."

During that week, the life at Fort Buffalo continued on in an uneasy atmosphere. The Kiwotas, obviously upset, made several angry appearances at the agency to inquire after the beef issue. Each time, the Indians were sent away while armed dragoons kept a close eye on the proceedings.

Colonel Wheatfall was anxious to get into action. He had his men of the territorial militia set up a bivouac behind the trading post. Since they could not provoke or attack the Indians so close to Fort Buffalo without challenging Major Devlin's federal authority, they refrained from interfering or taking part in any of the activity.

Wheatfall, with five years of military service under his belt, instilled a slightly different kind of discipline on his men. He taught them the rudiments of drill, and although they didn't really look the part of soldiers, the buffalo hunters did learn how to tramp around in unison, keeping in step and maintaining a loose, but cohesive formation while doing so. Finally, after teaching them to ride in as close a manner to the army as possible, the colonel broke camp and, taking his rag tag troops, disappeared from sight. He led his militia unit to an unknown place or places on the prairie.

Major Devlin didn't know whether to be happy about being rid of the riffraff or to worry about what they might be up to under their villainous leader.

Gilbert Paxton, excited and enthused about his own work, took no notice of other goings-on in the vicinity of his mission school. Exactly a week from the day he visited Fred Jeffries, the reformer reappeared at the black man's residence. Jeffries was waiting for him.

"I already let the Kiwotas know we're coming over," the scout said. "The tribal counsel is gonna be waiting for us."

"Thank you most kindly, Mr. Jeffries," Paxton said. "Your efficiency is well-appreciated."

The pair made the ride to the village, crossing the prairie and leaving behind all signs of civilization. The Kiwotas were located at a bend in Castor Creek. They hadn't been there long, and the area was quite pleasant.

Jeffries glanced over at his companion. "You reckon them Injuns is gonna want to give this up to move into houses and work their butts off plowing and planting?"

Paxton nodded his head with an expression of supreme confidence. "Believe me, Mr. Jeffries, we know what's best for them."

Jeffries stopped and dismounted at the edge of the lodges. Paxton followed his example, and they walked into the village, leading their animals. They went straight to the center of the Kiwota camp to find three of the tribal leaders waiting for them.

War Heart, quiet and withdrawn for a long time, still looked the part of a fierce warrior. With him were the medicine man, Lightning Tree, and an older man called Many Snows.

After Jeffries and Paxton secured their mounts, they approached the trio. The scout spoke to them in the Kiwota language while other members of the tribe began to gather around. Several of the women bore healing wounds on their arms where they had slashed themselves as part of the mourning ceremony for the warriors killed by Devlin and his patrol.

"I greet you and bring somebody for you to meet," he began. "His name is Paxton." He then introduced the Indians to the reformer, using their names in English.

"I am pleased to know you," Paxton said for Jeffries to translate.

"What does he want?" War Heart asked.

"He wants to be friends with the People," Jeffries replied.

"Why?" War Heart asked. Although he had considered Running Wolf as having about as much sense as a rutting buffalo bull during the mating season, he had always harbored a great affection for the young man. The veteran war chief had been greatly saddened by his death.

"He wants to help you and make your lives easier," Jeffries said. "He has built a school where he wants your children to live and learn. He can teach them many things so they can walk the white man's road."

"Why?" War Heart once again asked.

Jeffries turned to Paxton. "War Heart wants to know how's come you're gonna take them kids down the white man's road?"

"Tell him that some day all the Indians will follow the white man's road," Paxton said. "We offer them a better life in which they can produce their own food and not have to depend on hunting to keep from starving. We will teach them many skills that will allow the entire tribe to have an easier existence out here. Soon, instead of lodges, they will all live in comfortable houses."

Many Snows laughed after the words were translated. "How can we move around? Nobody can put a white man's house on a travois."

Paxton replied that the Kiwotas would not move again. They would settle permanently in one spot and be happy there. The Indians' reaction to the words was a mass expression of astonishment.

War Heart frowned. "Why don't you try to teach us to live in the lakes or rivers? That is as silly as staying in one place and never leaving it."

Paxton, well-trained by his organization, decided to go to the heart of the matter. "Tell them that for every family that sends a child to our school, we will give them a cow."

Jeffries was surprised. "The government ain't been able to do that, Mr. Paxton. How're you gonna get any cattle?"

"We can," Paxton said confidently. "And tell them that they needn't send any children over until they get their animals. Along with that, we have flour, sugar, coffee, and tobacco we will give them with the cattle."

Jeffries translated the words, and the hungry Indians now took interest. The Kiwotas talked among themselves for a few moments with the spectators making appropriate comments at them.

Many Snows asked, "Will you give us whiskey?"

"No!" was the firm reply.

A few more questions were asked until they all fully understood the children would have to live at the school and stay there. Finally, they all agreed, yet the medicine man was not completely happy.

Lightning Tree stood up and looked into Paxton's face. "There are serious things Indians must do or their souls will die," he said. "They must purify themselves from time to time. When young people are ready to become adults, there are spiritual things that must be done or they will have weak medicine. That means illness or death in battle and bad hunting for everyone. How can the children go through those ceremonies if they are living over by the soldiers and the agency in your lodges?"

Paxton smiled after Jeffries told him what the shaman had said. "Tell him that the children's spiritual needs will not be neglected."

Jeffries was not happy with the answer. Before translating, he asked, "Are you talking about the Indian side o' them things, or what your mission's idea is of religion? This can get real serious 'y'know."

"I understand, Mr. Jeffries," Paxton said. "Please use my own words and tell them that such matters will not be ignored during their education."

Jeffries frowned. "I ain't sure what you mean by that, Mr. Paxton."

"Just tell him that, please," Paxton again requested.

"If you make me a part of shaming or lying to these folks, I'll take it real bad," Jeffries said in a serious tone.

Paxton smiled. "Then, you must learn to trust me, too, Mr. Jeffries. Please translate my words to them."

Jeffries turned and answered the question. As he spoke, Paxton felt a surge of satisfaction. The first step in the reformation program had gone quite well.

Chapter 16

The Kiwotas' response to Gilbert Paxton's call for students was better than he had expected. More than a hundred and twenty lodges offered children for the school in exchange for live beef and the rations of flour, sugar, and coffee along with a generous supply of tobacco. Since the mission's school capacity was only fifty students, Paxton was able to take his choice of which of the youngsters would become students there.

He knew that desperation for food drove the Indians to send their children for an education, rather than a sincere desire to adopt civilized ways. But the schoolmaster took consolation in the fact that the result would be the same. The Kiwotas would be lead down the white man's road.

Paxton chose a pleasant area within a grove of trees to meet the children one by one. By using Fred Jeffries' interpreting skills, the mission teacher interviewed all the children, asking them questions and popping quick lessons on them in learning English words. Those that responded the best were chosen. After three days of testing, Paxton had thirty girls and twenty boys picked. Paxton had hoped to have an equal number of both sexes, but the people at the Mission of Indian Reform had advised him that the girls always offered more potential as students than the lads. The latter were a rough-and-tumble group raised in a warrior culture in which their independent thoughts and actions were admired. The young females, on the other hand, learned early to conform and be obedient.

Paxton wasn't all that surprised that most of the young males were either sullen or didn't take his questions seriously. The majority, bored with the procedure, paid scant attention to the teacher as their eyes kept turning to the inviting open country where fishing, hunting and other diversionary opportunities awaited them.

The girls, as was expected, were more eager to please. They looked on the oral examination as a game and responded in a positive way to the compliments given them on their participation when they gave correct answers or quickly mastered the words of English Paxton used to test their linguistic dexterity.

A few of the boys, however, had naturally quick minds that even their attitudes could not cover. These normally would have been those who would excel as leaders on the hunt or warpath when they reached adulthood. Paxton was particularly anxious to bring them into his program. Among those chosen was a bright boy of twelve summers named Swift Rabbit.

Paxton made his choices and informed the parents of the chosen children. When he took his leave, he told them that he would not return until he had the presents of food and cattle he promised through the Mission of Indian Reform. This was a carefully calculated move on his part. It was of the utmost importance to develop a bond of trust with the tribe. He wanted to prove that he spoke truthfully and had uttered no false promises to the Indians. The tribe took the children back to their lodges, and life got back to normal for them as they waited.

Two weeks after the interviews, Paxton returned with a large farm wagon driven by his handyman, George Fenwick. It was ladened with barrels of the promised commodities. Trailing behind, with Fred Jeffries and a couple of off-duty dragoons acting as drovers, came the small herd of cattle for distribution.

The families of the children destined for the white man's road presented themselves with their offspring. It was almost like a trading operation in the way that as each child stepped forward, the parents or guardians received one cow and the other items. The boy or girl was placed in the back of the wagon as the adults walked off with their prizes.

It took only an hour to make the swaps. When the cattle were gone, the soldiers returned to Fort Buffalo. Then, with the fifty little Kiwotas crammed into the back of the wagon, Fenwick whistled at the team of mules and flicked the reins, turning the vehicle around for the return journey to the school. The Kiwota youngsters, solemn and patient, stood clinging to each other in silence as they traveled toward an entirely new world.

Rachel, Paxton's wife, was waiting for them when the group reached the mission. After Fenwick brought the wagon to a halt, he hopped off and lowered the tailgate. The adults helped the children to the ground. Mrs. Paxton ushered the boys off to one side and the girls to another.

Paxton addressed the group in English, saying, "We welcome you to our school. I am Mr. Paxton and this is my wife, Mrs. Paxton. Mr. Fenwick is also a member of the staff who will assist you in your education. We are going to have a busy time as we spend the rest of today settling in."

Jeffries stood by to make sure there were no misunderstandings in communications. When he translated the greetings, he had to substitute the words "uncle" and "aunt" in place of "mister" and "missus" since no such words existed in the Kiwota tongue.

With that task done, the scout stepped back to see how the job of enrolling the children would be done. As Jeffries watched the proceedings, he felt a sudden and very strong sense of misgiving. Although the Paxtons seemed pleasant toward the children, in fact outright affectionate, Jeffries sensed that something in those children's lives was about to be ripped away like the scalp from a fallen enemy.

Paxton and his wife gently pushed both groups of children into a single line. The youngsters, completely uncomprehending of what was going on, broke the formation several times as their curiosity caused them to begin to wander off to look at the buildings. The grips on their arms as they were put back into place became firmer and firmer until exclamations of pain were heard. But finally, the Kiwota youngsters understood they were to remain as they had been arranged.

When that had been accomplished, Paxton walked up to Jeffries, saying, "Thank you very much for your services today. We won't be needing you for a while."

Jeffries, his uneasiness increasing, looked at the strange sight of Indian children lined up like soldiers. "I can stay around for a while longer, Mr. Paxton."

"It won't be necessary," Paxton assured him. "You may leave now. Don't worry, you'll still receive your fifty dollars a month whether your services are used full-time or not."

"I ain't worried about that," Jeffries said. "But how're you gonna be able to talk to these kids 'less I tell 'em what you're saying."

"We have our proven methods, don't worry," Paxton said.

"I can stay for a while," Jeffries said.

"You are dismissed, sir!" Paxton said firmly.

Jeffries took one more quick glance at the children before going over to his horse and swinging up into the saddle. Then, not wanting to take another look at the boys and girls, he rode back across the prairie to his home.

Now, speaking in English in loud voices, Paxton and his wife led the two groups of children to their respective dormitories. It was the policy of the Mission of Indian Reform to see that its students were exposed completely to English at the earliest possible moment, even if they would not understand the words.

Under the plan, the girls had a building all to themselves while the bunks for the twenty boys were set up behind partitions in the classroom. All the children tramped into their quarters without protest as they numbly obeyed the white adults.

The first activity of the day was to be much more difficult for the lads than their female counterparts.

Paxton, with Fenwick's less-than-gentle help, used shouts and sign language to get the young males to stand along one wall of the room. A single chair sat in the middle of the chamber. One by one, the boys were led to the chair where a pair of clippers wielded by the handyman quickly shed their heads of braids. He cut the hair down so short that no combing would be required. Only one boy showed any serious resentment. Swift Rabbit received a couple of hard clouts before he accepted his fate and allowed his glossy black locks to be shorn. Once he had been taken care of, the remaining boys submitted without argument.

When the barbering activity was finished, Fenwick had to sweep up the large piles of hair himself. An attempt to get a couple of the boys to do the job failed. Neither could quite comprehend what the strange-looking sticks with the stiff grass on the end were for. Because of not having much time, Paxton and Fenwick gave up that game, and the handyman did the cleanup himself.

The next order of business was to get the boys to strip down to the buff. They were puzzled by the procedure, but felt no particular shame or embarrassment. After all, most had run around naked as youngsters during the warm moons, and any swimming activities also required getting out of one's clothes in front of others.

Each boy was taken individually to a large box where the two men picked out a couple of jackets and trousers that would fit the student. Then hats, shirts, underwear, socks, and shoes were added to the issue. Then the boy was sent back to his place by the wall while the next took his turn.

Confused and pawing through the strange garments they recognized as white men's clothing, the naked boys remained silent. Some now felt a sort of threat in this new environment and wanted to leave. But a certain amount of fearful curiosity kept them in their places.

Once more Paxton and Fenwick spoke in loud, unintelligible words at the lads. Again, through gestures, they imparted their instructions. The boys understood and began donning first the long underwear. Although scratchy and uncomfortable, a couple of cuffs on the head dispelled any resistance to the strange apparel. Next came the trousers and shirts, the latter buttoned all the way up to, and including, the collar.

The shoes proved even more difficult.

Most of the boys, once they understood the heavy, stiff items were to be worn like moccasins, put them on without the socks. These had to be removed, then the socks pulled on, with all twists taken out. Several lads thought that should be enough footgear for anybody, and decided not to try the shoes. Shouts and slaps put an end to that nonsense. Within a half hour, all the Kiwota youngsters felt the discomfort of the unaccustomed foot coverings. All the fittings were not perfect, so Paxton and Fenwick made sure that if the proper size was not available, at least the suffering Indian had a pair too large rather than enduring the painful pinching of a smaller size.

Finally, shorn and dressed, the twenty lads were taken out in the same kind of line in which they had entered the building. Their native garments stayed piled up on the floor, where Fenwick would later gather them up for burning.

The girls were already outside when the boys made their reappearance in the yard. Rachel Paxton had had an easier time and been able to tend to the dressing of the young females without assistance. Their hair was left as it was, but they now wore simple calico dresses and, like the male students, uncomfortable shoes. The two groups of Indians stared at each other. The girls could not comprehend why the boys' braids had been cut off. Even under the hats they wore, there was something alien and almost sinister in their appearance because of the short-cropped hair.

The next order of business was instruction in the sanitary facilities of the mission.

Two outhouses had been located near the rear of the buildings. Gestures and shouting conveyed the lesson that one was for the boys and the other for the girls. It took more effort to make the little Kiwotas understand that they were expected to relieve themselves through the holes in the seats; but finally they not only understood, but several demonstrated the acquisition of the knowledge by tending to nature's call.

The next thing on the agenda was the evening's meal. Although it was three hours before the actual eating was to be done, the activity was as much for teaching as nutrition, including the preparation, setting of tables, serving, eating, and finally the clean-up.

All duties were organized along strict lines of sex with the girls tending to the cooking and serving while the boys did the more physical chores of hauling water, handling the arranging of the chairs and tables, and chopping wood for the stove.

The actual eating of the meal took a long time. The use of knife, fork, and spoon had to be demonstrated many times by the three grown whites, enforced by slaps on the hands of youngsters who preferred their own style of using—or not using—the utensils. But finally, after a hectic period, the meal was consumed and the clean-up begun.

Once more, the boys and girls had decidedly different chores. The girls cleared the tables and washed up while the boys moved the furniture and went about sweeping and mopping the floor, finally grasping the purpose of a broom. The whole affair was an unpleasant time for all concerned as more punishment and angry correction was given than praise.

The end of supper marked only the finish of one ordeal and the beginning of yet another. The next lesson down the white man's road was not only the making of beds, but sleeping in them inside the buildings in which they were located. The boys marched off to their sleeping quarters behind the partition in the classroom while the girls went to their dormitory.

The bedclothes used by the Mission of Indian Reform consisted of course wool blankets and muslin sheets and pillow cases to be placed on straw-filled mattresses. Once more the girls adapted quicker and more easily than the boys. Paxton and Fenwick slapped and yelled until the boys had their beds made up in an acceptable manner. After that followed a stripping off of clothing and the issue of nightshirts to everyone. With that accomplished, the children were ordered to bed, and lanterns were turned off.

The air in the enclosed rooms seemed stuffy to the Kiwota youth. The whites believed that there was harm and sickness in the night air, so they kept the windows shut.

Swift Rabbit threw the covers off and lay on the sack, staring at the ceiling. He rubbed his hands over his nearly shaven head and felt the strange sensation. Now his hair was even shorter than his white friend's, Fox, the son of the soldier chief Looks Ahead. He wondered what Fox would think if he could see him in his white man's clothes and wearing the heavy shoes and wide-brimmed hat given him that day.

The children, used to sleeping in the open, stayed awake until the early hours of the morning when physical exhaustion from the day's hectic activities finally lulled them into slumber.

It was a short night for the little Kiwotas.

Rachel Paxton took her time and gently woke the sleeping girls. She went to each individually, giving the child a warm smile and a gentle shaking if the Indian closed her eyes again. The girls, used to responding quickly to grandmothers and mothers to attend to chores, were up and ready for their first lessons in washing within a very few minutes.

The scene was entirely different over in the classroom where the boys slept. Indian warriors were fierce fighters and tireless hunters, but when not occupied with those activities, they tended to be physically lazy. They slept late, let the women handle the drudgery, and pretty much went through each day as they damn well pleased. This was the custom of the young males as well. If they weren't busied by exclusively male pursuits, they also sat around and rested, idly watching their sisters and other female members of the family do the chores.

This part of their lives was about to go through a drastic change.

Paxton and Fenwick went behind the partition and called out for everyone to wake up. The response to the disturbance was less than they had hoped for, so both men charged into the sleeping area, yelling and physically rousing the sleeping boys. The lads came awake in alarm. Such early-morning behavior generally meant danger from a surprise attack by tribal enemies. The young Kiwotas leaped from their beds and started to run, but the two adults stopped them in their tracks.

Several boys, including Swift Rabbit, were sent to draw water for washing up. When they arrived at the mission well and found the girls doing the same thing, they were mortified. All refused, throwing down their buckets. Men might perform such chores while out on hunting or war parties, but never when in the village and certainly never at the same time women tended to such tasks. This adherence to tribal customs and tradition enraged Fenwick, who pummeled and pushed the lads back to the classroom dormitory.

Paxton saw no sense in trying to reason with the boys. Not only would they be unable to comprehend his words, but they would stubbornly resist doing anything they deemed women's work. It was time to get very serious abut reeducating the youngsters and bringing them onto the white man's road.

Paxton went to the teacher's cabinet behind the desk at the head of the classroom. He retrieved two thin, but strong hickory sticks. He kept one and passed the other over to Fenwick.

The education of the Kiwota boys went into full gallop with each blow of the instruments on their bare buttocks.

Chapter 17

Colonel Ned Wheatfall and his ragtag militia fell behind in their schedule to have a confrontation with the Kiwota Indians. No matter how hard they tried, the buffalo-hunters-turned-soldiers could not find a situation in which a confrontation could be manufactured.

When Wheatfall first heard that the Mission of Indian Reform would be giving cattle, flour, sugar, coffee, and tobacco to the Indians, he had paid the matter little heed. Even though his second in command, Captain Red-Eye Morgan, expressed worry over the situation, Wheatfall had laughed.

"Aw, hell, Red-Eye!" Wheatfall told him. "Giving a few o' them Injuns cows and some tobaccy ain't gonna make do differ'nce in the whole bunch still going hungry. They'll be out in small groups looking for buffalo like they did in the old days. Then we'll hit one or two of them little bands and really stir things up."

But what Wheatfall hadn't counted on was War Heart sticking to the treaty out of respect for the man he called Looks Ahead. The Kiwota war chief was willing to stretch the benefit of the doubt as far as it would go where his former enemy was concerned. It was through his strong influence, along with the bitter lesson learned from Running Wolf's adventurous excursion, that even the most excitable young warriors stayed under control.

Another thing Wheatfall hadn't taken into consideration was the Indian custom of sharing. Each family who received an issue of goods from the Mission of Indian Reform gave some to others who hadn't. That way, a few weeks of beef and other staples kept the entire tribe's bellies filled.

Aside from the never-ending and demanding task of keeping wandering herds of buffalo turned away from the area, the militia had additional duties, one being the constant and futile search for opportunities to attack the tribe, which took up much of their time.

Wheatfall and his men rode through several hundred square miles of the Buffalo Steppes Reservation in an aggressive attempt to locate the isolated bands of desperate Kiwota hunting groups they expected to be out there. But the militia found the country to be empty. The situation continued for another month until the strength of the summer sun, and a lack of rainfall, baked and parched the part-time soldiers. They had to slake their thirst, and that of their horses, in creeks and streams that grew smaller with each passing week.

The last days of July found Wheatfall and his men, angry and nearly worn out, up on the northwest portion of the steppes. The hot, dusty, frustrated militia soldiers had settled down to camp in a wooded area bordering an unnamed lake. Although the bivouac consisted of military tents and accoutrements issued from quartermaster stores, there was no martial look about it. The hunters-turned-soldiers set up their sleeping arrangements in an unorganized, haphazard fashion as they settled down to wait and grouse about the situation.

Wheatfall knew that he faced the very real potential of a violent mutiny. The hunters might be wearing uniforms, but they were nothing like soldiers, who would be obedient under difficult conditions for long periods of time. These were lawless, independent, unreliable cutthroats who had been cast out from the best parts of society and, in some instances, even the worst. Wheatfall was going to have to see that things got better or a bad situation sure as hell would get worse.

Leaving Red-Eye in command, Wheatfall made a quick, direct trip to the reservation agency to have Wheeler Coburn send word to Senator Osmond Torrance about the deteriorating circumstances he now faced.

Back at Fort Buffalo, on the other hand, Major Matthew Devlin was able to breathe a bit easier because of the way things were going. Another half-issue of cattle for the tribe had come in from Fort Snelling. Those beeves, along with the food drawn from the mission, further calmed Indian tempers. Although no buffalo had appeared, the tribe was far from starving. Several weeks previously, the major had removed the twenty-four-hour, fifty percent duty order. That put his own troops in better moods. There was still the usual problem with desertions, but not to any great extent that the strength of the garrison was threatened.

Gilbert Paxton was also finding everything going his way. The school curriculum at the mission was on schedule under his heavy-handed supervision with the help of George Fenwick. But the students were far from happy. Even the girls felt the heavy oppression and confinement of the white man's discipline.

The first time members of the tribe came to visit their children, they were shocked at the change in them. The girls in their dresses and the boys with short hair wearing suits caused some consternation among the Indians.

In addition, the youngsters were forbidden to speak

in Kiwota. Immediate physical punishment was the fate for any student caught even uttering an exclamation in Kiwota during play. During the tribe's visit to the school, the children fearfully spoke to their elders in English when the Paxtons or Fenwick were within earshot, then reverted to whispering in the tribal tongue when the opportunity presented itself. The elders, confused by this conduct, unable to understand the words, and unused to subterfuge of any sort, were alarmed. But the potential issue of additional gifts kept them calm.

Using English was not really all that difficult for the Indian students. The acquisition of the new language was easy for young minds whose speaking habits were not yet deeply ingrained. But it was done at the expense of their native tongue. The total exposure to English, in many cases, had begun to make it the preferable way to speak.

Even their Indian names had been taken from them. An alphabetical list of first names for both girls and boys had been drawn up. They were allotted to assigned desks where the children sat, without regard to the child's personality.

Everything in the young Indians' lives was regulated, overseen, and subject to the mission's rules. Most civilized children would have seen the place as an extremely strict institution, but to the Kiwota children, it was a cruel place in which their natural desires to enjoy and admire the world around them had been crushed.

Every boy had experienced at least a dozen whippings and other punishments. The record holder was Swift Rabbit, now called Samuel, who bore marks of the whip on his back that would leave him scarred for life.

War Heart and others voiced concern about the

change in the youngsters, but Paxton was ready for that. He decided to move ahead of time, and made another gift of foodstuffs and tobacco. In addition, more cattle arrived from the Mission of Indian Reform in early August, and he saw to it that the beeves were quickly distributed. This, coming so close on the heels of the regular government issue, meant the tribe had more than enough to eat for the first time in many months.

Even the elder Many Snows argued against those who wanted to take the children out of the school. "Now, for the first time in many moons, we do not have to kill dogs for meat," he counseled his people. "Even the elk have not been numerous enough to feed us. Therefore, let us leave things as they are, and see how it will all turn out."

The tribe agreed, settling down to enjoy the larder that would carry them into the first days of September. With the fall season approaching, however, and winter not far away, the old fear of the Moons of Cold Hunger came upon them once again. With no buffalo at all that summer, the influx of the extra cattle would not meet many of the Kiwotas' needs. Even if the elk had been plentiful, they would not give the Indians all that they required.

The bison supplied more than meat. The animals' carcasses provided cups and ladles from the horns; bowstrings, rope, and halters from the muscles and sinew; knives, arrowheads, and tools from the bones; and robes and clothing from the hides among other things necessary for survival and a comfortable life.

Once more Many Snows gave advice to his people. "Let us go out and search the buffalo in small groups. If a herd is found, we will all come together to kill the animals in it."

A young hunter asked, "What if we have to leave the reservation, Many Snows?"

"We are desperate for buffalo," the old man replied. "Therefore, do what you must."

Another few weeks drifted by. Although the weather was still blistering hot, the days had grown shorter. Now, with even War Heart willing to ignore the treaty under those desperate conditions, numerous hunting bands were ready to go out and find buffalo, no matter where.

A couple of mornings later, things were not going well for Colonel Ned Wheatfall. He noticed his men getting more restless with each passing day. Only his most loyal followers, the ones he'd made officers in the militia, displayed any patience with the situation. Things finally came to a head when the entire band, armed and scowling, approached the campfire where Wheatfall and his staff were preparing breakfast.

Within an instant, the militia colonel leaped to his feet. He drew his revolver with one hand and his knife with the other. He faced the crowd, standing shoulder-to-shoulder with Captain Red-Eye Morgan, and Lieutenants Pockets Dugan and Dan Lilly. Scared and angry as hell, the quartet faced off against more than forty angry men.

The mob also sported drawn pistols or buffalo rifles along with a smattering of issue carbines. One man stood out in front of the others. His name was Dink Martin, and the fury in his expression and voice seemed to increase his naturally large stature.

"You're bringing this all on yourself, Wheatfall!" he sputtered. "We told you yesterday we wanted you to pay us off. If you give us the money we got coming, then ever'body walks away and 'live and happy."

Wheatfall licked his dry lips. "You ain't getting

nothing 'til it's due you. We ain't finished our work out here."

"There ain't no more work to be did!" Martin shouted. "They ain't gonna be no Injun war. Them Kiwotas is big, fat, dumb, and happy with all that stuff they're getting from the government and that mission feller. We ain't gonna see none of 'em out here, and you can bet your ass that no man jack in this bunch is gonna sit around on his ass 'til the snows come."

A couple of the men on the side made a slight move to get around the back of Wheatfall, Morgan, Lilly, and Dugan. Red-Eye aimed his pistol at them. "Take another step, you son of a bitches, and I'll put a bullet through you."

"You can't get us all," Martin said.

"We can damn sure get you," Wheatfall said.

"And we can damn sure get *you!*" Martin retorted. He, like all the rest of the men, was primed to fire.

Wheatfall decided to take it from another angle. "There's lots o' money to be made out here. You been paid pretty good so far, ain't you?"

"There ain't no women out here," a disgruntled hunter shouted. "You said we'd have squaws, but even they ain't been made available to us."

"That's on account o' the Injuns has been slow about getting out here," Wheatfall said. "When they do, you'll have plenty o' their women."

"We're wasting time," someone shouted. "If this thing falls through, we won't get another damn cent!"

"Sure you will," Wheatfall said. "We're far from finished."

Pockets leaned toward Wheatfall and whispered, "Maybe you better pay 'em off, Ned."

"Not on your life!" Wheatfall said. "If'n I did, which I cain't, the senator'd be all over my ass."

"What senator?" Pockets asked.

"Just shut up," Wheatfall snapped. "You don't have to worry about no senator 'cause it ain't none o' your business."

"Things ain't going worth a damn," Lilly complained.

Red-Eye didn't have much confidence either. "They're gonna make a move pretty quick, Ned."

"It's gonna be all over for us," Pockets added.

"Rider coming!" someone in the crowd shouted.

Wheatfall didn't take his eyes off Martin. "Who is it?"

Lilly looked and replied, "It's Earling Denmore."

Within moments the drumming of hooves and Denmore's shouts could be heard.

"Injuns! Injuns!"

Now everyone looked around, expecting to see a crowd of Kiwotas riding down on them. But the view around the camp stayed clear as Denmore rode on in. He scarcely took notice of the unusual gathering as he reined in hard and looked out over the crowd.

"There's a Injun hunting camp about five miles to the east," he announced. "Twelve bucks and a bunch o' squaws and kids." He looked at Wheatfall. "Ain't that what we been waiting for?"

"It sure as hell is," Wheatfall answered.

Martin grinned. 'That's more like it." He shoved his revolver back into its holster.

Wheatfall fired, the bullet striking his antagonist in the middle of the chest and throwing him back against the men standing directly behind him.

"What the hell did you do that for?" one of the men asked, kneeling down to look at Martin. "Damn! He's dead!"

"Let that be a lesson to all o' you son of a bitches. Don't start getting big ideas about who's running things around here!" Wheatfall said. "I ain't taking no guff from nobody! Now get ready to ride out. We got work to do."

Pockets Dugan looked down at the dead man. "What're we gonna do with him? If'n them dragoons from Fort Buffalo find him, there'll be big trouble."

"Big trouble?" Wheatfall asked. He laughed loudly. "There sure will be. But not for us. "Ol' Martin there was killed by Kiwotas."

Red-Eye Morgan laughed. "Then, let's go get even with 'em for it."

"That's exactly what we're gonna do," Wheatfall said. "Saddle up, damn it!"

Minutes later, with Earling Denmore in the lead, the pack of territorial militia galloped out of camp, heading over the prairie with their weapons locked and loaded, not only with powder and ball, but also with murderous intent.

At exactly that same moment, more than a thousand miles away in Washington City, another situation had arisen that would affect the Kiwota tribe and the lives of its people far out on the Buffalo Steppes.

Senator Osmond Torrance stood at the window of his office looking down at the street scene below. He was in a thoughtful mood as he slowly enjoyed the excellent cigar which wreathed his head with a pleasant smokey aroma.

His secretary, Howard Puffer, approached him and offered a snifter of expensive brandy. "Have you sorted it out yet, Senator?"

Torrance took the glass and sipped the liquor. "Not quite, Howard," he answered. "One must be very careful in a situation like this.

"You should keep in mind that you already own that land," Puffer said. "A thousand prospectors could stake a thousand claims, but it wouldn't mean a thing. The entire Medicine Hills section of the Buffalo Steppes has been legally claimed by you since we filed the papers just before DeWitt Planter's tragic death."

"I haven't forgotten that," Torrance assured him. "No one will be able to dispute my ownership or make trouble for me over it."

"Of course not," Puffer said. "No record of that government geologist's find up there exists."

Torrance turned away from the window and walked back to his desk and sat down. "I'm going to have to do something, though. Things are just moving too slow out there. If Ned Wheatfall can't stir up anything, then there may not be any good opportunities for a while. I want to have the situation under my control when next year's spring rolls around. It is most imperative that I am able to get the Torrance Mining Company into full operation."

"Well, sir," Puffer said. "Permit me to point out to you that if you do something now, it will guarantee that when the warm months arrive on the Buffalo Steppes, there will be very little time before quite a ruckus starts by an influx of prospectors."

"You're right!" Torrance exclaimed. He stood up. "I want you to go to New York and see our friend Ambrose at the *Herald*. Tell him that gold has been discovered in the Medicine Hills of Dakota Territory. I want you to make a personal call on him to make sure the news is reported exactly as I want it." He took another pull on his cigar and a sip of the brandy. "By God! That should cause quite a stir around the country."

Puffer nodded in agreement, saying, "The real tumult will be out there on the Buffalo Steppes."

"Yes," Torrance said, smiling. "And it will be most violent."

Chapter 18

Many Snows walked slowly across the length of the small hunting camp. Every joint in his old body ached with each narrow stride he took on his spindly old legs. He tried not to show the discomfort he felt, but everyone who stopped their activities to gaze at the elder member of the tribe could tell that the two-day ride on horseback had been a real punishment for the oldster. Yet, in spite of the pain, he was glad he had made the trip. It had been a wonderful experience to once again be away from the main village and out in the open countryside. Deep in his heart, Many Snows knew it would be the last time he would ever ride out on the prairie on a hunting expedition.

"Grandfather!" a young warrior named Two Horses called to him. "Come and sit with me. We can visit."

Many Snows appreciated both the respect and the courtesy of the salutation and the kind invitation from the man who was actually no kinsman. But he shook his head. "Thank you, Grandson. But I have much to attend to. Later we will smoke a pipe and talk together."

"If we are lucky, we will eat buffalo liver together, Grandfather," the warrior said. "We young men will use our strength and your wisdom to make sure that happens."

Many Snows smiled. "We will all do our best, and the People can share the best parts of many large bulls."

"Everyone will look forward to that, Grandfather," Two Horses replied.

Many Snows went back to where his son-in-law and daughter, Calling Dove, had set up their lodge in the hunting village. This group of people from the tribe was one of several that had gone out in a determined effort to find buffalo. Normally, Many Snows would have stayed back, but the warm weather gave him energy and took the pain from his joints. That was the reason the old man decided he would be able to go out one more time before he died. Although the demands of hours on horseback were more than he had bargained for, he enjoyed being out in the open in a small group rather than being surrounded by many tepees in the regular village.

When he was a young warrior, they had called him Two Kills from the day on which he killed a pair of Pawnee warriors in a single charge. Only a few seasons previously the People had begun to call him Many Snows because of his advanced years. He didn't particularly like the name, but he didn't blame them. His braids were gray and his dark face heavily wrinkled from a lifetime spent in the sun, wind, and various temperatures of his environment. His muscles had shriveled and his eyesight deteriorated. All that was left was his personal dignity and wisdom. When he accepted all that as good, Many Snows knew he had become a traditional elder of the People.

He also knew he had truly reached advanced years when, during the telling of the story of Two Kills at the council fire one evening, most of the people there didn't realize he was the warrior who had performed the brave deed. Those who had witnessed it had passed over to the Spirit World a long time before.

The elderly Kiwota thought perhaps there was one man in the tribe older than he. A confused, skinny fellow called Beard because of excess facial hair, lived with his grandchildren. Many Snows could recall when Beard was a warrior and used to go out on the same hunting and raiding parties as he did. But it was difficult to recall whether the man had been an older warrior or not. Many Snows could not even recall Beard's name from his youth. It was just as well. Now and then the wrinkled old man could be seen walking around the village calling out names of warriors long gone, to go with him to steal horses or fight the Pawnee. One of his granddaughters would eventually come and get him, taking the babbling, disconcerted oldster back to their lodge. He was a bad-tempered ancient, but most of his surliness came from the pain that caused him to limp. A scar, from either a bullet or a lance head, marred one hip. The old wound was stiff, and whatever glory it had gained him in the past meant nothing in the present.

Many Snows sat down at the fire where his daughter tended to a pot of elk stew. He sniffed, saying, "It smells good."

"It is too bad the elk is not as sustaining as the buffalo," Calling Dove said. "Or offers the People as much." She glanced outward onto the prairie. "Now we cannot find a herd because of the bad white men. Too many things have changed for the People. It should stay the same, and we could live like the old ones did."

Many Snows was aware that nothing ever stayed the same for the tribe. He could remember the father of his grandfather telling him what it was like for the People before the white man. These were referred to as the "old ones" by the younger generation.

From the old ones who were ancient when he was young and called Two Kills, Many Snows learned what it had been like when there were no horses or guns or iron weapons and tools. The People walked the prairie with their possessions transported by travois-pulling dogs. Not much could be loaded on the contraptions; so lodges were smaller, and the People had fewer possessions.

But the mighty horse changed all that.

Warriors could range farther and faster once the horse was conquered. More could be hauled by the newly acquired animals than by the smaller dogs. This gave the People the luxury of larger tepees and more possessions. They ate better and were richer. They could also range farther to make war, so long-lasting feuds with the Pawnees and other enemies developed as killings, rape, and horse stealing increased in intensity and violence.

On the more peaceful side, the horse also provided the People with more leisure time. It was during hours of inactivity that old tales and legends were told and retold. Much of the religious tradition of the People, normally observed by only a few, became well-known by all. Thus, the tribe developed a spiritual side to their beings.

"Nothing stays the same, Daughter," he said. Sometimes changes are for the best."

"Maybe when you were young," his daughter said. "But not anymore."

Many Snows thought about the mission school and the strange sight of Kiwota boys with short hair and white man's clothing. The girls looked different in the cloth dresses they wore, and all the children spoke the white man's tongue.

"Maybe you are right, Daughter," he finally conceded. "But when we once more have plenty of buffalo, things will get back to normal. War Heart will see to that."

"The People are losing their trust and confidence in War Heart," the woman remarked.

"They are stupid," Many Snows said. "War Heart has a good head. He knows when to wait and when to act. If he thinks something must be done, he will see that it is done. If it were not for the wisdom and bravery of War Heart, the soldier chief Looks Ahead would have defeated us much sooner with his strong medicine."

Calling Dove dipped a gourd into the stew. "Here, Father. Eat and be quiet."

Many Snows took the food and gratefully chewed the meat softened by the long boiling in the stock. When one was missing most of one's teeth, it was good to have something that could be eaten without discomfort.

The old man sank deep into thought as he ate and stared out over the countryside that had been his home for the entirety of his long life. He remembered many things as he slowly took his nourishment. There had been the glory of intertribal warfare, furiously frightening moments of frustration when the Pawnees were able to press their advantages, and gentler memories of his three wives and the children they bore him. He had been lucky as a father, since more than half of those babies had lived past infancy.

Many Snows also recalled the first meetings he'd had with white men. He had thought them loud, hairy, strange creatures with wondrous knowledge and remarkable tools and weapons. Those fellows had been easy enough to get along with. They had only wanted to hunt, trap, or trade. Many of the Indian women had been willing to lay with them to get presents of beads and mirrors. It had been a good time then, with those first white men. No land grabbing had taken place, and everyone got along fine.

Then the other type of white man arrived. These were the ones who wanted to settle down in an area of open land and call it their own, not allowing anyone else to even travel across it, much less settle down to camp for a while. Many Snows had always thought that concept of ownership of earth ridiculous. One might as well point to a star in the night sky and say, "That one is mine. No one else may look at it." That was when the trouble with the whites had started, the old man recollected. The raiding had been easy on those isolated, unpleasant settlers. The men had been killed, the women raped, and their children either slain or taken into captivity.

The battles became more serious later on when the soldiers arrived. They were clumsy fighters and did not always do well. Many Snows—or Two Kills, as he was known—and his fellow warriors could pick and choose the times they wanted to fight. The white army fought back viciously, gaining ground in the long war because they had more soldiers than the Indians had warriors. It seemed that for every bluecoat killed, three more would appear in tribal country.

But eventually the great white soldier Looks Ahead came to fight the Kiwotas. He was a different sort of soldier chief, who fought the Indians like an Indian. He sprang from nowhere when he wanted to, killing off many warriors before pulling back out of harm's way. He cared for his soldiers like they were his own sons, making it hard to kill them. Finally, even the leader War Heart was defeated. Many Snows had to admit, however, though the Kiwotas hated Looks Ahead, they also respected him because he always spoke the truth.

The old man finished his stew, remembering once again the first time he met with whites. He vaguely wondered what his final contact would be like.

The shadows lengthened as the sun went faster across the autumn sky. Many Snows enjoyed the warmth of the season that comforted his joints. The Moons of Cold Hunger were unkind to old men. With his belly full of elk stew and his daughter humming as she tended her camp tasks, the elderly Indian settled back against some rolled-up buffalo robes. Before long he nodded off into a light nap, but eventually sank into deep slumber in which he dreamed of riding a galloping horse across what seemed to be an endless prairie.

He awoke with a start, uttering an exclamation.

"Father!" Calling Dove cried in alarm. "What is wrong with you? Are you ill?"

"I had a bad dream," Many Snows said.

The woman frowned in worry. Bad dreams were taken very seriously by the People. "What did you dream about, Father?"

He took a deep breath. "I dreamed I rode a war horse I had many summers ago. He was strong and powerful, so I let him run as fast as he wanted. But as he ran, he grew weaker and began to starve until his ribs showed through his skin."

"What could that mean?" his daughter wondered.

Many Snows ignored the question. "Finally, he could barely walk. Then a war party of hairy white soldiers ambushed me from a dark cloud that lay across the land." The old man sighed. "Then I woke up."

"Did they kill you in the dream?" Calling Dove asked.

"I think so," Many Snows said.

"That was a bad one," the woman remarked.

"Yes," Many Snows agreed. He lay back again on the buffalo robe. "It is the worst dream I ever had."

The sudden sound of approaching horses startled them both. Many Snows struggled to his feet and saw the hunting party from the village approaching. A dozen warriors, all in the prime of their lives, brought their animals to a walk as they closed in on the village. Then each dismounted and led his mount to his lodge. From their conduct, all could tell they hadn't located a herd.

Many Snow's son-in-law, a solemn man called Swift Elk, turned his horse over to his wife. After checking the stew pot, he walked over and sat down beside the old man.

"We saw sign," he said. "But it was many suns old."

"Which direction did the animals go?" Many Snows asked.

"To the north and west," Swift Elk replied.

"That is good!" Many Snows exclaimed. "They will be coming back this way. There is no good grazing to the west of Medicine Hills."

"Then, why would they not go farther to the west?" Swift Elk asked. "They are not bound to stay on the reservation like the People."

"But this is their home," Many Snows argued. "If the white hunters do not run them off, they will come back here and graze." He stood up and pointed outward. "See the grass? It is thick and undisturbed. That will draw the buffalo back here. There will be a great hunt."

Swift Elk was thoughtful for several moments. "Perhaps you are right. They have eaten for a long time in other parts. The old bulls will remember the land of the People and bring the herds to us before the first snows."

"We must be patient," Many Snows counseled.

"I will tell the others what you said," Swift Elk said.

Like all Kiwotas, he was brought up to respect the elders of the tribe. "They will heed your words and wait for the buffalo."

Calling Dove returned from feeding the horse. She dipped up some stew for Swift Elk. After handing it over to her husband, she asked, "Do you want more, Father?"

"My stomach is troubled; I cannot eat," Many Snows replied.

"Are you ill?" Swift Elk asked between slurps of his supper.

Calling dove answered for him. "He had a bad dream."

"I dreamed I rode a dying horse and that soldiers attacked me from a cloud that lay on the land," Many Snows said.

"He thinks they killed him," Calling Dove said in a serious tone.

"Let us not speak of such things," Swift Elk said. "When we return to the village you can ask the medicine man about it. If the dream is bad, he will help you purify yourself and keep the bad spirits away."

"Yes," Many Snows agreed. "I must do that."

Before retiring for the night, the hunters met and worked out the next day's activities. Then, as the fires died out, everyone eventually withdrew to the interior of their lodges to rest up for what was hoped would be a successful buffalo kill.

Many Snows went to his blankets and robes in the far side of the tepee and settled down. He didn't like to let on, but he was extremely tired. The ride and all the camp activities had worn him out. It was only from great effort that he was able to hide the fatigue that dogged his ancient body like a pack of wolves at a dying old buffalo bull.

The oldster went to sleep fast, but his slumber was

not restful. Once again he dreamed of riding the dying horse as it weakened in its run across the prairie. The cloud across the earth appeared again, and the hairy white soldiers charged out of it to attack him.

Many Snows' eyes popped open.

He glanced toward the opening of the lodge and could see that the dawn had begun to break. A slight grayness invaded the blackness of the night. The old man had to urinate. At his age, that was something to be attended to immediately or he would lose control. He painfully got to his feet and shuffled toward the exit. Bending over to get through the small gap in the tepee's cover was agony, but he got outside and gradually straightened up. After a couple of breaths, he limped slowly to a spot behind a tree and tended to his business, urinating in weak spurts from his flaccid penis. At one time even the sight of a pretty woman would cause the member to swell out erect and proud, but those days were certainly over with.

Many Snows finished, then turned to go back and get more sleep. A flash of blue caught his eye at the edge of the camp. Then another, another, and yet another.

"Soldiers!"

He bellowed out the word so loud and strong that it surprised him. But he didn't have time to reflect on the strength in his voice before the firing started. Many Snows found even more hidden strength as he rushed back to the lodge. Already some of the sleepy warriors, with weapons in hand, appeared outside their lodges. His son-in-law was also there, holding a carbine. The old man bowled over his daughter as he went into the tepee and retrieved the bow and quiver of arrows he had brought with him from the village.

He quickly gathered up the weapons and headed for

the opening, but Calling Dove blocked the way. She shrilly asked, "What are you doing, Father?"

"We are being attacked!" he shouted over the growing thunder of detonating weaponry outside.

"Let the young men fight," his daughter begged.

He ignored her and went back outside. Several dead women and children could be seen scattered among the lodges. The soldiers, well-armed, were moving through the small village shooting at everyone. Many Snows fit an arrow to the bow and sent it flying in the direction of the soldiers. He didn't know if he hit the man he'd aimed at, for a cry behind him attracted his attention. He turned in time to see Calling Dove collapse to the ground, the front of her dress soaked in blood. Her open, staring eyes gave evidence of her death.

Infuriated, Many Snows stumbled forward on his old legs. Now he could see that the warriors were badly outnumbered and that many had already gone down. But at least a handful of soldiers also lay on the ground in grotesque positions of instant, violent death. The old man shot his arrow and hit one man, causing the bearded fellow to bawl in pain as he fell to his knees. The old man prepared to send another arrow into the enemy, but a blow from behind caused him to stumble forward and fall face-first to the earth. He turned over and could see the distorted face of a soldier aiming a pistol at him. The old Indian didn't have time to hear the detonation of the weapon before the bullet crashed into his skull, taking away his life in one measureless instant.

It was Many Snows' last contact with white men.

Chapter 19

The persistent shout of the sentry broke into Major Matt Devlin's concentration as he read the quarterly report recently prepared by the post quartermaster.

"Corporal of the guard! Post number one!"

Devlin tried to renew his concentration on the complicated document.

"Corporal of the guard! Post number one!"

The major gave up the effort, getting to his feet to walk to the window. He unlatched it and pushed it open.

"Corporal of the guard! Post number one!"

He glanced toward the guardhouse and could see the corporal of the guard quickly buckling on his cartridge belt and rushing toward the calling sentry at the front gate of Fort Buffalo. An off-duty guard, lounging in front of the building, idly watched the activity.

"Trooper!" Devlin yelled out.

The dragoon looked toward the headquarters building and snapped to attention when saw that it was his commanding officer calling to him.

"Yes, sir?"

"Get inside and tell both the officer of the day and the sergeant of the guard to accompany the corporal," Devlin ordered. "As soon as they find out what the hell is going on, they are to send someone to me as quickly as possible with a full and *accurate* report."

"Yes, sir!" The soldier saluted and went inside to tend to the instructions.

Immediately, two more figures could be seen running toward the front gate. Devlin went back to the report, disgruntled that his concentration had been broken. Facts and figures on government property had to be perused very carefully before a signature was applied. Many an officer had met his administrative Waterloo from signing incorrect supply reports as proper and accurate. Not only would he be censured for inefficiency, but monetary charges could be levied against any shortages of items on the list.

"Now, let's see," Devlin said to himself as he began to read aloud. "Six drum cases, one hundred lantern wicks, two hundred linen collars, fifty curb bits, fifty watering bridles, one dozen barracks chairs. . . ."

Several more minutes passed before the corporal of the guard reappeared, running toward headquarters. This time he bounded up the building's steps and stopped momentarily at the sergeant major's desk to deliver a quick, important message. Immediately the senior noncommissioned officer knocked on Devlin's door and stepped inside.

"Sir!" he announced. "The officer of the day sends his compliments and wishes to inform the commanding officer that the territorial militia detachment is approaching the post with dead and wounded."

"Oh, goddamn it!" Devlin swore.

"Yes, sir!" the sergeant major replied.

Devlin grabbed his cap and rushed outside, turning toward the gate. He walked rapidly, noting the gathering of dragoons and wives and children.

"Make way!" the sergeant of the guard yelled out. "Make way for the post commander!"

Devlin walked up in time to see the ragged column of Wheatfall's militia less than a half mile away, approaching slowly. As they drew closer, it was obvious both men and animals were dust-covered and tired.

"They got dead slung over horses, sir," the sergeant of the guard said.

"So I see," Devlin said. He knew that whatever had happened to Wheatfall and his men would prove unsettling for everyone on the Buffalo Steppes.

Within a quarter of an hour, Wheatfall led his troops up to the gate. He signaled a halt and dismounted, walking over to Devlin. He stood there for a moment, then said, "I got a salute coming. Militia or reg'lar army don't matter in this case."

Devlin gave a quick, careless salute. "Welcome to Fort Buffalo," he said.

"Thanks, Major," Wheatfall said. "Here's how a ex-sergeant who is now a colonel salutes." He rendered a snappy example of the military gesture, saying, "Colonel Wheatfall of the territorial militia begs to report to the post commander that me and my soldiers was attacked by Injuns of the Kiwota tribe early yesterday morning."

"I notice you have some wounded men," Devlin said. "See they're taken to the post hospital. You come with me—" Then he added, "Colonel."

"Sure, Major," Wheatfall said. He turned. "Hey, Pockets. See that the boys who's hurt is took to the doc." He gestured at his second in command. "Red-Eye, take care o' my hoss."

"Sure, Ned," Captain Red-Eye Morgan responded. He rode up and took the reins.

Wheatfall looked at Devlin and smiled. "Well, let's get down to business, Major."

The two walked across the post back to headquarters. They went directly to Devlin's office, where the major invited Wheatfall to take a seat.

"Got any coffee?" Wheatfall asked. "It's been a terrible day so far."

"Sergeant Major!" Devlin bawled. "Get hot coffee in here." He sat down. "Give me a verbal report *now!*"

"A Kiwota war party raided our camp at dawn yesterday," Wheatfall said. "They killed a half dozen of the boys and hurt a few more afore we drove 'em off."

"Am I to assume that this was an unprovoked attack?" Devlin asked.

"You bet!" Wheatfall said. "We was just sleeping out there in our bivouac, minding our own business, and them damn Injuns snuck in and hit us without warning."

"Did you inflict any casualties on the hostiles?" Devlin asked.

"You bet we did," Wheatfall said haughtily. "We killed a bunch of 'em and drove the others off. I didn't count 'em, but they was plenty dead out there. I didn't want to hang around and have the whole damn tribe down on my neck, so I skeddadled back here to Fort Buffalo."

An orderly appeared with a pot of coffee and a couple of tin cups on a tray. He set it down on the desk and made a hasty withdrawal. He didn't like the scowl on Major Devlin's face.

"Are you sure you did nothing to provoke those Indians?" Devlin asked.

"We didn't do nothing a'tall," Wheatfall claimed. "I tole you we was asleep in our bivouac. How'n hell is that gonna get Injuns mad at you, huh? Maybe the boys was snoring so loud it disturbed them damned-to-hell redskins."

Devlin chose to ignore the sarcasm. "What about before you went to sleep that night," he said in measured tones. "During the previous few weeks or days, did you or your men do anything at all that might enrage the Kiwotas? Did you interfere with their hunting of buffalo? Did you pick a fight with any of them?"

"We ain't even seen 'em, Major," Wheatfall said. "So they ain't got no reason to do us dirt like they done."

"Very well," Devlin said.

Wheatfall pulled a pint bottle of whiskey from his inner pocket and poured a generous shot into his coffee. "Care fer a bit o' flavoring?"

"No, thanks," Devlin said. He went to the door and opened it. "Sergeant Major, get a stenographer and you come along, too, as a witness." He went back to his desk and sat down. "I'll make out an official report to go back to Fort Snelling."

"By God, Major, you don't sound like you believe me," Wheatfall said casually.

Devlin, a furious frown on his face, pointed a finger at the militia officer. "You listen to me, Wheatfall! I'm going to get to the bottom of this, understand? I don't trust you or your friend Senator Torrance any farther than I can toss a government mount."

"That's downright unfriendly," Wheatfall said calmly. "And disrespectful, too."

"I'm not fooled a bit," Devlin said. "There is something going on in regards to the Buffalo Steppes. A United States senator doesn't casually wander out to the frontier and poke his nose into army and Indian business simply to keep himself amused. And he doesn't pull strings to get some miserable buffalo hunter appointed a colonel in the territorial militia."

Wheatfall took a swig of his coffee. "You're gonna be real sorry for them words someday, Major." He knew better than to press the issue, since even he didn't know the real motives behind Torrance's interest in the area. Because of his ignorance, there was always an outside chance he could spoil things without meaning to.

Sergeant Major O'Rourke came into the office trailed by a private carrying a pad and pencils. They immediately situated themselves, with the noncommissioned officer off to one side and the clerk seated at the side of the desk where he could easily hear both Devlin and Wheatfall.

The clerk's name was Evans. He positioned himself with the pad on his knee and the supply of sharpened pencils in his pocket. "I'm ready, sir," he announced.

"I am going to have Colonel Wheatfall tell of the incident of the attack on his command," Devlin said. "Will you be able to take it down if he speaks slowly enough?"

Evans replied, "The colonel may speak at a normal speed, sir. I have mastered Isaac Pittman's *Stenographic Sound Hand*, and will be able to record all spoken words."

Devlin was doubtful. "Are you sure, Evans?"

"Certainly, sir," the clerk replied. "This is an excellent phonetic system developed in 1837, so it is quite efficient and modern."

Sergeant Major O'Rourke interjected. "He's not exaggerating, sir. I've seen him at work. Not to worry. He'll have ever' single word uttered without losing a thing."

"Very well," Devlin said. He looked at Wheatfall. "Well, Colonel, you can start at the beginning."

"Sure," Wheatfall said. "But first let me fix some more coffee." He poured himself another cup, laced it with whiskey, then settled back to relate his version of the attack on his command by Kiwota Indians.

"Now," he began. "Me and the boys—my command o' territorial militia, that is—has been out on the prairie performing patrol duty for quite some time now. We ain't seen much o' the Injuns, but did run across some trail of small war parties now and then. Or maybe they was hunting parties. Who knows? Anyhow, we didn't figger there was any danger. After all, there's a treaty and ever'thing. . . ."

Wheatfall spun his tale as the young soldier Evans recorded every word spoken. According to the militia colonel, the life of his unit had settled into simple routines of patrolling and camping with a bit of hunting to keep fresh meat in their diet. Three days previously, they had settled down in a bivouac on Castor Creek some forty miles to the north of Fort Buffalo. It had been an uneventful time with no contact with any other people in the prairie country. Then, the morning before, just before dawn, a large war party of Kiwota Indians attacked them after killing the two men on guard duty. It was a hard-fought battle in which six of his men were killed and eleven wounded. Wheatfall was unable to determine how many Indians were killed because the survivors took their dead with them. After the battle ended, he ordered his men to break camp and get to the safety of Fort Buffalo as quickly as possible.

"We rode up to the front gate there and you met me," Wheatfall concluded. He finished his coffee. "That's the end o' my report."

"Just where on Castor Creek did the attack occur?" Devlin asked.

"I don't know," Wheatfall said.

"You said you were forty miles north of here," Devlin pointed out. "So you must have a good idea of the battle's location?"

Wheatfall shrugged. "I was just guessing at the forty miles."

Devlin reached in his desk and pulled out a map of the Buffalo Steppes. "Show me on the map where your command was attacked."

"I cain't read maps," Wheatfall replied smugly. "You might as well show me a pitcher o' the moon."

"Then, how do you know you were on the reservation?" Devlin asked.

"On account o' we was west of the Des Lacs River," Wheatfall said. "South o' the Medicine Hills and north o' Fort Buffalo. That's smack on the Buffalo Steppes, by God!"

"Can you identify any of the hostiles?" Devlin asked.

"It was kind o' dark that early in the morning, and the fighting was hot and heavy," Wheatfall said.

"Did you recognize War Heart?" Devlin asked.

"Cain't say that I did," Wheatfall answered.

"What about Swift Elk?" Devlin inquired. "Medicine Bull? Crooked Horn? Standing Tall?"

"I told you, Major," Wheatfall insisted. "I didn't see no Kiwota that I could point out to you. If'n I could, don't you think I would?"

"I don't think so," Devlin said.

Wheatfall shot a glance at Evans. "Did you get that? did you write that down?"

"Don't worry about Evans," Devlin said. "Another question. How many Indians attacked you?"

"I didn't count 'em," Wheatfall said. "I was too busy shooting at the son of a bitches."

"Well, do you think it was a war party of troublemaking young warriors or a concentrated effort of the entire tribe?" Devlin asked.

"It was the whole dang bunch, you bet!" Wheatfall said. "Them Kiwotas has got theirselves on the warpath, no doubt o' that."

"Then, how did you fight them off?" Devlin asked. "The Kiwotas can field at least two hundred fighting men."

"Me and the boys is damn good at killing Injuns," Wheatfall said.

"I want to go to the site of the battle," Devlin said. "As soon as possible."

"I don't remember exactly where the fight was," Wheatfall said.

"Do you mean to tell me that an experienced frontiersman and buffalo hunter like yourself cannot go to a certain point on Castor Creek?" Devlin asked. "Particularly one where you'd camped for several days and fought a battle?"

"I ain't never bragged on being no kind o' expert," Wheatfall said. "I been getting more'n more forgetful as time goes by." He cackled. "Ain't that plumb awful?"

"You're leaving your story with a lot of weak points," Devlin remarked.

Wheatfall scowled. "Are you calling me a liar?"

Devlin turned to Evans. "Let the record show that I do not believe Colonel Wheatfall."

"I don't give a shit what you think," Wheatfall said sullenly. "All I want to know is what're you gonna do about this?"

"I'm not going to discuss that with you," Devlin said. "You are dismissed. I want you to take your command and bivouac at the rock ford on Castor Creek. Do you know where that is?"

"Sure," Wheatfall answered. "It's less'n a mile from here."

"You can find that, but not the spot where you were allegedly attacked by Kiwotas, huh?" Devlin said.

"Listen, damn you!" Wheatfall growled.

"I said you're dismissed, Colonel," Devlin said. "Get the hell out of my office."

"You bet I will, you son of a bitch!" Wheatfall said, finally losing control. "And you wait'll Senator Torrance gets through dragging your ass through the mud."

Devlin waited for Wheatfall to leave. "Did you get that, Evans?"

"Every single word and syllable, sir," the clerk assured him.

"Fine," Devlin said. He smiled over at Sergeant Major O'Rourke. "I guess you know what you must do."

"Yes, sir," the sergeant major answered. "I'll have the post back on fifty percent alert, twenty-fours a day."

"Meanwhile, I'm going to visit the post hospital," Devlin said.

"Don't tell me you're concerned about them wounded militiamen, sir?" O'Rourke commented in a tone of puzzlement.

"Why, certainly, Sergeant Major," Devlin said. "They're a dandy bunch of fellows."

The major left headquarters and walked past the barracks to the building used as the post medical facilities. When he went inside, he found the surgeon finishing up the chore of dressing wounds.

Devlin asked, "How're they doing?"

"Pretty well under the circumstances," the doctor replied. He was a drunk named Elliott. He had experienced several run-ins with Devlin over his drinking, and disliked the post commander.

"No serious cases at all?" Devlin asked.

"Not a one, Major," Elliott asked. "Why?"

"Let's have a look at them," Devlin said.

"These are my patients, sir," Elliott said. "They are under my control. That is army regulations."

"And excellent regulations they are, Dr. Elliott," Devlin said. "I believe they also permit me to visit patients in the post hospital. After you, if you please."

The surgeon took him into the ward where a half-dozen militiamen relaxed on beds. All were bandaged, but obviously none suffered any great pain.

Devlin smiled, and loudly asked, "How're you doing, men?"

All replied in the affirmative.

Devlin eyed them all, then took the surgeon by the arm and led him outside. "Did you notice that fellow on the far end?"

"I suppose," Elliott said. "What about him?"

"He's a serious case," Devlin said.

Elliott shook his head. "No he's not. None of them—"

Devlin gritted his teeth in anger. "I said *he is a serious case*. You are to have him remain behind because of infection or something."

"What in hell are you talking about?" Elliott asked.

"Now, now, Dr. Elliott," Devlin said with a grin. "I really hope there isn't going to be additional trouble between ourselves." He smiled even wider at the surgeon. "The man's arm is infected—*infected!*"

Elliott looked at Devlin for a second or two, then nodded. "Of course, Major."

"Get those others back to their unit as quickly as possible," Devlin said.

"Actually, I can have them back to duty by this evening," Elliott said.

"Fine," Devlin replied. "I really appreciate your cooperation, Dr. Elliott. Say! Why don't you join me in the back of the sutler's store tonight about eight o'clock. We can have a few drinks together. On me, of course."

Elliott smiled broadly. "Why, thank you for the kind invitation, Major. I'll be there."

Devlin went back outside. Dragoons were forming up in front of their companies as swearing irritated first sergeants began putting them back on full alert.

Chapter 20

Freddie Devlin, his eyes wide open, listened intently for noises in the house as he lay, fully clothed, beneath the blankets on his bed. The only sound he could hear was the steady breathing of his sleeping siblings nearby. Freddie didn't know what time it was, but the harvest moon in the Dakota sky was visible through the window. It indicated to the boy that it was not too far past midnight.

A few more moments of carefully listening convinced Freddie that no one was up and moving around. The twelve-year-old eased himself out of bed, being careful not to awaken his younger brother and sister. After grabbing the packed haversack from its hiding place behind the dresser, he went to the window and slowly pushed it open. He climbed across the sill in a cautious, deliberate manner, dropping to the ground.

After a few moments of peering around in the moonlight, he began a swift and silent trek that took him past A Company's barracks and the stables. He knew the location of the sentry post in the vicinity and was able to avoid it as he continued on toward the limits of Fort Buffalo.

The next obstacle the boy faced was getting past guard post number one. That would take some careful timing since the renewal of having half the troops on duty at all times meant extra sentries on duty there. Freddie reached a place in the shadows next to the commissary building. A few moments of observation soon enlightened him as to the guards' routine. As soon as the one who walked the post between that building and the gate reached the place where he turned and began pacing back, Freddie made his move.

The twelve-year-old scurried without a sound off the post and continued out into the shadowy countryside of the open prairie. He hadn't realized it at the time, but as he made his unauthorized departure from military property, his father hadn't been at home.

At the time of Freddie's activities, Major Matt Devlin slowly sipped from his tumbler of whiskey as he sat across the table from the surgeon in the back of the sutler's store. This was Fort Buffalo's unofficial officers club, where off-duty rankers in the dragoon squadron could come and relax with a bit of card playing, drinking, and conversation.

Elliott, grandly but sleepily drunk, had just made what he considered an important pronouncement regarding the proper medical care of troops on the frontier when the evening's heavy drinking finally caught up with him. He stopped speaking and closed his eyes, then slowly lowered his head to the table and passed out.

Devlin, who had been drinking lightly, shook Elliott to make sure he was really unconscious. Satisfied, the major got to his feet and left the establishment by the back door. He found Sergeant Major O'Rourke, Sergeant Dawson, and Private Evans waiting for him.

O'Rourke asked, "Is the sawbones out, sir?"

"Like a lantern in a hard wind," Devlin said. "Now we can get to work."

The quartet of dragoons walked across the post to

the hospital and went into the building. All the beds were empty save one. On that bunk, Earling Denmore of Wheatfall's militia unit snoozed comfortably. He was the militiaman picked by Devlin for Elliott to diagnose as having an infected wound. Denmore had his bandaged arm across his chest. Devlin leaned over the man and shook him.

"Wake up!"

"Huh?" Denmore opened his eyes and looked at the four soldiers in the lantern light. He immediately came fully awake. "What're you fellers doing here?"

"We've come to fetch ye, laddie boy," O'Rourke said. "Now off the bunk and into yer clothes lively-like, hey?"

"I cain't get outta bed," Denmore said. "The doc says I got a infection in my arm."

"Would ye like yer bloody neck broke, then?" O'Rourke asked with a smile.

"Not likely," Denmore answered in a surly tone.

"Then, off the bunk!" Sergeant Dawson interjected.

Denmore, whose arm really didn't bother him too much, did as he was told. As he dressed himself, he asked, "What do you want with me? The other jaspers got sent back to camp right after they fed us."

Devlin said, "We want to have a talk with you. What's your name?"

"Denmore," he answered. "Earling Denmore."

"Hurry up, Denmore," O'Rourke said.

In less than ten minutes, they left the hospital and were on their way to headquarters with the hapless militiaman being pulled along by the burly sergeant major.

The group passed several sentries, and Devlin responded to the salutes as they continued on. More military pomp in the moonlight followed their arrival at headquarters, but they were finally cloistered in Devlin's office.

Captains Bernie Blanchard and Paul Teasedale were there along with the contract scout Fred Jeffries. Denmore, completely confused as to the reason for the gather, nodded to Jeffries, whom he knew from the past.

"Howdy, Earling," Jeffries said.

"What's going on?" Denmore asked him.

"I reckon that's what ever'body wants to find out," Jeffries said.

Denmore now fully sensed the hostility from the others. "Y'all had best let me get back to the hospital! You fool around with me and they'll be cutting off my arm afore you know it."

O'Rourke gave him a shove toward a chair. "Shut up! Yer arm is just fine, so don't give it no extry worrying about. And ye'll do no more talking 'til ye're told to!"

Denmore was seated at the chair in front of the desk where Devlin took a seat. Evans situated himself in his usual stenographic position with pads and pencils. The two noncommissioned officers each stood slightly behind the militiaman. Jeffries and the two officers made themselves comfortable by sitting down on a bench next to the wall.

"State your name," Devlin said to the reluctant guest.

"I already told you my name," Denmore said.

O'Rourke gave him a clout on the side of the head. "Give the major yer name, damn yer eyes!"

"Ow!" Denmore complained. But he answered, "Earling Denmore."

"Where and when were you born?" Devlin went on.

"I was borned in Pendleton County, Kentucky," Denmore said. "I don't remember when."

"How old are you?" Devlin asked.

"I reckon I'm 'twixt thirty and forty," Denmore surmised.

Devlin looked at Evans. "Put his birth date as sometime between 1815 and 1825." He turned his attention back to the wounded man. "Are you a member of Colonel Ned Wheatfall's detachment of territorial militia?"

"You know—ow!" Denmore exclaimed when he received a punch from Sergeant Dawson. "Yeah! I'm in Wheatfall's militia."

Evans, taking every word, even recorded the exclamations of pain as he rapidly worked at his skill in shorthand.

"Tell me about the fight with the Kiwotas the other morning," Devlin said.

Denmore hesitated, but he wasn't sure where he stood with the major. "Well, Wheatfall chose me to scout, so I used to go out ever' day and look around for Injun sign. I finally found some and I went back and told Ned about it."

"What sort of sign did you find?" Devlin asked.

"Tracks of a hunting party," Denmore said. Then he added, "I knowed it was a hunting party on account o' they had travois and women and some kids with 'em. Injuns do that, don't you know? They'll split off in little groups like that when they're looking for buffalo. When any is found, then they all get together and go after the herd."

"Yes, I understand," Devlin said patiently. "So what happened after you told Wheatfall about the hunting party?"

"Well, sir, he—uh—he said we was prob'ly gonna have a fight with 'em," Denmore said uneasily.

"That's what he said. I recollect that he said we might gonna be having a fight with 'em or something like that."

"Did you have a fight with that hunting party?" Devlin asked.

"Yeah," Denmore responded.

"Who started the battle?"

"They did," Denmore said.

"Tell me about the fighting," Devlin said.

"Well, now, let me think," Denmore said slowly. "Well, now, we fought 'em and they killed some of our fellers and we killed some o' them."

"Did the Indians run away after the fight?" Devlin asked.

"Nope," answered Denmore.

"Did you militiamen run away?"

"We didn't have to run, on account o' we won," Denmore said with a grin.

"If the Indians didn't run away and you and your friends didn't run away, what did you do?" Devlin asked. "Sit around and have tea together after the fighting ended?"

"Hell, they wasn't no Injuns to have tea or nothing else with," Denmore said.

"Why not?" Devlin asked.

"Well, now, we killed 'em, I reckon," Denmore said.

"*All* of them?" the major wanted to know.

"Ever'one," Denmore said smugly.

"The women and children, too?"

"Damn right!" Denmore said. "The squaws and papooses got theirselves killed along with the warriors."

"Did all the women get killed in the battle?" Devlin asked.

"Not all of 'em," Denmore replied. "Not ever' single one of 'em, no."

"Were they raped?"

Denmore shrugged. "Some fun was had, yeah."

"Then, they were killed after being ravished, correct?"

"That's what's generally done with squaws," Denmore said. "They do it to our women, don't they?" He eyed the frowns of the men looking at him. "Hey, I didn't kill none of 'em myself."

"I didn't say you did," Devlin said. "But they were killed by somebody after being ravished, weren't they?"

"I said so, didn't I?" Denmore said.

"Now, in this battle, how many Indians were there?" Devlin asked.

"I don't know," Denmore replied. "I never did no counting. I got shot in the arm, so I was taking it easy toward the last o' the fight."

"When did you attack the Indians?" Devlin asked.

"Just at dawn while they was sleeping," Denmore replied.

"So they didn't attack you?" Devlin went on. "The Kiwotas didn't start the fight, hey?"

Denmore started to answer, but he stopped. For a few moments his eyes darted back and forth, then he said, "They attacked us."

"You said you attacked them."

"No, I didn't neither!" Denmore insisted. "I said they started it, didn't I?"

"So they attacked you, right?" Devlin said.

"You bet!" Denmore said, relieved.

"Kiwota men, women, and children attacked you," Devlin said. "Is that what you're telling me?"

"The men attacked us," Denmore said.

"Then, how did you come about killing women and

children?" Devlin asked. "How were you able to rape those women?"

"Because they was there."

"Where?" Devlin asked.

"In their camp."

"How did you kill them if they were in their camp and the warriors attacked you?" Devlin inquired.

Denmore knew things were going bad for him. "Let me think about this."

"Sure," Devlin said. "You think for a few minutes; then you make a statement to me about what happened."

A full five minutes passed before Denmore cleared his throat and said, "The Injuns attacked us, and we follered 'em back to their camp and kilt 'em all."

"How many places out on the steppes are there dead Indians?" Devlin asked.

"One," Denmore answered. "Where we kilt 'em. Where else would they be?" He chortled. "Dead folks don't move around, y'know."

"If the Indians attacked your camp and you followed them back, then there should be dead Kiwotas in *two* places," Devlin told him.

"Yeah," Denmore said. "They're in two places."

"If I go out there and find dead Indians in one place, that will mean you're lying to me," Devlin said.

Denmore didn't say anything.

O'Rourke interrupted, speaking to Devlin. "I got to remind you that if Denmore's lying, we'll have to shoot him, sir."

Denmore turned and faced the dragoon. "What the hell do you mean—shoot me?"

"For lying to an officer," O'Rourke stated falsely. "If a soldier lies to an officer, he gets shot for it."

"Shit! I ain't no soldier!" Denmore pointed out. "I ain't never been in the army like Wheatfall."

"Well, bucko, you're in the army now," O'Rourke countered. "You're a legal-enlisted militiaman on duty, and that makes you a soldier."

Denmore looked back at Devlin. "Hey! There ain't none o' this my fault, y'know!"

"Listen, soldier," Devlin said, leaning forward. "All you have to do is tell me the truth and I'll see that nothing happens to you."

"Nothing at all?" Denmore wanted to know.

"Not even a single day of jail time," Devlin promised.

"I'm going to hold you to that," Denmore said in a sullen voice.

"I'll see that you become an official witness for the government," Devlin said. "That means nobody can put you in jail. Not even the highest-ranking officer in the United States Army."

"In that case, you listen to me," Denmore said. "I found that hunting camp, and I told Ned about it. He got the boys together, and we hit them Injuns at dawn. We kilt ever' damn one of 'em, too, just like I said. We had fun with the squaws that didn't die right off. When we finished with 'em, we bashed their heads in. In the end, they wasn't one buck, squaw, or papoose that walked, run, or crawled away from there."

"Will you sign a statement to that effect?" Devlin asked.

"If'n I don't get shot or have to go to jail," Denmore said.

"You won't, don't worry," Devlin said. He gestured to Evans. "Write this up as quickly as possible. Denmore will sign it as will everyone in this room as witnesses."

"Yes, sir," Evans replied. "I got ink and paper out at my desk. It won't take me long."

Devlin reached in his desk and pulled out a bottle of

whiskey and a glass. He shoved them across to Denmore. "Treat yourself to a snort, Denmore."

"Damn! Goddamn!" Denmore said, pouring himself a drink with shaking hands.

Devlin got up and motioned the two officers to follow him. The three went outside the office. Captain Bernie Blanchard said, "Congratulations, Matt. It looks like you'll have Wheatfall in plenty of trouble."

"I want to go farther than Wheatfall," Devlin said. "That son of a bitch Senator Osmond Torrance is who I really want to hang."

Captain Paul Teasdale shook his head. "Wheatfall will never implicate him. He won't have any reason to. All that's going to happen is that Wheatfall will be kicked out of the territorial militia. Killing Indians isn't crime enough to go to jail, much less be executed for."

"I have an idea how to get Wheatfall to tell all he knows in front of witnesses," Devlin said. "It'll be tricky, but worth the try."

"How're you going to do that?" Blanchard asked.

"Have you ever wanted to go to jail or be dishonorably discharged from the army for being an accessory to a crime, Bernie?" Devlin asked.

"Hell, no!"

Devlin smiled. "Then, you don't really want to know what I've got on my mind, do you?"

"I don't think so," Blanchard said.

"Me neither," Teasedale echoed.

While everyone waited as Private Evans wrote out Denmore's statement, young Freddie Devlin sat hidden in a stand of spruce trees. In the bright moonlight, he could easily make out the Mission of Indian Reform school less than fifty yards away. His legs had begun to cramp, and he stood up to relieve the discomfort when he spotted the figure moving toward him.

Five minutes later, Swift Rabbit—known as Samuel

in the classroom—joined him. He carried a cloth sack with him. "I had trouble getting out," he said in English. "Mr. Fenwick kept coming around."

"Not me," Freddie said. "Ever'body at my house was sound asleep." He pointed to the bag. "What'd you bring?"

"I got some apples," Swift Rabbit said. "That's all I could find in the kitchen. I tried to get to the smoke house but never could."

"I got some bread and jam," Freddie said.

"We'd better get moving," Swift Rabbit suggested. "We'll have to get some distance between us and here before the sun comes up."

The two boys left the trees and headed in a more-or-less direct northwesterly direction, trotting across the flat country. They continued the pace for an hour until settling down to a walk.

The plan to run away had been hastily hatched between the two during several sessions held between the mission school and the one for the children of Fort Buffalo. Gilbert Paxton had arranged the joint class and recreation time to give his charges a fuller exposure to civilization by allowing them to study, play, and converse with white youngsters.

"You said you had a pretty good idea what we was gonna have to do," Freddie said. "I reckon we ain't gonna be able to go to your village, are we?"

"Nope," Swift Rabbit said. "They'd send me back to the school."

"Do you have a plan?" Freddie asked.

"Yeah," Swift Rabbit answered. "We can find a Sioux village somewheres to spend the winter. If I can get some stuff like arrows and a couple of bows and other things we'll need, then we can live out on the prairie."

"Yeah!" Freddie said. "No more studying or books.

232

We can fish and hunt all we want. And do things Injuns do, huh? Just what do you Injuns do anyhow?"

"We'll be warriors," Swift Rabbit said. "After the winter is over, we can go down and raid the Pawnees."

"Yeah!" Freddie exclaimed.

"We'll steal horses and women," Swift Rabbit said.

"How come we're gonna steal women?" Freddie asked.

Swift Rabbit shrugged. "I don't know. That's what warriors do. I suppose they can keep our clothes mended and cook for us."

"Sure!" Freddie said. "That's a fine idea."

Dawn was still a bit more than an hour away as the two friends trudged on toward their adventure.

Chapter 21

War Heart signaled over to his friend Medicine Bull, then turned and did the same to Crooked Horn. While the two kept the majority of the men in the war party with them, War Heart took another twenty and rode toward the east. It would take the group a short while to reach the point where the vegetation along the creek called Castor by the white men was thin enough to allow horses to enter the water and cross to the other side.

Back at the spot where Medicine Bull and Crooked Horn waited was an easy ford in which only the hooves of the horses would be wetted by the shallow water. But they didn't want to cross there because of the commotion such an action would make. A loud disturbance would alert the camp of soldiers located on the other side.

As War Heart led his band, he could barely contain the fury that dominated his entire being. The death of Swift Elk, a friend and companion of countless war and hunting expeditions, had cut him even deeper than the loss of Running Wolf. But at least Running Wolf's passing could be attributed to the young man's quest for glory and vengeance. The unfortunate Swift Elk had died in a massacre brought on by a cowardly attack on a small hunting camp by the same whites who had driven away the buffalo all that summer.

Because the assault had occurred on treaty land, such treachery was completely unexpected. Many women and children had also fallen in the swarms of bullets fired by the whites. And yet another terrible blow to the tribe was the loss of the venerable old man Many Snows. His wisdom and guidance would be sorely missed by the tribe.

When War Heart reached the break in the trees along the creek, he abruptly turned and rode down the bank into the water with his twenty companions close behind. The horses had to swim a bit; but the distance was short, and they quickly gained the other side, bounding back up onto level ground.

Now they were on the same side of the creek as the soldiers' camp. Experiencing the excitement of a coming battle, War Heart led his warriors back toward the west and the enemy camp, anticipating the clash to come.

It was past dawn, with the sun a quarter of the way up in its journey to the apex of midday. This was normally too late for a surprise attack, and that was exactly what the Indian tactician was counting on, as well as taking advantage of any sense of security the enemy might have because of the proximity of the soldier fort.

War Heart rode on until he sighted the familiar portion of the tree line that marked the ford. After signaling a halt to the others, War Heart let his horse slowly walk onward. He took advantage of a dip in the ground to circle slightly to the south, then came back up where some waist-high vegetation grew. At that point he could easily see the whole of the camp. The soldiers lounged about doing nothing as he had been told they would. War Heart had been correct in his assumption. Being this close to Looks Ahead's fort made them feel safe and secure with no need to post guards.

The war chief rode back toward his warriors. He glanced at the sky to judge the wind since noise could be easily carried by a brisk breeze. It blew toward them from camp, and that pleased him. He also noted the clouds in the northern sky. They consisted of a thick, wintery vapor, and the air had a coolness to it. Perhaps winter would come to the People's country earlier than usual that year.

So much the better to get this day's bloody task done quickly.

When War Heart reached the others, he gave terse orders. "Standing Tall, take some men and go to the south. I do not want any soldiers to escape in that direction."

"I understand," Standing Tall said. "No soldiers will pass." He pointed to a half dozen of the warriors, then led them off in the proper direction.

"Come, warriors of the People!" War Heart said. "We avenge our dead!"

The line of Kiwotas, now joined by those waiting across the river, bounded forward, gathering speed as they rushed across the open country toward the camp of the unsuspecting enemy. The hooves of their horses pounded the ground, and now the men began to shout out their battle cries to strengthen their personal medicine for protection and to make them better killers.

The soldiers looked in stupefied fear and surprise at the line of warriors charging into their camp. They scrambled for their weapons but were too late as the Indian horses galloped through the bivouac, kicking over camp utensils, tents, and sending individual soldiers sprawling to the ground. Bullets and arrows knocked others down. When the Indians reached the other side, they turned, sweeping back through the white men.

Pockets Dugan, drunk as a lord, bellowed hoarsely as he staggered around firing ill-aimed shots at the attackers. A warrior charged up behind him and was able to come to a complete stop before delivering a deliberate blow with an ax. Dugan's head split down as far as his nose, and an eye popped from its socket. He still managed to keep to his feet as instinct and nerves caused him to walk uncertainly for some ten yards before finally falling.

A quartet of more intelligent fellows formed up back-to-back to cover each other. Three had carbines and one a Hawkens buffalo rifle. They began to score on the Indians with slow, deliberate aiming at easy targets. Three Kiwotas, with the same instinctive fighting sense as the whites, made a sudden, unplanned charge. Only one was shot from his horse while the other two swept in and took out three of the defenders with arrows and tomahawks. The fourth, losing his head, made a run toward another group of his friends but didn't get far before being hit almost simultaneously by a half-dozen arrows. He collapsed to begin dying slowly in the prairie dirt.

Another small group of the soldiers managed to get to their horses and make an escape through the ranks of Indians by damning caution and riding bareback. One lost his seat and fell to the ground. He scrambled on all fours but was trampled when one of the warriors rode over him. A couple of quick turns and repetition of the act left the man resembling no more than a bloody pile of smashed meat in the grass.

His five companions cheered their luck, but soon found they would not make it. Standing Tall and his fellow warriors, waiting to cut off any escape attempt in that direction, made short work of them, sending a shower of arrows that cut down men and animals alike.

By then the surviving whites had instinctively drawn together in the center of the bivouac. Ned Wheatfall, Red-Eye Morgan, and Dan Lilly stood in the middle of the frightened defenders, firing frantically and uselessly at the Indians who now taunted them and kept far enough away to make a difficult target.

Finally Wheatfall and his men, out of ammunition and unable to get to their gear where more was stored, stood stock-still to see what would happen. Frightened out of their wits, and sweating heavily, they looked wide-eyed at the Indians who slowly approached.

"What're we gonna do?" Red-Eye asked of no one in particular.

"Shut up!" Wheatfall snapped.

"What're we gonna do? What're we gonna do?" Red-Eye kept asking. "What're we gonna do?"

One man figured the best thing to do was to simply run. He foolishly made a rush toward the warriors in an attempt to get between them. The Kiwotas laughed, and a couple let him through, then chased after him and finally caught up with the panic-stricken fellow to deliver death blows with the butts of their long guns.

War Heart bellowed a loud cry that brought all action by the Indians to a halt. Giving orders in the Kiwota tongue, he pointed to some warriors and then at some of the captives.

The Indians put arrows to their bows and loosed several into the helpless men.

War Heart once more yelled out instructions, and more of the defenders went down filled with numerous arrows loosed into the tightly packed mass. Only Ned Wheatfall and one other man were left. The war chief rode forward, his painted face twisted with fury. He had yet to fire his musket, so it was loaded and ready. He pointed at Wheatfall's trembling companion and pulled the trigger. The man somersaulted with the violent impact of the lead ball, going faceless to his death.

Wheatfall, going into shock from fright, simply stared at the Kiwota and breathed in quick, shallow gasps. War Heart reached down and grabbed him by the collar of his militia colonel's jacket, then began riding back toward the north where the tribe's latest village had been located for the previous couple of weeks.

Other warriors rode up and cuffed and kicked at the struggling prisoner. War Heart kept his hold on Wheatfall, who soon lost a boot after going close to a mile in the Indian's strong grasp. Large prairie stickers soon impaled the bottom of his foot, causing increasing pain and bleeding, this in addition to the several rocky areas he was forced to trod.

Wheatfall was a natural fighter, and he resisted at times in an attempt to break free; but numerous sharp blows from bows and coup sticks on his head and shoulders put an end to his struggles. He spent the rest of the morning and part of the afternoon going through the torment before the war party finally reached the Kiwota village.

The reception was loud and violent. Furious Indian women slapped, scratched, and spit on Wheatfall. He tried to cover himself, but still received more physical punishment. His near exhaustion made any self-defense on his part almost impossible.

Finally War Heart reined in when he reached the council lodge, letting loose of the hapless captive. Wheatfall collapsed to the ground. He tried to keep from moving and to catch his breath in order to regain as much strength as possible. He knew the Indians would deal him a slow, torturous death. He wanted to be able to get to his feet and fight and run so that perhaps an arrow or blow from a tomahawk would take his life away quickly and with as little pain as possible.

Wheatfall suddenly leaped to his feet. He started to run, but stopped. "What the hell?" he muttered.

Major Matt Devlin, Fred Jeffries, and Gilbert Paxton stepped from the council tent.

"Did they catch y'all, too?" he asked.

Devlin shook his head. "We are not prisoners, Wheatfall."

Wheatfall whirled around, looking at the Kiwotas who surrounded him. "Something is going on," he said. "What is it? Goddamn you to hell, Devlin!"

"You are a prisoner of these Indians, Wheatfall," Devlin said in a loud, clear voice. "If they thought I would punish you, they would give you to me."

"Then, tell 'em you're gonna punish me, for the love of God!" Wheatfall pleaded.

"I have no reason to," Devlin said. "And I won't lie to these people."

"Sure, you can lie," Wheatfall said. "Tell 'em you're gonna hang me up by my wrists and lash me bloody. Tell 'em you're gonna throw me in jail forever." He clasped his hands together. "Help me, Devlin. Please! They'll roast me over a fire. You know they will."

"I would say you're right about that," Devlin said. "It's strange why they'd do that, when you take into consideration that they're cheerfully willing to allow Mr. Jeffries, Mr. Paxton, and me to return safely to Fort Buffalo."

Paxton, a bit horrified by the whole thing, asked, "Colonel Wheatfall, why do these Indians wish to torture you?"

"Oh, God!" Wheatfall cried out. "Because I killed a bunch of 'em the other morning."

"You said they attacked you," Devlin said. "I cannot punish you for defending yourself."

"Listen to me," Wheatfall begged. "It was a hunting camp with men, women, and children. We snuck up on 'em. . . ."

He frantically and quickly confessed to the unprovoked sneak attack and mass killing of the Indians in the small band.

He even told of raping the women before killing them.

Paxton's face paled. "You mean you ravished, then murdered those poor Indian women?"

"Yes! Yes!" Wheatfall almost shrieked. "You can get me on that, can't you, Devlin?"

"That would probably be considered retribution for past Indian crimes by any court," Devlin said. "Therefore I cannot possibly have you court-martialed on that alone. What made you do it? Did someone put you up to it?"

"Yes, goddamn it!" Wheatfall shouted. "Senator Osmond Torrance hired me to raise hell out here with a bunch o' my old pards from my hunting days. He wanted us to rile these Injuns so's they'd go on the warpath and get the treaty broke."

"Will you be willing to make a statement to that effect in front of other witnesses and sign it?" Devlin asked.

"What the hell do you think, Devlin?" Wheatfall asked. He staggered over and grabbed the army officer's jacket. "I can tell you things about that son of a bitch Torrance that'd curl your hair! And I will!"

Devlin turned to Jeffries. "Tell War Heart we will see that not only Wheatfall is to be punished, but also the powerful man who paid him to cause all the misery to the Kiwota people."

Jeffries spoke to War Heart in a voice loud enough for all the Indians to hear. When he finished, War Heart slipped off the back of his horse. He walked up to Wheatfall and spat on him, then spoke a few words to Devlin.

Jeffries translated, saying, "War Heart wants you to know that he believes you, Looks Ahead. He really feels that if you're able to take over Fort Buffalo and the agency, then things'll get better for his people."

"Tell him I'll do my best," Devlin said. He grabbed

Wheatfall's arm and pulled him over to where horses and Paxton's wagon waited. As Wheatfall climbed up into the back of the vehicle, he had to endure a bit more physical roughing and pummeling from the Indians, but the whites were able to safely leave the village and head out over the prairie for Fort Buffalo.

Wheatfall sat in the back of the wagon while Devlin and Jeffries rode alongside. He looked at the major and asked, "Are you gonna put me in jail?"

"You'll go to the guardhouse, Wheatfall," Devlin said. "Remember, you're a military prisoner, not a civilian."

Wheatfall, hurting like hell, grimaced. "Did you send them Injuns over to our camp?"

"Nope," Devlin answered in a matter-of-fact tone.

"But you knowed they was gonna come after us, didn't you?" Wheatfall asked.

"If I did, and failed to respond to save you and your men, I would be derelict in my duty," Devlin said.

Jeffries laughed. "Yeah! You'd be going to the guardhouse yourself, wouldn't you, Major?"

"I sure would," Devlin said. "That wouldn't be very good for my career, would it?"

Wheatfall fully realized Devlin had known of the Indian attack on his men before it happened. Angered now, the buffalo hunter bared his teeth at the army officer.

"You son of a bitch!"

Chapter 22

Major Matt Devlin found out about the disappearance of his son Freddie when he returned to Fort Buffalo with Ned Wheatfall in custody. Beth was frantic with worry and had already gotten Sergeant Major O'Rourke to send several men around the post to find any spot where a twelve-year-old boy might hide. But the effort had been futile.

Under the circumstances there was nothing Devlin could do but comfort his distraught wife as he set about having more sophisticated search parties organized to hunt for the missing lad. Meanwhile, the harried major still had to go about the business of getting information and statements out of his prisoner. As much as he wanted to, the major could not take the time to personally lead the search for the missing boy. He delegated the authority to his trusted officers and sergeants to see the job was done as quickly and efficiently as possible.

However, after a week passed, Devlin's initial fears subsided to irritated worry when he learned from his wife that some bread and jam were missing from the family kitchen. Also, when received word that one of the Indian boys at the mission school, a particularly lively young fellow named Swift Rabbit, had also run away, Devlin knew what had happened. While there was no denying the danger of the open, wild country, both boys were capable, strong, and healthy, and one was an Indian who'd spent his entire life in the wilderness.

While squads of dragoons searched for the boys, Devlin began the task of getting testimony from Wheatfall. One of the guests invited to attend the confession was Major Harold Pendergrass from Fort Snelling. Getting him there meant keeping Wheatfall locked up for three days under constant grilling and threats, but that paid off, too. It softened up the militia colonel and made him fully realize the hell that awaited him if he reneged on his promise to cooperate.

After Pendergrass arrived at Fort Buffalo, he was quickly but thoroughly appraised of the situation. Then it was time for the official statement to be made in Devlin's office. Because of the importance of the revelations about to be disclosed, three more persons were invited to attend the session. Gilbert Paxton and the two captains from the dragoon squadron were seated in the room to add to the list of official, credible witnesses.

When both the room and everyone concerned were ready, Devlin had a couple of guards bring Wheatfall into his office. Once more, the skillful young Private Evans was put to work with his shorthand skills.

When Wheatfall came into the office, he had no intentions of lying or trying to cover up. When first brought back from the Kiwota village and jailed, he was shocked to learn that his old pal Earling Denmore was also an inmate of the guardhouse. The other buffalo hunter was kept in a separate cell and unable to communicate with him. It didn't matter. Wheatfall knew damned well that Denmore would have already blabbed like a drunken politician on election night about everything that had gone on during the gang's time as both hired guns and territorial militia.

Another thing also made Wheatfall cooperative. He harbored a very real fear that he might be turned loose and eventually be back in Kiwota hands. When Devlin started asking questions, the prisoner talked so much and so fast that even Evans was sore put to keep up. The militia colonel and buffalo hunter left out no details as he implicated the senator, Harvey Puffer, and the agent Wheeler Coburn in a scheme to break the treaty with the Kiwotas and drive them to war. He explained how the senator was able to arrange for a shortage in the beef issues, and had told Coburn to do everything in his power to keep Kiwota tempers boiling over. The fact that innocent lives might be lost did not concern the office holder.

Using the statement as evidence, Devlin personally took a detachment of dragoons over to the agency trading store. He entered unannounced, finding Wheeler Coburn lounging at his stove behind the counter. The autumn weather had turned decidedly cooler, and the agent was snug and comfortable.

Devlin smiled at him. "Looks like winter is closing in, Coburn."

Coburn nodded in agreement. "I reckon I'll be all right again, though. Let the blizzards come."

"It's going to be sort of rough on the Kiwotas, isn't it?" Devlin asked. "No buffalo, and the beef issues are getting smaller and later all the time."

Coburn grinned. "I'll turn in a report on that, Devlin."

"No, you won't," Devlin said. "Under my authority as the military commander of the Buffalo Steppes, I am arresting you for fraud against the United States Government and the endangerment of the peace on the aforementioned Buffalo Steppes."

Coburn, so surprised he lost his arrogance, got to his feet. "Just what the hell are you talking about, Devlin? You're sure 'nuff gonna get in trouble." He was taken aback when Devlin didn't show the slightest inclination to back down. "I'll tell Senator Torrance, by God!"

"Senator Torrance is going to be in enough trouble himself," Devlin said. "He'll be too busy trying to keep himself out of jail to lift a finger for you."

"What the hell are you talking about, Devlin?" Coburn demanded to know.

"You'll soon find out," Devlin replied. "Let's go."

A couple of the dragoons went around the counter and grabbed the agent, dragging him along as Devlin led them back to Fort Buffalo.

Wheeler Coburn, when presented with the statements made by Wheatfall with some backup by Earling Denmore, knew the only thing that would save him from a stiff prison sentence was to cooperate. He became yet another willing government witness and added more damaging information as the amazed audience listened to testimony that revealed corruption in the Indian Bureau and the treacherous influence of a crooked senator.

When the episode was finished and Private Evans had filled no less than five pads with his scribblings of shorthand, everyone involved was exhausted. Although they were promised recommendations for leniency, Wheatfall, Coburn, and Denmore were still held in the post guardhouse as material witnesses in a government case. Arrangements would be made to take them to Fort Snelling, Minnesota, and then farther east where the real power of the federal courts would be brought into the case.

Major Harold Pendergrass, charged with making the arrangements through the judge advocate general to press the case, made a hasty departure from Fort Buffalo. He shook hands with Matt Devlin just before leaving for Snelling and points east.

"Best of luck to you, Devlin, old man," he said with

a warm smile. "This is going to be a real coup for the army over both crooked politicians and that corrupt Indian Bureau. The departmental commander is going to be dancing with joy when I bring him the news of these hearings."

"It can't end there," Devlin told him. "We've got some serious wrongs to right where the Kiwota tribe is concerned. After all, it was the tricks pulled through Torrance's influence that caused the shortage of beef and those hunters keeping the buffalo clear of the reservation."

"I already have some recommendations to make along those lines," Pendergrass said. "You can be sure that both the army and the federal government will approve. Public opinion will force them to."

"Do you think this will get in the newspapers?" Devlin asked.

"I'll see that it does," Pendergrass promised.

"What are those suggestions of atonement you're going to recommend?" Devlin wanted to know.

"First, of course, is an immediate issue of beef cattle to make up for the shortages in the past," Pendergrass said. "Then I'm going to get authorization to allow a large hunting party of Kiwotas to leave the reservation with dragoon escort to do some serious buffalo hunting. That should take care of them through this winter."

"That's fine," Devlin said. He looked out at the weak scattering of snowflakes drifting down around them. "But you'd better hurry before the first blizzards arrive."

"I shall," Pendergrass promised. "And I imagine you would like to join those search parties out looking for your son without further delay. So I'll bid you goodbye and see you at the trials."

The two officers shook hands; then Pendergrass climbed up into the army wagon for his journey while Devlin rushed to the stables where a horse was already waiting for him.

Chapter 23

The snow had been falling for two days and a night, leaving two feet of the powdery substance across the entirety of the Buffalo Steppes. Three horsemen, with a packhorse in tow, rode slowly across the white terrain. The hooves of the animals broke through the thin, frozen crust of the frigid covering with each step, and the vapor from their nostrils spurt forth with each breath they exhaled.

Major Matt Devlin huddled in his heavy blue army overcoat. The civilian fur cap he wore was pulled down over his ears. Just ahead of him, Fred Jeffries was dressed in the type of thick, blanketlike jackets worn by French-Canadian trappers in cold weather. The rest of his garb was Indian, including buffalo leggings and knee-high moccasins. War Heart was dressed similarly, but had a blanket pulled tightly around him. Of the three, he seemed to bear the cold temperature with the least discomfort.

This was the third time the trio had been out trying to locate Freddie Devlin and Swift Rabbit. None expected to find the boys alive anymore, but it was hoped their bodies could be retrieved before the cold drove the ravenous pack of wolves onto the Buffalo Steppes looking for food. If the boys' bodies were found by animals, there would be nothing left to bury except some gnawed bones not carried away. If, however, Indians discovered the remains, they might have been properly buried.

Back at Fort Buffalo, the agency, the mission school, and the Kiwota village, all was well. The buffalo hunt a few weeks earlier had been undertaken by the Kiwotas with soldiers along to escort them. The affair, arranged through the permission of the department commander at Fort Snelling, had been successful. Hundreds of buffalo fell to arrows and bullets, and the women and girls had spent several long days in ceaseless butchering. The meat, hides, and other useful parts of the bison were carted back on travois. Meanwhile, the back issue of cattle had also arrived and were wintering in shelter at the agency. Gilbert Paxton, undertaking an extra job as the official reservation agent, made sure the count was correct when the beeves arrived. Now the Indians would be able to come and take a few at a time whenever fresh meat was needed or desired.

When the news reached the Buffalo Steppes about the newspaper stories on gold being discovered in the Medicine Hills, Devlin took direct action. He went straight to War Heart and, with Jeffries supplying his usual skills in translation, explained the situation. Devlin promised that the dragoons would clear out all illegal prospectors. War Heart, still trusting Looks Ahead, agreed to leave the enforcement of reservation policies to the army. That way there would be no trouble that might escalate into a full-scale war between Indians and interlopers.

While things were straightened out on the frontier, judicial proceedings against Senator Osmond Torrance moved slowly. A thorough investigation by certain of his political enemies brought out the fact he had illegally put a claim on land in the Medicine Hills of the Buffalo Steppes where the gold was reported discovered. Further inquiry about how he found out about the precious metal's presence in Indian country promised to be most interesting. An unusual event occurred, however, when his secretary, Harvey Puffer, looted the senator's safe of thousands of dollars and disappeared to parts unknown. Reports of sightings of the thieving aide in Europe surfaced several times, but no real information on his whereabouts was substantiated. Meanwhile, Torrance was settling in for the fight of his political and professional life, and things did not look good for him.

Devlin, with faith that justice would prevail, turned his mind from the case and mourned the loss of his oldest son. He would never forget Freddie and his devil-may-care pranks and playfulness. Beth took it hard, but having to care for the two remaining children gave her strength. The only thing that kept Devlin going was wanting to bring his boy's body back home for a burial. He wanted a grave with a tombstone so that the loss would be more bearable.

War Heart, for his part, also wanted to retrieve Swift Rabbit's corpse. The boy was a nephew, and if he were devoured by wolves, certain ceremonies could be performed by the medicine man that would guarantee the youngster being whole in the spirit world of the dead. Being dismembered by a hungry animal was not the same as mutilation by an enemy. Animals were the People's gift from the Great Spirit and did not do evil or mischief simply to be bad or cruel.

Now, still moving across the frigid terrain, the trio continued their sad quest. Suddenly, Jeffries pointed to the west. "A campfire, see?" He said the words again in the Kiwota tongue for War Heart's benefit.

A wisp of smoke could be seen curling upward from

a ravine. It was obviously an Indian camp. The smoke was intermittent, showing care was being taken that it would not attract attention unless someone was actually looking for it.

War Heart muttered a few words that Jeffries translated as, "It's probably a Sioux camp. They'd be out here this time of year to hunt elk or deer before the snows got too deep and dangerous. They may have information about the boys' corpses."

The three men, with the packhorse trailing, pushed on. They skirted a stand of leafless trees looking stark and dead in the dreary winter landscape. After rounding the dormant vegetation, they turned into the ravine.

"Pa!"

Freddie Devlin's loud call caused his father to rein in and stare in a strange emotion of happiness and anger.

"Freddie!"

Swift Rabbit appeared from the snow cave behind the small fire. He looked at the three men, then at Freddie. "Boy! Are we in trouble!"

"You certainly are," Devlin said. He dismounted and struggled through the snow until he reached his son. He picked him up and gave him a hug.

"Put me down, Pa!" Freddie yelled out in embarrassment. "I'm too big to be lifted up like a baby."

War Heart, satisfied that the boys were hale and hearty, dismounted and glanced at their camp. He looked at Devlin and spoke a few words.

Jeffries said, "War Heart is telling you that he sees a lot of Sioux stuff in their cave. There's bows and arrows, a buffalo robe, and other things."

Devlin, now with Freddie standing in front of him, kept his anger under control. "Just what do you mean by running away like this? Your mother took it very hard, young man."

"Me and Swift Rabbit ran off to live out here on the prairie all by our lonesomes," Freddie said.

"Yeah," Swift Rabbit said. "I wanted to get away from that mission school."

"But that wasn't the main reason we lit out," Freddie explained. "We're good friends and didn't want to have to fight each other when we're grown up."

When War Heart was told what the boy said, he replied through Jeffries, stating, "I think that children sometimes see things better and brighter than adults."

"What were you two planning on doing?" Devlin asked.

"Like we said, Pa," Freddie explained. "We was just planning on staying away from other folks and hunting and fishing."

"The way life is supposed to be," Swift Rabbit interjected.

Freddie now had something else on his mind. "Are we gonna get a whipping, Pa?"

"You bet you are," Devlin said. Then he added, "If your mother allows it."

"I'll get a whipping," Swift Rabbit complained. 'I always get the switch at that school."

"I'll talk with Mr. Paxton," Devlin said. "If Freddie doesn't get whipped, I'll see that you don't.'

"Paxton don't whip us," Swift Rabbit said. "It's that Mr. Fenwick."

"I'll still keep you from that switch you told us about," Devlin promised. "But you'll both be punished somehow."

"Yeah," Freddie said, downcast.

"Gather up your stuff," Devlin said. "You two can sit on the packhorse for the trip back to Fort Buffalo."

War Heart spoke through Jeffries. "Maybe the boys will not have to be enemies after all."

"Maybe you and I won't either," Devlin told him. "But you'll have to be patient when the white men come next summer to look for gold in the Medicine Hills. They won't care if it's against the treaty for them to be there or not."

War Heart replied, "You said you will chase them away for us. If you say that, I believe you."

"Then, we are not enemies," Devlin said.

It didn't take the boys long to prepare for the trip back. Jeffries helped them aboard the packhorse, then mounted his own. The group turned back toward the south, where Fort Buffalo waited them.

After they had been traveling an hour, War Heart looked at Devlin. He took a deep breath, then spoke as best he could in English:

"Looks Ahead, we friends."

"Goddamn right we are," Devlin said.

Jeffries translated the phrase for the Indian as, "Through the strength of the Great Spirit we will remain so."

The travelers continued across the snow-covered terrain. The wind died down, and the sun edged out from the clouds, casting a sparkling light that glittered and danced across the Buffalo Steppes.

Epilogue

Spring on the Buffalo Steppes brought the usual mud, but in that year of 1856 the sun came on early and strong. The ground firmed up nicely, and everyone was able to get out into the open country without the worry of being mired down in boggy soil.

On one misty morning, not long after the first shoots of fresh grass had begun to appear, Major Matthew Devlin rode his favorite horse across the awakening prairie. He had made arrangements to meet Fred Jeffries just north of the mission school. As he drew close he could see the scout on horseback. His Cheyenne wife, Moon Deer, was also mounted, but she also held the reins leading to another horse that pulled a travois stacked with their belongings.

Devlin rode up and halted. "Good morning, Mr. Jeffries," he greeted him. The army officer knew better than to attempt to speak to the scout's wife.

"Good morning to you, Major," Jeffries said.

Devlin sighed. "I wish I could talk you into staying, Mr. Jeffries. I could really use your help now that those illegal prospectors have started to show up in the Medicine Hills."

Jeffries shook his head. "Thank you just the same, Major, but I really got my mind made up. You ain't gonna need no scout for that work, and the Kiwotas ain't gonna go on the warpath as long as you keep the area clear. So, I'm gonna get out of this scouting business and head up to the high country and spend the rest o' my days in them mountains."

"That sounds a lot like what Freddie and Swift Rabbit wanted to do," Devlin said.

"Well, now, I got to admit I kinda got the idea from them," Jeffries said. "But I really been thinking on it for some time." He pointed to the buildings a short distance away. "That's what made up my mind."

Devlin was puzzled. "Mr. Paxton's mission school? I don't see what that's got to do with your decision to leave."

"I scouted for the army 'cause I think the Injuns need to be helped along," Jeffries said. "A good reservation is 'bout the best they can hope for. I know how it's gonna be when folks start getting pushy 'bout needing farm land."

"Well, hell, Mr. Jeffries," Devlin said. "The Kiwotas do have a good reservation. They're drawing rations from the government and the Mission of Indian Reform, and they're able to hunt enough buffalo to get by, too."

"They ain't being destroyed by the reservation," Jeffries said. "They're gonna be wiped out by Paxton and that school. To make it even worse, he thinks he's really helping them along."

"He is," Devlin insisted. "Those Indian children are learning to read and write, acquiring good work skills, and being given spiritual guidance, too."

"That's what's gonna destroy them as a people," Jeffries said. "I don't know how to really explain this, but you don't help nobody by ripping out his soul. Turning those boys and girls away from their tribal religion and beliefs means that Paxton is gonna cut out their hearts. The Kiwotas won't even exist in another twenty or thirty years. They'll just be another bunch o' lost Injuns, preyed on by liquor and a life God didn't put 'em on the earth for."

Devlin was taken aback, but he was ready to defend himself. "I'm a better friend to War Heart than that."

"You want to be," Jeffries said. He shrugged. "What the hell? It can't be helped. Well, I got to go, Major. It's been nice knowing you."

They shook hands. The army officer watched Jeffries and his wife ride toward the northwest, heading for the purple shadows of the distant mountains. After a while he turned his gaze toward the mission school. The children, in orderly lines, marched from the classroom into the dining hall.

Devlin had to admit to himself that the sight made him uneasy, too. He turned away, riding back across the open country. He chanced to glance to the north and could see shadowy figures in the mist that swirled across the ground. They were obviously Kiwota warriors on some early-morning hunting expedition. After a few moments he recognized the silhouette of War Heart among the Indians. Suddenly, Devlin remembered something the Kiwota had said to him while they were camping overnight during the search for the two boys:

"Some day, Looks Ahead, my people will fade from the earth like the snow during the Moon of Awakening. We will be gone. We will not even be shadows on our own land."

The dragoon officer continued to watch the Indians until, finally, they disappeared into the mist. He tried to catch sight of them again. But they were gone.

Devlin pulled on the reins of his horse and rode back to Fort Buffalo.